THE HIDING PLACE OF THUNDER

A NOVEL BY

KEITH REMER

The Hiding Place of Thunder

v2.0

Enlighten Press, A Division of Enlighten Communications, Inc.
Norman, Oklahoma

ISBN: 978-0-9825085-1-0

Library of Congress Control Number: 2009942171

PRINTED IN THE UNITED STATES OF AMERICA

For Carrie, my lovely wife

Acknowledgements

My thanks and appreciation goes to the following: to Stacy and Doug Shelton for believing in this project; to my beautiful daughter, Sloan, for the use of her face on the cover; to my friend and an amazing artist, Kendall James for the artwork and photography; and to James Wilcox for his editing expertise.

"YOU CALLED IN TROUBLE,
AND I RESCUED YOU;
I ANSWERED YOU IN
THE HIDING PLACE OF THUNDER…"

Psalm 81:7

Chapter One

"Put the bat down, Herman, and stop calling me a son of a bitch."

"This here is my bat, and you are standing on my land. So don't go tellin' me what to do, Burl. Besides, if I was to put this here baseball bat down, it'd be kind of hard to knock yer head off with it...You goofy son of a bitch!"

Burl Hansen leaned back against the fender of his car and crossed two beefy arms over a barrel chest. "Herman, don't make me come over there and take that damn thing away from you."

Herman Grambs puckered his crusty lips and deposited a glob of thick black tobacco juice between Hansen's cowboy boots. "Some says you the biggest and baddest son of a bitch in this county Burl. But you ain't near big enough or bad enough to take away my bat!"

Hansen unfolded his arms and pointed a thick index finger at the feisty little welfare recipient. "It's hard to make me angry Herman, but you're about to do it. You got about three seconds to throw that…"

A sudden beeping sound from within his car interrupted Hansen's threat.

"What is that noise?" Grambs piped.

"It's my cell phone," Hansen grumbled as he pushed away from the car's fender. "You don't move. I gotta see who's calling."

"I ain't goin' nowhere. Hell, I live here…you son of a bitch!"

Hansen grabbed the phone, pushed the talk button and barked, "This is Burl."

"Hi, honey."

Hansen grimaced at the sound of his wife's voice. She seemed to have a knack for calling at the most inconvenient times.

"Who is it?" Grambs asked.

"It's my wife."

Grambs cupped a hand around one side of his mouth and hollered, "Howdy, Vicki!"

"Herman Grambs says 'Hello,'" Hansen relayed, then grumbled back to Grambs, "Vicki says 'Hi.'"

Turning his attention back to his wife, Hansen asked in his typically gruff manner, "Whatcha need, Vicki?"

"Do you know what a *bar mitzvah* is?" The sweet voice sounded distressed.

"A what?" Hansen countered.

"A bar mitzvah. I just watched one on T.V. It was on the Discovery Channel."

"A bar mitzvah? Yeah, yeah, it's some kind of Jewish ceremony," Hansen said, doing nothing to conceal his agitation. Before Vicki gained a chance to respond, Burl covered the phone with his hand and hissed at Grambs, "You better throw that bat down!"

"You better kiss my ass!" Grambs hissed back.

"It's a ceremony," Vicki continued, "performed when a Jewish boy turns thirteen that..."

"Oh, hell, not this again!" Hansen bellowed, and immediately wished he hadn't. Vicki hung up without another word. Despite his renowned terse disposition, Burl Hansen didn't relish hurting his darling wife's feelings. He felt really rotten, and feeling rotten did nothing to improve his already tweaked temperament.

Hansen crammed the small phone into the rear pocket of his jeans and stomped around to the back of his car. He popped the trunk and pulled out a twelve-gauge pump shotgun, violently jerked the slide forward and back to chamber a shell and whirled to level the barrel at Herman Grambs' midsection.

"Drop that bat Herman, or I'm going to drop you."

The bat hit the ground and both of Grambs' hands went high into the air over his head. "Goddammit Burl," he whined, "I used to like you back when we was in high school."

"Everybody liked me back in high school Herman. I was a star linebacker."

"Yeah, you was a hell of a football player and a real

nice feller, too. Now that you're the county sheriff though, you've become a sure enough asshole!"

"Is that right? Well let me tell you something Herman. I liked you a whole lot better before you started exposing yourself to young girls!"

"Young?" Herman squealed. "Hell Burl, she was fifteen if she was a day!"

At the moment, Hansen needed no more than a simple spark to ignite his anger. Vicki's feelings were hurt, and the mere mentioning of a *bar mitzvah* had turned Hansen's thoughts to a fourteen-year-old boy way back east in Boston, Massachusetts. Anytime and every time Hansen thought about this boy, his mood darkened.

"Herman, I want you to get in the car, and I want you to shut up. If I have to listen to one more word from your hillbilly mouth, I'll probably pull out your nasty tongue and beat you to death with it."

Herman Grambs never seemed real smart, but he now proved to be no idiot. He crawled into the car and managed to keep his mouth shut.

Darrell Baker prepared to cross the street in front of the Pushmataha County Courthouse when Sheriff Hansen pulled up in his cruiser. Newly implanted in the town of Antlers, Oklahoma, the high school junior knew few adults other than his teachers, but he knew of the sheriff. Although Burl Hansen presently served as a small time cop in a God-forsaken land of hicks and rednecks, he'd once been phenomenally famous in Darrell's home town of Chicago, Illinois.

Darrell's grandparents lived in this out-back country nearly all their lives. Long before Darrell wound up here with his next of kin, he'd known Antlers to be Burl Hansen's home town and where the famed hero chose to return after he retired from the National Football League.

This once awesome linebacker and a few other standouts from the Chicago Bears had attracted Darrell Baker to football. Universities across the nation already vied for Darrell's tremendous passing arm. His grandparents and others assured him the recent tragic change in his life and the subsequent move to this backwoods dive would not hamper his lifelong dream of being a professional quarterback. Darrell only hoped in the next four to five years, there would be a greater presence of African-American quarterbacks in the professional ranks.

Because Hansen pulled his car into a parking space just feet away from him, Darrell stopped in his tracks. He'd never been this close to a sports legend. Darrell measured six-three and weighed two hundred and ten pounds. However, the man unfolding from the driver's seat of the muddy cruiser made him feel small. Darrell guessed Hansen to be at least six-six and real close to three hundred pounds. The former Bear sported a significant belly, but the rest of him still looked capable of running down quarterbacks and crushing them at will.

Once he'd performed the arduous task of getting out from beneath the steering wheel, Hansen adjusted the ball cap on his head and tucked his flannel shirt into his jeans. Preoccupied with a boy in Boston he'd never even laid eyes on, Hansen failed to notice the young man standing on the curb just a few feet away.

"You're Burl Hansen."

The sheriff's hand grasped the rear door handle to let Herman Grambs out of the back seat. Instead, he dropped his hand and turned to face the big teenager. "Yeah, I am. Who are you?"

"My name is Darrell Baker. I'm from Chicago, and I grew up watching you play football."

The athletic looking young black kid named Baker set off bells in Hansen's mind. Then he remembered. "You're Teddy and Martha Hallum's grandson."

"That's me," the boy nodded.

Hansen offered Darrell his right hand. "I heard what happened to your mama. I'm sorry."

"Thanks," Darrell replied as he shook hands with Hansen.

"I also hear you are one heck of a quarterback."

"I do what I can," Darrell grinned.

"That's what they say. I'm anxious to watch you play. When I get a few spare minutes, we need to sit down and swap game stories."

"Cool," Darrell nodded, his grin widening.

Hansen turned back to the rear door of his car wondering if the boy in Boston possessed any athletic abilities.

Darrell Baker stepped out of the way as Sheriff Hansen opened the passenger's door. The man in the back with the tangled mess of thinning hair and scraggly beard did not look at all happy. But neither did Hansen.

"Come on Herman, I don't have all day," the sheriff barked.

"Don't rush me, you son of a bitch. I'm a by-god tax-payin' citizen and I pay your goddamned salary! So you got just as long as I want to take to get…"

Hansen grabbed his prisoner by the scruff of the neck to interrupt the declaration and jerk him from the back seat. The sheriff took several steps before lowering the man enough so his feet touched the ground.

"Ohhhhhhhhhhh, my neck! You have done broke my fuckin' neck!" the stained and crusty man bellowed.

The sheriff maintained his grip, shaking the much smaller man like a rag doll. "Shut up, you ignorant bastard or I will break your neck, both your arms and your legs, too! Just shut the hell up!"

"Okay! Okay!" the prisoner managed through chattering teeth.

As Hansen shoved his captive in the direction of the courthouse, the man's eyes made contact with Darrell. "What the hell you lookin' at, tar baby?"

Darrell thought the entire state of Oklahoma would be flat and bare, but he was wrong. The Kiamichi Mountains, with thick forests of pines, surrounded the southeastern county of Pushmataha. He heard the state referred to as the Heartland and the Bible Belt. He thought the people from such a place would be less hateful, hostile, and color conscious than the people of Chicago, but he was wrong about that, too.

"He's looking at an idiot, Herman," Sheriff Hansen said before kicking the man in the butt with the side of his boot. "Now get your ass moving."

The grungy man in Hansen's custody had been the first person in Antlers ever to verbally assault Darrell. He wasn't, however, the first racist the newcomer encountered. Mannerisms, looks, and subtle attitudes of some classmates had Darrell believing that Antlers High housed more than its fair share of bigots. It didn't help that Darrell was one of only six blacks in the junior class of ninety-eight students. Still, the majority seemed to have no problems with him being a minority. Most had been cordial, and one in particular had been downright friendly. Darrell's reaction to this particular person had no doubt prompted most of the racist attitudes.

Shelly Rafell had gorgeous blonde hair and bright blue eyes. She introduced herself to Darrell during the second hour of his first Monday in the new school. Her approach had been blatantly flirtatious, and what started as friendly banter culminated in a date the following Friday. At Antlers' one and only movie theater, Darrell Baker and Shelly Rafell kissed and cuddled. Later, in Shelly's new Camaro, Darrell went where other boys had quite obviously already been. Darrell and Shelly's hand-holding the next week at school raised more than one set of eyebrows.

The fact that some didn't approve of the relationship didn't bother Darrell one little bit. He approved of it very much, and no matter what anybody else said or thought about it, Darrell intended to take just as long as Shelly agreed to give.

Darrell didn't move from his place on the curb until his hero and the cracker disappeared into the courthouse. Then he set out on his after school trek home. Darrell didn't intend to walk much longer. Having to walk in his old neighborhood in inner-city Chicago was one thing. Practically everybody there walked or took the subway. Walking in Antlers, though, proved altogether another thing. No self-respecting high school junior in Antlers walked anywhere. They drove. As soon as Granddaddy finished teaching him how, Darrell would be driving as well.

In less than ten minutes, Darrell made it to the outskirts of town. With only a few blocks left between him and his grandparents' place, a white car pulled alongside and slowed to a near stop. Darrell stooped to peer into the front passenger window and immediately felt relieved to find an attractive red-head smiling at him.

"You wouldn't by any chance be our new football star now would you?" The woman's smile broadened as she brought the late model Ford to a complete stop.

Darrell stepped up to the car and leaned in for a closer look. The contrast between the woman's very white skin and her long red hair appealed to him. The tight and very short skirt riding high on bare, shapely legs practically took his breath away. "I'm Darrell Baker, and I do play a little football."

"You are a tease, Darrell Baker. The word around town is you play a lot of football, and play it very well."

Darrell shrugged his broad shoulders and offered his best smile. A large set of very dark sunglasses covered much of the woman's pretty face, making it hard to determine her age. If Darrell had to guess, though, he would put the woman in her early thirties. Her smile really turned him on.

"Word gets around fast in this place," Darrell chuckled.

"Oh honey, you got that right," she giggled, "and if the word was to ever get out that I saw our new football hero walking and didn't offer him a ride, well, I'd probably be thrown out of the football booster club! You climb in this car, Darrell Baker, and let me give you a ride," she said, patting the seat beside her.

Darrell didn't argue and wasted no time squeezing in next to her.

"My goodness, you are such a huge young man," the woman cooed as she blatantly scanned every inch of his body. "Your arms are as big around as my legs," she exclaimed before leaning toward Darrell to pat his left bicep, "and hard as a rock!"

Her blouse gaped as she leaned, and Darrell zeroed in on more than a fair amount of cleavage. Only after nearly swallowing his tongue did he manage to mumble, "I work out quite a bit."

"I guess you do," the woman sighed, as her hand went from patting to caressing his arm. "Tell me, Darrell Baker," she continued as she picked up his left hand and placed it on her cream-colored thigh, "have you got time for a little ride before I take you wherever it is you're going?"

"Uh, yeah, sure, I got some time."

The woman slammed the Ford into gear and gunned away from the curb as Darrell stroked her soft thigh. Being on foot in Antlers, Oklahoma, wasn't such a bad thing after all.

"Oh, by the way, my name is Shannon," the woman in the red wig lied.

The Baker boy moved his hand only a few inches

under her hiked up skirt and started working to get a finger into her panties. "Nice to meet you, Shannon," the teen beamed.

Knowing she had several miles to drive, Shannon spread her legs just enough to keep the boy occupied, then she pushed down harder on the gas pedal.

It became quickly apparent that Baker wasn't going to be content just probing and poking around her panties. When he started trying to work the undergarments down her thighs, she faked a giggle. "I do like what you got in mind, Darrell, but not while I'm flying down the road at seventy miles an hour. You just wait 'til we get stopped and I'll help you get those panties out of the way!"

"I hear that," Baker grinned as he moved his hands from beneath her skirt to the buttons of her blouse.

Before he could free her breast for the whole passing world to see, the woman hiding behind the sunglasses thought of something that might slow him down. "Tell me, Darrell, why in the world would anyone leave a big, glamorous city like Chicago to come to our little wide spot in the road?"

It worked. Baker let go of the buttons and straightened in his seat. "Oh, uh, well, I stayed there with my mama, and she, uh, died."

The woman acted surprised and faked a look of pity. "Oh, no, honey! That's terrible. How did she die?"

"Cancer," Darrell sighed, turning his head to look out the window.

Realizing how quickly the memory of the loss extinguished the boy's burning desire, the woman fought back a smile. She now only needed to keep Baker's mind on his dead mother and off her tits just a couple of more miles. She didn't want the black bastard pawing at her when she parked the car under the dense clump of trees next to the Kiamichi River.

Sometimes Darrell found comfort in believing his mother still watched over him from her place in heaven. Yet there were some things he just didn't want Mama seeing. Shannon evidently sensed his pain and embarrassment because he'd been quiet for several minutes.

"I'm sorry," the pretty woman finally said before slowing to pull from the paved county road onto a narrow, graveled surface not much more than a trail. "I didn't mean to make you feel bad."

Darrell turned back to her, his eyes falling victim to her wonderful legs and large breasts. "Hey, it ain't your fault. Don't worry about it," he shrugged.

"I can't help but worry about it. It was my big mouth that made you start thinking about your poor dead mother," Shannon pouted as she navigated down the winding, rutted pathway. "I'll tell you what I'll do, though. When I get this thing parked, if you're still willing, I'll use my big mouth to help you stop thinking about her."

A stirring in Darrell's jeans pushed Mama from his mind. "Couldn't we just pull over here?"

"I know a special place that's very secluded," she purred.

A quick look around the rough, hilly countryside revealed nothing but a wall of pine trees. Darrell couldn't imagine a more secluded place, but he kept his eyes peeled in anticipation. Within minutes, they paralleled a narrow rushing river. A few minutes later, Shannon slowed to a near stop, pulling the car off the road and parking beneath a clump of trees on the bank of the river.

Darrell grew anxious to experience Shannon, but felt it much more exciting to let the hot woman make the first move. Turning to face her, he watched as she put the car in park and turned off the engine. From the way Shannon acted and the things she had said, Darrell expected her to literally spring at him, but that didn't happen.

Before facing Darrell, the woman slowly turned her head to look out the windows in every direction. Darrell couldn't see her eyes because of the sunglasses, but her lips looked to be clenched tight and the muscles of her jaw were flexing. Shannon suddenly looked very nervous, and it wasn't hard to figure out why. Darrell had no doubt grown white women carrying on with underage black boys wasn't something taken lightly in Pushmataha County, Oklahoma.

By the time Shannon turned her face toward Darrell, her lips were all but frowning. Darrell started to ask her why when she suddenly burst into a beaming smile and let out a gleeful sounding laugh. She removed her sunglasses revealing dancing, wonderful blue eyes. However, they weren't looking at Darrell. Shannon obviously found a great deal of joy in something outside Darrell's window.

Infected by the smile, Darrel donned one of his own and turned to see what wonder caught Shannon's eye.

What made the woman smile made Darrell Baker clinch in horror.

Chapter Two

"Why doesn't Daddy go to church on Wednesday nights?" six-year-old Sandy Hansen asked her mother.

"He don't go," nine-year-old Bret Hansen inserted, "'cause he don't wanna go. Same reason he don't go on Sunday mornings and Sunday nights."

"Shut up, Bret! I'm not asking you," the little girl squealed.

"You shut up!" Bret screeched in return.

"You both shut up," Vicki Hansen said to her children without raising her voice.

"How come he doesn't go to church with us, Mama?" Sandy persisted.

Vicki continued to work patiently at braiding her squirming daughter's long auburn hair. "We have this discussion at least once a week, honey. Like I've told you a dozen times before, your daddy works late most Wednesday evenings, just like he is tonight. Sunday is normally the only day he takes off, and he has to catch up on all the ranch work. Please be still, Sandy."

"If it's all right for Daddy not to go to church," Bret piped up, "then it should be all right for me not to go to church either."

"I didn't say it was all right for your father not to attend church, Bret," Vicki asserted, dryly. "I just told you the reasons he doesn't. And I will not tell you again to go change your shirt."

"I like this shirt."

"It doesn't match your slacks, Bret. Go change it."

"Bret never matches," Sandy chimed in.

"Shut up, Sandy!"

"You shut up, Bret!"

"You both shut up," their mother exhaled.

Vicki worked to finish her daughter's hair while thinking about her husband. She didn't know an all-around finer man than her Burl. A hard man and often harsh, Burl nonetheless proved to be a good husband and father. Still, there were things Vicki would change about her mate if she could. First and foremost, she would alter his views and attitudes about one of the most important aspects of her life. If she could, she would have Burl attending church with her and the children. If she could get Burl in church, Vicki believed it wouldn't be long before he, too, could appreciate the peril of one teenage boy in Boston.

After booking Herman Grambs, Hansen spent three hours trying to catch up on some of his department's administrative requirements. He currently toiled through his second year of a four-year term and decided long ago being a sheriff wouldn't be such a bad job if it wasn't for all the paperwork. On this "red tape bullshit," he laid the blame for his typical twelve-hour days. He feared calculating his salary against hours worked would prove he earned well below minimum wage standards. The possibility of such would bother Hansen if he intended to make a career in law enforcement — which he most definitely did not — and if he hadn't made some outstanding investments during his lucrative years in pro football.

After completing as much paperwork as he could stomach, Hansen drove the twenty mile trek to his beloved Arrowhead Ranch and the Hansen home. As usual, it took him just over two hours to feed his large herd of registered Black Angus cattle.

With the cows tended, Hansen worked another hour on a cutting horse that cost him twice the price of the average home in Pushmataha County. By the time he made it into the house, his wife and children were back from Wednesday night services at the Oak Avenue Baptist Church in Antlers.

Bret rushed to meet him at the back door. "Hey, Dad," the boy said as he ran to greet his father, "You know, I was thinking, if I didn't have to go to church on Wednesday nights…like you…I could help feed the cows like I do every other night." Bret finished the declaration with a proud nod of his head and a sly grin.

"I guess you ran that idea past your mother?" Hansen asked as he swooped the boy into his arms and made his way to the refrigerator.

"Well…yeah," Bret said, settling into the crook of his father's right arm.

"What did she have to say about that?" Hansen said before twisting the lid off a bottle of beer with his teeth. "Did she think that was a splendid idea?" he snickered.

"Nope. She said I have to go to church," Bret pouted, but then with a surge of enthusiasm he added, "but you could make her let me stay home!"

"Yeah, sure, and when I accomplish that magnificent feat, I'll start turning all our cow shit into gold," Hansen chuckled and lowered the boy back to the floor.

Bret worked his way through a long and woeful, "Awwwwwwww, Dad," when his younger sister bounded into the kitchen.

"Mama was crying at church tonight," Sandy declared.

"Ohhmmmm, Sandy, she told us not to say anything about that," Bret scolded.

"That would be lying," Sandy fired back.

"No it wouldn't. Lying is when you say something that ain't true."

"Nuh uh!"

"Uh huh!"

On his way out of the kitchen, Hansen bent to kiss his daughter on the head. Shaking his head and chuckling, he left his children to their debate.

When her husband walked into the living room, Vicki looked away from the television screen and up at Burl.

"What are you watching?" he asked before flopping down beside her on the sofa.

Looking back at the television, Vicki studied the program for a second or two before responding. "I don't even know what's on."

Burl draped a huge arm around Vicki's shoulders and pulled her close. "You're watching TV, but you don't know what's on?" he teased.

"I wasn't watching it. I was just looking at it." Vicki sighed as she snuggled into her husband's side and closed her eyes. Vicki felt like hiding and could think of no better place than in her husband's arms.

Burl placed a finger beneath Vicki's chin and gently lifted her face up and toward him. "Hey, open your eyes."

"Why?" Vicki asked without obeying.

"I wanna see if you're still angry about how I acted when you called me this afternoon."

"I'm not angry," she said.

"Come on, baby," Burl cooed, "look at me."

Vicki opened her eyes and looked at her husband's ruggedly handsome face.

Burl stroked her cheek and with a sympathetic gaze all but whispered, "You've been crying."

"You can't tell that by looking at my eyes because they are not red. Which one of your little big-mouthed children ratted me out?"

"Sandy thought not telling me would be dishonest."

"I warned them both to keep quiet. I ought to just spank her little butt!" Vicki tried to be upset with her daughter, but couldn't pull it off.

"Aw, Honey, it probably really upset her to see you cry. It isn't something you do very much of."

Vicki closed her eyes again and tucked herself back underneath her husband's arm. Lately, she'd cried quite often, but Burl just didn't know about it.

After sitting silently for a few seconds, Burl softly asked, "If it makes you feel so bad you have to cry, why do you even go to church?"

Vicki felt her defenses going up, so she made a conscious effort to keep an edge off her words. "Going to church does not make me cry."

"Then what did make you cry?"

She detected the tone of his voice fading from inquisitive to challenging. She sat up and looked at him. A wide, furrowed brow, arched eyebrows, and a smirk confirmed it. She scooted from beneath his arm to the far end of the sofa.

Vicki jabbed an index finger in his direction, "You know what made me cry," she said, raising her voice an octave. "You know good and well that I've been thinking about Jacob."

Burl flinched and averted his dark brown eyes. Vicki knew he didn't like hearing the boy's name. It seemed easier on Burl to refer to him as the boy back east or the boy in Boston — if he even referred to him at all.

"Yeah, well," Burl grumbled before taking a swig of beer, "church just always makes it worse."

Vicki looked hard into her husband's eyes and struggled to keep her voice down. "I don't have to go to church, Burl, to know Jacob is not being properly raised."

"Oh, come on, Vicki," he exhaled with a shake of his head. "That boy has been raised by very wealthy *parents* in a very religious home."

"A Jewish home," Vicki emphasized through a sudden blur of tears.

Burl set his beer bottle on the floor and exposed both palms to his wife. "Okay. Okay. Let's just stop this. We both know it isn't going to lead to anything but a fight."

After a few seconds of sniffing and wiping at her eyes, Vicki dropped what she knew would be a bombshell…a nuclear one at that. "I want to meet him," she practically whispered. "I want to see what he looks like. I want to get to know him. I want to go to Boston, get him, and bring him here."

Burl stared at her incredulously for several long moments. When he determined she meant what she said, his expression softened and the hard lines of his face turned sympathetic. "Oh, Baby," he moaned as he reached out and took both of her hands into one of his. "You got to know that can't happen."

"Why not?" she reasoned. "I just want him here for the summer." She began to sob.

"His parents would never agree to such a thing."

"How do you know that?"

Letting go of her hands, he brought his up to rub his tired looking eyes. After a few seconds, he sighed long and hard and ran both hands through his mop of thick, reddish hair. "I think it's a very, very bad idea for all concerned," he exhaled.

Vicki had already prepared reasons to support and justify her stance. Before she could compose herself enough for a rational delivery, the phone rang, bringing a noticeable look of relief to Burl's face. The giant man wasted no time grabbing the nearby phone.

Hansen normally felt irritated by the frequent evening and late night phone calls that took him away from his family. However, as he grasped the receiver and brought it up to his ear, he hoped this one would do just that. By all estimations, this evening at home held no promise of being a pleasant one.

"Hello," Hansen grumbled.

"Hope I ain't pulling you away from a hot piece of ass!"

The voice belonged to Chuck Turner, Hansen's best friend and the chief of the Antlers police department. Sadly, there stood very little chance of this call getting him out of the house. "Not even close," Hansen sighed in disappointment.

"Well, hell man, don't let it get you down. The night's still young. Little Vicki might decide to pounce on you before it's over."

"She just might at that," Hansen said as he cut his eyes to the petite brunette glaring at him from the couch.

"Well, that would figure. Here in a little while you'll be snuggled up with the prettiest woman in a three-county area while I'm out here on the mean streets of Antlers, performing a public service."

Hansen glanced at his watch. "It's nearly ten, Chuck. Why is the chief of police still working?"

"That's what I called about. We've got a kid that's been reported missing. I personally think he's probably just out with some buddies, but we're looking around for him all the same. Thought I'd see if you can spare a deputy or two to check some of the hot spots outside the city limits."

"Sure I can. Who's the kid?"

"Teddy Hallum's grandson. His name's Darrell Baker."

"I'll be damned," Burl said, "I just met that boy today."

"You did? Where was he at and about what time was it?"

"Let's see, I guess it was somewhere between three-thirty and four. He was out in front of the courthouse. I assumed he was heading home from school."

"Yeah, well, he never made it. But like I said, I reckon he's just out and about. I ain't real worried about it."

"You're probably right," Hansen nodded, taking a moment to think. "Okay. I'll get out there with a couple of deputies and help you look for him."

"Hell, Burl, ain't no sense in you messing up your evening. Just send a couple of deputies."

Vicki now wore a scowl. "Yeah, all right. We'll get right out there."

Hansen heard a confused "Huh?" just before hanging up the phone.

Hansen cradled the receiver and turned to his wife. "There's a teenage boy missing from town. A new kid that doesn't know the area or any of the people. Chuck's pretty worried about him and wants me to give him a hand." Hansen hated lying to his wife, but if a white lie could temporarily postpone the inevitable conversation and ensuing ugliness, he could live with it. Besides, a little time to reconsider what she wanted might bring her back to her senses.

"Do you think the boy is okay?" she asked, obviously worried.

"I don't know," Hansen said as he put on what he hoped would pass as an equally worried look. In actuality, he had to agree with Chuck Turner. Darrell Baker probably just lost track of time while out with new friends, learning a few things Okies do for fun.

Shelly Rafell turned on her dome light and glanced at her watch. With a loud and frustrated sigh she pulled down the sun visor and checked her makeup in the lighted mirror before extinguishing the dome light. It was 11:40 and she had been sitting in the Wal-Mart parking lot for fifteen minutes. Darrell Baker said he would meet her at 11:30. If he didn't show up, Shelly intended to be some kind of pissed. After all, slipping out of the house after her mom went to sleep put Shelly at great risk. If her mom found out she'd snuck out, she would be in serious trouble and in light of their mother-daughter confrontation earlier in the day, if her mom found out *why* she had slipped out, Shelly would be good as dead.

Bored by the emptiness of the huge parking lot and Antlers' late-night radio programming, Shelly's mind turned to the fight she had with her mother. Her mom basically ambushed her the moment she walked in from school, and Marlene Rafell had not been timid or subtle in her attack.

"Is it true you've been dating a black boy?" Marlene screamed as Shelly came through the front door.

Shelly could tell by the look on her mom's face and the pitch of her voice that telling the truth at this juncture would not work to her advantage. "I went to the show last week with a black friend, Mom, but it wasn't a date. We were just hangin' out together."

"Oh, yeah?" Marlene spat. "I guess you consider kissin' and holdin' hands at school with the black bastard just 'hangin' out together too? Well, do you?"

"That's ridiculous, Mom!" Shelly retorted. "I haven't been kissing and holding hands with any boy at school. Who's telling you this shit?"

"Don't you never mind who's telling me," her mother snarled. "I got eyes and ears all over this town and they're seldom wrong. And you watch your filthy mouth when you talk to me, young lady!"

It took Shelly several minutes, but she finally managed to maneuver her mom to the point where she didn't know whether to believe her daughter or her undisclosed sources.

"Well, I'll tell you right here and now, Shelly Rafell," Marlene huffed as she obviously struggled with doubts, "the best thing for you to do is just stay away from them negroes. You ain't got no business even being around them...It just ain't right...it ain't natural."

Shelly spent the rest of the day scheming about how she could secretly maintain her relationship with Darrell without her mom finding out. Marlene made it clear that any association — no matter how slight — with an African-American male would result in Shelly losing her car. Her mother hated the car anyway because it had been a gift from her dad — one of Marlene's most hated ex-husbands.

Sitting behind the wheel in the Wal-Mart parking lot, Shelly gave the interior of her Camaro a visual once-over. "Damn," she hissed as she slapped the steering wheel with the palms of her hands. Her mother could be so unfair. It was such an amazing car, and Darrell was such a hot guy. It seemed just unfathomable to forsake one for the other.

Shelly deeply contemplated which she would give up if push came to shove when someone rapped on her passenger window. The noise startled her, but she smiled before turning toward the window. When she realized the person peering into the car wasn't Darrell, her smile faded, but it didn't completely go away. With a push of a button she lowered the passenger window.

"I haven't seen you like in forever," Shelly grinned. "Get in and talk to me. I'm waiting for a friend."

Hansen pushed his chair away from the desk, stretched his arms high overhead and erupted into a long, hard yawn. He had stayed out until a little past midnight looking for the Baker kid. He crawled out of bed at five, completed his chores, and arrived at his office by seven. Having two hours of paperwork under his belt, he could hardly keep his eyes open now. He thought about getting up and stretching his legs when a dispatcher stuck her head in his office.

"Chief Turner is on line two, Sheriff."

Hansen pushed the blinking light on his phone and hoped his friend had some good news about Darrell Baker. "I guess you're just now getting to your office," Hansen taunted. He never tired of ribbing Chuck Turner about his liberal work hours.

"I was up 'til nearly three, asshole," Chuck returned dryly.

"The next time you talk me into a law enforcement job," Hansen chuckled, "I want one like yours." Hansen held Chuck responsible for prodding him to run for county sheriff. The previous sheriff, Bob Morgan, had spent thirty illustrious years in the job before giving it up for retirement. Chuck had been less than enthused about the hopefuls who threw their names into the hat and pursued Hansen like a duck after a June bug. Because the county seat was in his town, Chuck wanted a sheriff he could trust and depend upon.

"Hey, mister smartass," Chuck huffed to Hansen's comment, "do you want to jack with me over my office hours or do you want to hear how I solved the case of the missing football star?"

"You found Baker?"

"We didn't find him, but we know what happened to him."

"Is he okay?"

"Hell, he's a damned site better than just okay."

"How's that?"

"You know Marlene Rafell's daughter Shelly, don't you?"

"Yeah, I know who she is." Hansen graduated from high school with Marlene. Her last name way back then had been Hammonds. It had changed at least a half-dozen times since.

"Well, when Marlene got up this morning the girl was gone. Come to find out, Shelly and Darrell got the hots for each other, and Marlene told Shelly to keep her young and fine ass away from the homeboy. So the way I see it, that young 'gangsta' is out there someplace right now doing all kinds of nasty things with that good-looking little blonde." Chuck paused long enough to catch this breath, then added for emphasis, "Yeah, I'd say he's damned okay!"

Hansen shook his head, "Spoken like a true pervert and bigot."

"Call me what you want, but the streets of Antlers, America, are once again safe to walk. Another crime mystery has been solved and all that good ol' horseshit!"

"What are you going to do about finding the kids, Sherlock?"

"We've entered them into NCIC. I've alerted the highway patrol and now you. Tell your deputies to keep their eyes open for Shelly's new Z28, red, with Texas tags PNE 378. How about some breakfast?"

"It's nearly lunch time," Hansen said. He couldn't

dismiss the two kids as easily as his old friend. He hadn't been a cop long enough to have calluses on his emotions.

"Okay. I could do a burger. Meet me at Flodell's?"

"See you there in about ten," Hansen said without adding a good-bye.

Chapter Three

Jacob Swiretynsky wrung his hands and popped his knuckles to relieve the residual tension before grinning at his opponent. "Are you ready to throw in the towel, Dad?"

"Quite ready, Son," Joe Swiretynsky all but panted. After wiping his damp brow with the back of his hand he added, "That was a most tedious bout. You were kicking and punching with such speed and accuracy, that I simply could not counter. Every time I would strike or kick all I would connect with was thin air. Congratulations, Jacob."

"Thank you, Dad," Jacob grinned as he brushed a lock of sandy blond hair out of his green eyes. "Would you like to play a game of football?"

"No thank you, Jacob," the elder Swiretynsky said as he laid his joystick aside and rose from the couch. "Video kickboxing is mentally and physically taxing enough. Video football would absolutely exhaust me!" The elder Swiretynsky did not usually smile much, but he did now.

Before his father could exit the sitting room of Jacob's bedroom suite, the boy jumped to his feet. His eyes danced with hope of an improbable occurrence. "Have you ever been in a real fight?"

The question registered a predictable response of inquisitiveness on Doctor Swiretynsky's normally dignified face. "That is a peculiar question, Jacob," he said, gently tugging at his nub of a chin.

"I'm just curious. I have never been in an actual fight so I have no frame of reference as to what it might be like."

"I am a physician, my dear boy. Like yourself, I was raised in a most civil environment of exclusive neighborhoods and private schools. I have never been presented with the opportunity of engaging in fisticuffs, nor have I ever desired to brawl in the streets."

"Have you ever been hit or kicked?" Jacob wondered aloud.

"Jacob, are you having problems with a bully?"

"No, sir. I'm simply curious," Jacob said, lowering his head. His boring but safe life in the Back Bay area of Boston produced nothing as exhilarating as a bully.

"You have been watching entirely too much television, Son," Joe said with a wave of his hand before turning to walk away.

"One more thing, Dad," Jacob hailed his father a second time. He paused, trying to assess a way of broaching a subject he'd wanted to mention to his father for quite some time. Considering the nature of the topic, there would be no better opportunity to bring it up. He pressed on reluctantly, "If I were to attend public school next year, I would be old enough to try out for the football team. Because of my size, I think I could make a formidable lineman."

Joe turned once again to face his son, making a visible effort to consider the proposal before beginning to chuckle. He looked his son directly in the eye. "Your girth, my son, is undoubtedly better suited for less physically aggressive endeavors. Besides, there is no chance on God's green earth that you'll attend a public school next year or any other year thereafter." Joe looked his son directly in the eye to emphasize his conviction.

"But, Dad, football would help me to…" Jacob began.

"Jacob, football is entirely out of the question," Dr. Swiretynsky interrupted with a tone of finality.

"*Okay,*" Jacob thought as he shrugged his shoulders. Now he would not feel guilty taking this matter over his father's head to a higher and much more accommodating authority. Jacob seldom heard the word "no" from his mother.

"I ain't never seen you in a suit and tie," Bret Hansen said to his father.

"And you *ain't never* going to either," Hansen replied to his son, who sat in his Sunday best on the seat of the ancient tractor while Hansen made minor repairs.

"Not all the boys wear suits and ties to Sunday school. Charlie Davis don't," Bret said begrudgingly.

"Uh-huh," Hansen grunted as he toyed with the John Deere's carburetor. The tractor was getting fire, but it wouldn't start, which Hansen hoped meant a simple fuel-line problem.

Bret flipped at his tie with the middle finger of his right hand. "Charlie makes fun of me for wearing this crap."

"Uh-huh," Hansen mumbled, paying more attention to the carburetor than his son.

"If he makes fun of me today," Bret huffed, "I might just kick his ass!"

"Don't be kicking ass in Sunday school, Bret," the father ho-hummed. Then as an afterthought he added, "And don't be saying ass either."

"You say ass," Bret smirked.

"I say a lot of words you better not be saying, and you just said ass a second time after I told you not to be saying it. If I hear you say it again before you're at least, I don't know... eleven...then I'll be kicking your *ass*. Understood?"

Bret exhaled loudly, "Yeah."

Hansen looked up from the engine and forced a scowl at his son. "Yeah? Where're your manners, boy?"

"I meant yes sir," Bret half-grinned.

"I thought you did," Hansen half-grinned back.

For the next few minutes Hansen made what he hoped were the right adjustments while Bret played with the steering wheel and made engine noises through pursed lips. All was relatively peaceful until Vicki walked up.

"Go get in the car, Bret. It's time to go," she directed.

"You sure you don't need for me to stay and help you with this old piece of junk, Daddy?"

"Do what your mama says, boy."

"Awwwwwww, Dad!"

Hansen pulled his head out of the engine compartment and watched his son climb down from the seat.

"I'm going, but I get the front seat," Bret declared.

"Your sister is already in the front. You get in the back," Vicki countered.

"Oh, man!" Bret stretched the two words into a ten-second whine. "I have to go to church, wear this crap, and sit in the back seat, too? I hate my life!"

"Go hate it in the back seat of the car, Bret," Vicki ordered.

Bret stomped off. "Real funny, Mom."

Hansen watched his son kick rocks and sticks and anything else in his path as he made his way to the car. After expressing a true fondness for his son in the form of a chuckle, Hansen turned to face his wife.

Three days had passed since Vicki expressed her desire to meet the boy in Boston. To say the least, their relationship had been strained since that evening and Hansen spent little time looking at his wife. Seeing her now in her Sunday finery caused him to marvel at her pretty face. Often when they were cross with one another, or just too busy with life, Hansen would forget what a beautiful wife he had. They were the same age — thirty — but he always thought she looked much younger. Sometimes he attributed her youthfulness to the thick, dark hair that fell past her shoulders. At other times, he believed it to be the lively spark that danced in her emerald green eyes.

Hansen snapped back to the issue at hand when Vicki struck a defiant pose, placing her hands on her slender hips and planting her shapely legs shoulder width apart.

"When I get home from church, we're going to talk," she said decisively.

They would talk. Or more likely, they would fight. And although she stood just mere inches above five feet and weighed slightly over a hundred pounds, Vicki Hansen could be a most able opponent. "Fine," was all he could muster for a response.

When the family car pulled from the drive, Vicki waved a solemn good-bye. Sandy blew a kiss, and Bret stuck out his tongue. Hansen scowled and aimed a big index finger at the boy. When they were out of sight, he started chuckling again.

Several minutes and twice as many expletives later, Hansen got lucky and the antiquated tractor struggled to life. After a couple of minutes of belching plumes of black smoke, the old engine leveled off and came as close to purring as the thirty-year-old machine would ever be capable of. When Hansen felt the engine had adequately warmed, he coerced the gear shift into second and began maneuvering around the farm implements scattered throughout his equipment yard. Overly dry conditions and high March winds had Hansen concerned over the possibility of fire hazards. He intended to plow a wide swath of ground in the pastures surrounding his home and out buildings to serve as a firebreak.

Within minutes Hansen aligned his tractor with and backed up to his breaking plow. While the tractor idled in neutral, he crawled down to hook up the piece of equipment. Kneeling to make his connections, Hansen's gaze fell on the old plow. Settling back on his haunches, he considered the terribly rusted condition of the plow and remembered a time when it looked pristine.

The first time he'd looked at the breaking plow it had been brand new, bright shiny yellow, and hooked up to the very same tractor Hansen prepared to hook it to now. That had been fifteen years earlier and both the tractor and plow belonged to Lester Templin. The memories of that day, now a decade and a half in the past, still caused him to nearly grow sick to his stomach.

On that long ago day he looked at the plow because he couldn't bear to look at the man sitting on the tractor. Lester Templin was a good, hard-working man who treated Hansen with friendship and respect. Hansen could still remember the shame and sorrow he felt then and he would never forget how his teenage voice quivered.

"Mr. Templin...I got your daughter pregnant."

The words hit the older man like a fist to the gut. His body went slack and his shoulders drooped as his throat emitted a long and agonizing moan. Templin turned, and without a word, climbed up on the tractor and pulled away, but Hansen saw the moisture in his eyes.

It would have been easier for Hansen had Lester Templin responded with anger instead of pain. Hansen ran beside the tractor for nearly a hundred yards shouting promises to the man he held in such high esteem.

"I'll marry her, Mr. Templin...I'll work hard to support her and the baby...I'll do right by her...I promise I'll always take care of her and treat her good!"

It didn't exactly turn out that way. Burl Hansen and Vicki Templin weren't allowed to get married until they turned nineteen. By that time their son had been living with his adopted parents in Boston for four years.

With a fingernail tempered from hard work, the sheriff of Pushmataha County flicked a peeling chip of faded yellow paint from the rusty old plow. It clearly needed some maintenance. It was not the only thing at the Arrowhead Ranch in need of a little fixing and patching up.

Vicki walked into her front door to be greeted by the scent of aftershave. She only had a few seconds to wonder why before Burl stepped from the living room into the small entryway. She couldn't keep the consternation from showing on her face. At one o'clock on a Sunday afternoon, her workaholic husband stood in the house wearing the closest thing he had to dress clothes.

"I thought I'd take you and the kids out for Sunday lunch," he shrugged, almost sheepishly.

"I have a roast in the crock-pot," Vicki responded in near shock.

"We can have it for dinner."

Vicki came close to turning loose a smile when a plausible reason for the most unusual behavior struck like lightning. "Burl, I hope you are not attempting to woo me out of trying to get Jacob for the summer," she said, pursing her lips.

Her husband gently placed one of his huge, callused hands on her elbow and guided her to the living room couch. He didn't speak until they were seated. "Just how, exactly, do you intend to get him?"

Before Vicki could determine if the question intended to suggest the folly of her desires, Burl threw a palm into the air.

"I'm sorry," he said, shaking his head, "I meant to say…just how, exactly, do we intend to get the boy for the summer? What's our plan?"

Vicki arched her eyebrows. "Am I supposed to believe that you suddenly want this, too?"

"Why don't you just believe that I love you enough to try to make this happen for your happiness and well-being?"

On this matter Vicki wasn't about to look a gift horse in the mouth. Besides, she had to believe whatever reservations her husband held would vanish the moment their oldest child stepped into their lives.

"That's it?" Hansen asked his wife incredulously. "That's our plan?"

"What's wrong with it?"

Hansen hefted his significant bulk from the couch and started to pace. If he could keep his mouth shut, Vicki's plan would net no results. Hansen would be relieved, but Vicki would be gravely disappointed. Hansen would then have to live with knowing he hadn't done everything he could to make the dream come true for the woman he loved more than anything in the world.

"Well, let me see if I can get this right," he began. "You're gonna call these Sworzeny people in…"

"Swiretynsky," Vicki corrected.

Hansen paused a moment to study his wife's face. "How do you remember their name after all these years?"

"When a mother is forced to give a child away, she doesn't forget the names of the people she had to give him to."

Hansen felt pleased for not keeping his mouth shut. "Okay, so your plan is to call the Swiretynsky's and say, 'Hey, guys this is your son's biological mother. Remember me?' Then as they're gasping for air and grasping their chests because you have just popped into their lives, you say, 'I called to see if I could meet with you about Jacob spending the summer in our Southern Baptist home!' And that's when they say, 'Hell, yeah! Fly on up here and we'll have him packed and ready to go!'"

"If nothing else, you have the mechanics right," Vicki shrugged.

"Vicki," Hansen exhaled emphatically as he plopped back down beside her, "you've got to be prepared to do more than that."

"Do you have a better idea?" she challenged.

"I've got a suggestion that might put some teeth in your plan. Sure, start by asking for what you want, but be prepared for them to say no. And when they do, threaten with legal action. I doubt that we have a leg to stand on, but the bottom-line truth is, our child *was* taken from us, and we had no say about it. I'm sure we could hire a really big-time lawyer and have him waiting in the wings to attempt bluffing them into letting us have him for the summer."

Vicki reached out and placed a hand on Hansen's thigh. "I appreciate the suggestion and your willingness to help me make this happen, but Burl, I don't want it to get ugly."

"Baby," Hansen said, reaching out to squeeze the hand

on his leg, "do you honestly believe that you can get that boy for the summer without some really powerful outside help? Do you truly believe you can just call those people on your own, tell them what you want, and then get it?"

After a long and thoughtful moment, Vicki answered, "No, to your first question. Yes, to the second. I'm not doing this on my own, Burl. I do have some powerful outside help. A help that says, 'Ask and ye shall receive.' I believe with all my heart, honey, that Jesus Christ wants Jacob to spend the summer with us."

With the satisfaction of knowing he tried and a slight sense of relief over the fact he failed, Hansen pushed off the couch a second time and extended a hand down to his wife. "We can talk more about this later. Right now I'm starving to death. Let's head to town for that lunch."

Hansen helped his wife to her feet, feeling obligated to make one further point. "By the way," he grinned, "if I were going to try to get Jewish parents to let me keep their son for the summer...I don't think I'd use that Jesus-wants-it-to-happen crap as a selling point!"

Although she made a serious effort not to, Vicki laughed.

The voice calling his name seemed to be coming from the far end of a very long tunnel, and whoever or whatever kept hitting him in the face really started to piss him off. Then, with a start, Hansen awoke.

"What's wrong?" he blurted as he grabbed in the dark for the hand Vicki used to tap the cheeks of his face.

"It's Mike Meeks again," she said irritably before yawning long and hard. After cramming the phone into Hansen's hand she collapsed back onto her side of the bed.

"What time is it? Hansen groaned as he fumbled with the receiver.

"Nearly three," she slurred.

"Shit," he said, still attempting to align the phone with his ear. "What is it now, Mike?"

Deputy Meeks' earlier call had come just as the Hansens crawled into bed some five hours earlier. Max Bemo, a full-blood Choctaw Indian, had just whipped two white men. In the process, the very drunk and terribly mean Bemo tore the hell out of Joe Buck's Cafe and Convenience Store and Meeks wanted to know if Bemo's impending arrest could be put off until the following day. Hansen readily approved the request. He didn't want Meeks trying to arrest an intoxicated Bemo during the hours of darkness. Besides, if Bemo had to be taken in, Hansen wanted to be the one to do it. He had been the only cop in the county able to take Bemo to jail without a fight.

"I really hate bothering you in the middle of the night, Sheriff," Meeks apologized, "but I need to get your permission to call OSBI."

The initials of Oklahoma's state criminal investigative

bureau brushed the remnants of sleep from Hansen's mind. "What have you got, Mike?" he asked the youngest and greenest of his deputies.

"I'm up in the northern part of the county about five miles from Albion. Some coon hunters up here found a practically brand new Ford abandoned in the woods. The tag and VIN check hot. It was stolen from Hugo.

"The back half of the car has substantial fire damage. I think whoever stole it, Sheriff, tried to ignite the gas tank to blow it up. For some reason, it didn't work. I think they wanted to get rid of the car so they could destroy what I found in the front seat compartment."

Just when Hansen began to think the deputy paused for dramatic effect he heard the young man thumbing the striker of a cigarette lighter. Hansen sat on the verge of emphatically airing his curiosity when Meeks exhaled forcibly into the receiver and started talking again.

"I found a bunch of dried blood on the front seat, dashboard, and passenger floorboard. Then I found something down in the driver's side floorboard that really freaked me out at first because I thought it was a scalp, but it's really just a wig."

"A wig?" Hansen asked.

"Yes, sir. A long, red wig. It's got some blood on it, too."

"When was the car reported stolen?" Hansen asked to help arrange the pieces of the puzzle.

"Last Tuesday."

"I don't recall hearing of any major crimes involving a new Ford or people wearing a red wig," Hansen thought out loud before pointedly asking, "What are you thinking, Mike?"

"I been kind of wondering, Sheriff, if maybe the car wasn't used in some type of rape or abduction that ended up in a murder. Maybe the guy driving the car picked up a woman somewhere and when they started scuffling, her wig came off. Hell, really though, I don't know what we got here."

"Well, unless that happened in the last twenty-four hours or so there'd be a missing persons report," Hansen moaned as he sat up on the side of the bed. "But I can't see some guy pulling something like that in a car that's been reported hot for nearly a week. If something like that happened, it would more likely be within hours of the car being stolen, and if that was the case, we'd probably have already heard about the missing woman. Have you searched the area around the car?"

"As good as I can. It's awful dark out tonight and I don't have the best of flashlights. On top of that, the underbrush in the area is thick as a bitch."

"Okay. Go ahead and call OSBI and see if they want to process the car," Hansen said, stifling a yawn.

"Are you coming out, Sheriff?'

Hansen could tell by Vicki's smooth, rhythmic breathing that she had fallen back to sleep. The desire to join her proved much greater than his sense of duty in this particular case. "No. You can handle it, Mike. Until we get more, all we got now is just another stolen car."

Chapter Four

Hansen's second in charge, Undersheriff Pete Marsh, brought the weekly payroll in for the sheriff's review and signature at two p.m. At three, Hansen spread it across his desk and tried for the fifth time to complete the process. When the sixth interruption came in the form of a knock on his office door, the sheriff's response was not cordial.

"This damned sure better be important!" Mondays were never good days for Hansen and this one had been worse than usual. Still hanging out there on his list of things to do were the visits he needed to pay to all involved in the incident at Joe Buck's Cafe and Convenience Store.

Hansen's office door slowly creaked open a few feet, and the head jailer, Paul Winters, cautiously stuck his incessantly frowning face through the opening. "Excuse me, boss, but you wanted me to let you know how Herman Grambs' arraignment turned out."

"Well?" Hansen responded without patience for his least favorite employee. If the sheriff ever got concrete proof supporting his suspicions of how corrupt he thought Winters to be, he'd hang him out to dry.

"There wasn't no surprises," the jailer droned in his sullen way. "He was bound over for trial with the bond set at only twenty-grand. But still yet, that little pervert can't even come up with the ten percent it'd take for a bondsman to get him out."

Hansen anticipated as much. "I want to let Herman be a trustee. Do you have any problems with that?"

"You're the boss," Winters grimaced.

"Go get him and bring him here."

Hansen put the ten-minute interim to good use and signed his name to the payroll before Winters rapped on the door a second time. Even his knock sounded glum.

"Come on in," Hansen answered reluctantly.

Winters swung the door open and roughly shoved a disheveled Herman Grambs into the office.

"Dammit Winters," Hansen growled, "is that really necessary?"

"Sorry," he grumbled, "I'm just sick and tired of him calling me names."

"Go on out and shut the door behind you," the sheriff responded to his jailer. To Grambs he said, "Sit down, Herman."

"Why do you give a dirty damn about that asshole pushing me around?" Grambs sulked before slithering into a chair in front of Hansen's desk. "Hell, you the one kicked me square damned in the middle of the ass right in front of a jigaboo punk kid. I'd rather be pushed around a little than have that done to me!"

"And I guess you're going to tell me you didn't deserve getting kicked in the ass that day?" Hansen smirked.

"Nope. Sure didn't. You're just a son of a bitch!"

Hansen couldn't help but laugh out loud. Sometimes Grambs just struck him that way. "I like you, Herman. Always have. And seeing how it looks like you're going to be here quite a while, I'm going to offer you a sweet deal."

"How's that?" Grambs sneered.

"I'm going to give you a chance to work as a trustee. You do a little cleaning and fixing up around here, and I'll let you have full TV rights and pay you three dollars a day. That'll give you plenty of money for your chewing tobacco and whatever snacks you like."

"Yeah? So what if I don't want to be no damned trustee?"

"Well, then you get no TV, no chewing tobacco, and you can just sit in your cell and rot." Hansen picked up a pen and began working as if he couldn't care less about Gramb's reluctance.

Grambs considered his options for a few seconds before nodding his shaggy head and sighing, "Okay. I'll be your damned lap dog…you son of a bitch!"

"Two more things," Hansen said, dropping the pen

and narrowing his eyes to the meanest squint he could make. "First thing, don't ever call me another name unless it's sheriff, Hansen, Burl, sir or any combination thereof. Second thing, I want information."

"Information? What kind of information?" Grambs asked with a squint of his own.

"Anything you can get on anybody." Hansen didn't want Grambs to feel restricted to just prisoners. "Anything on any drugs or other paraphernalia coming into the jail, anything said by loose lips, anything that isn't right that I ought to know about."

"You want me to be a snitch?" Grambs said with an expression of disgust.

"Is that against your moral code?" Hansen grinned.

"My what?"

Hansen dismissed the joke with a wave of his hand. "No. I don't want you to be a snitch. I want you to be an informant."

"Oh, well, that's different…I think…but what if I don't hear nothin' to tell you?"

"Then you don't tell me anything. But I got others working, too. Don't let me find out that you're holding out on me."

"And what if I do?"

"Herman, do you remember that time you hit me with a rock when we was just kids?" Hansen grinned.

"Yeah, I remember," Grambs smirked.

"What you got back then won't even start to compare

to what I'll give you now." Hansen could tell he'd hit his mark by the way Grambs simply but seriously nodded his head. "And one more thing, old friend..."

"What the hell is it?" Grambs sighed.

"Start showering. You smell like something crawled up between the cheeks of your ass and died."

"I understand we have a new trustee," Undersheriff Pete Marsh grinned when he stepped into Hansen's office to retrieve the payroll documents.

"News travels fast in this old building." Hansen grinned at his lanky, good-natured second in charge. "How did you hear about it?"

"I know you will find this hard to believe, but I first heard Paul Winters grumbling something about Grambs not making a wart on a good trustee's ass. Then, Grambs stopped me in the hall and wanted to know if trustees got to wear a badge!"

Marsh started laughing, and Hansen couldn't help but join in. His undersheriff always had that effect on him. When Hansen's first and only term expired, he planned to do everything in his power to get Marsh elected in his place. Although many considered Marsh an outsider because he'd come to Oklahoma from Connecticut, Hansen knew of no better man for the job.

"You know Pete, Herman just wouldn't be Herman if

he wasn't so wonderfully ignorant. Here, I'm finished with the payroll," he said, handing the documents to his friend.

Marsh retrieved the papers just as Chief Chuck Turner stepped through the doorway.

"Well, looky here," Turner called out in a raspy smoker's voice, "I'll be damned if it ain't the head Pushmataha County mounty and his faithful Yankee, Ickabod Marsh!"

Turner's occasional comparisons of the undersheriff to the fictional headmaster never failed to amuse Hansen.

"Don't laugh," Marsh moaned with a smile, "it only eggs him on."

"Hell, Burl knows you look like Ickabod Crane," Turner snickered, "You are about as skinny as a stream of piss and the biggest thing on you is your Adam's apple!"

"You haven't seen everything on me," Marsh deadpanned as he turned to leave the office.

"And I don't care to either," Turner said as he reached out and playfully cuffed the passing undersheriff on the shoulder.

With Marsh on his way out, Hansen leaned back in his chair and looked up at Turner. "What are you up to, ol' buddy?"

Turner plopped heavily into the chair in front of Hansen's desk. The chair creaked a loud objection, and Hansen winced. Antlers chief of police wasn't nearly as tall as Hansen, but he came dangerously close to weighing the same and little to none of his bulk appeared to be muscle.

"I'm getting ready to call it quits for the day. Thought

I'd see if you want to do a little fishing this afternoon."

"Can't. I've got too much to do around that place of mine."

"Just thought I'd check," Turner said as he ran a palm over the sweaty bald crown of his head. "Damn, it's warm for March."

Hansen nodded in agreement before a voice erupted over the portable police radio attached to Turner's gun belt.

"Any unit on or around Main Street…there's a fight in progress on the northeast corner of Main and Broadway."

"Johnny Bottoms' service station is on that corner," Turner said as he hoisted himself to his feet.

The chief and Bottoms did a lot of hunting and fishing together, and Bottom's wife, Trisha, served as the two lawmen's favorite waitress at Flodell's Diner. "That's just three blocks from here," Hansen said. "I'll head over there with you."

A rough looking and heavily muscled man with a lot of tattoos and a ponytail sat on the sidewalk. He tried hard to get to his feet but looked noticeably dazed to the point of a rum-dumb state of helplessness. Hansen had never seen the man on the sidewalk, but he knew the man standing over him.

Butch Myers' famed hands were still formed into fists. Myers kept calling the downed man all kinds of foul names, taunting him to get back on his feet. Myers owned a couple of acres that butted up to the Arrowhead Ranch, and happened to be Hansen's closest neighbor, however, the two men were anything but neighborly. Myers openly and vehemently resented the successes life provided Hansen.

"You're such a bad talking mother fucker," Myers slurred at the stunned man. "Why don't you get up and back up some of your bad mouth?"

Hansen moved in closer, but not too close. "Looks like he's had enough to me, Butch."

"Get up, you pussy!" Myers bellowed, ignoring Hansen altogether.

The sheriff moved only one-step closer, being careful to stay at least an arm's length from Myers. Johnny Bottoms and Turner talked off to his side, but Hansen kept his eyes glued on Myers. The man had to be nearing fifty and hadn't trained in years, but still could pack a hell of a hard and quick punch. In the seventies Butch Myers had been just one of several nationally ranked heavyweight boxers touted as the "Great White Hope." That was before a practically unknown black fighter nearly killed him in the fourth round of a fight in Las Vegas. From that point life quickly went downhill for the Oklahoma boxer.

"It ain't Butch's fault this time, Chuck," Hansen heard Johnny insisting about Butch, who happened to be his first cousin.

"I don't know, Johnny, he looks pretty damned drunk again," Turner replied.

Turner and Bottoms stepped away together and whispered words Hansen could not hear.

Meanwhile, Myers didn't let up on his opponent. "If you don't get up, I'm going to jerk you up and knock you back down again, you worthless piece of shit. How would you like that?" Myers took a step in the tattooed man's direction.

Hansen didn't want to, but he stepped between them, "I said he's had enough, Butch."

"This ain't none of your goddamned business, Hansen. Get the fuck out of my way."

"Back off, Butch," Hansen warned, working to keep his voice calm.

"What are you going to do if I don't? You think just because you was some big shit famous football player that you can take me on? No, no, motherfucker, because I could've been famous, too. You know that, asshole?"

"Yeah, Butch. I know that."

"You don't act like you know. If you did, you'd get out of my way. You think just because you are so big and strong and younger than me that you'd have a chance against me? Huh? Look at that bastard on the ground. He's big and strong too and a hell of a lot younger than you. I put his ass down with three punches."

Hansen took just about all Myers' mouth he intended to take. "Last warning, Butch. Back off."

Turner quickly stepped up to Hansen's side. "Hey, big guy," he said in a tone of voice used to calm a dog ready to bite, "Johnny insists Butch didn't start this one and he's willing to get him out of here and take him home."

"Yeah, you big dumb fuck," Myers hissed at Hansen, "I didn't start this shit. I finished it."

"He is close to crossing a line he doesn't want to cross," Hansen grumbled to Turner.

"Oh, come on, Burl. We'll let Johnny handle this."

Hansen wanted him to go to jail and he wasn't happy about Turner's benevolence, but this was the city cop's turf. "Whatever," he exhaled, "It's your town."

Johnny Bottoms quickly grabbed his cousin by the arm and began tugging him away. They had not moved more than two feet when Myers turned to glare at Hansen over his shoulder. "There will be another time, mother fucker!"

Hansen slowly nodded his head in agreement.

Hansen just finished his chores when Johnny Bottoms' one-ton wrecker pulled into his drive. The last remnants of the sun's rays peaked through a purple and gold haze over the horizon.

"Howdy, Burl," Bottoms smiled as he climbed from the cab of his service truck.

"Hello, Johnny."

"Hey, man, I just wanted to drop by and apologize for

the way my cousin was acting this afternoon."

"That wasn't your fault, Johnny," Hansen said with a shake of his head. It would be difficult for Hansen not to like Johnny Bottoms. He seemed like just one hell of a nice guy.

"Oh, I know it. I just don't want you and Butch to get cross ways. You know he ain't a bad guy. He just gets kind of mean when he's drinking."

"He seems to be doing a lot more of that nowadays, Johnny. I'm afraid his drinking is going to get him in serious trouble. Still though, I don't have a problem with Butch. Butch has a problem with me."

"Yeah, I know, Burl, but you know how it is. Hell, he's just kind of bitter about how life's turned out for him. I just don't want to see things get worse between you two."

Hansen walked over and leaned back against the bed of Bottoms' wrecker. The last comment brought some rumors to mind. "How old is Butch's son now?" he asked while staring down the road in the direction of the Myers' place.

Bottoms scratched a handsome face with nails holding the oily black residue of a mechanic's work. "Randy? Well, let's see, I guess he's about fifteen now."

Hansen digested the information a few seconds before speaking his mind. "I hear he's really tough on the kid and on his own wife, too. It's rumored that he beats on both of them."

"Oh, that's bullshit, Burl," Bottoms said with a nervous

chuckle. "He wouldn't do that. Hell, those two is the only life he's got."

"I hope you're right, Johnny. I won't stand by and let a man whip up on women and children."

"I don't blame you. You wouldn't be doing your job if you did," Bottoms agreed with nods of his head. "And by the way, I want you to know I think you're doing a fine job as sheriff. You're the best we've ever had as far as I'm concerned. I voted for you, you know."

"Well, thank you for your support, Johnny," Hansen smiled wearily.

"I mean, I'm going to tell you, Burl, voting isn't something I take lightly. As Americans, now more than ever, we got to be damned careful who we put in office. Hell, man, we got the wars in Iraq and Afghanistan, we got Iran and North Korea trying to build nukes, we got neighbors like Cuba and Venezuela that hate our guts. I'm here to tell you that if we don't put the right people in office, this whole damned mess could come tumbling down around our ears."

Hansen cleared his throat in an effort to fight off a smile. It wasn't that Bottoms had said anything funny or that what he said wasn't true. It just surprised Hansen that Bottoms followed what happened in the world outside of Antlers. Hansen also felt slightly chagrined for underestimating what he'd considered just a "good ol' boy" with no interest outside of turning bolts and killing wildlife.

The man seemed insightful as well.

"You're surprised to hear that coming from me, ain't you, Burl?" Bottoms grinned.This time Burl couldn't contain the smile. "Well, yeah, Johnny, to be honest with you, it surprised me. I just didn't have you figured as a student of current affairs!"

"I do study it, Burl. I spend hours on the internet. Did you know the terrorists have hundreds of sleeper cells positioned all over these United States?"

"I've heard that. I don't know that it's true, but I've heard it."

"Well, I believe it's true. Let me tell you something else I believe. I believe that al-Qaeda and the Taliban and maybe even Hezbollah are selecting and training candidates to put in our public offices. But not outright and honestly. See, their candidates are going to look just like regular people. They are going to be undercover until they get in office. Then they are going to start tearing down our American ways. You watch, the first thing they will do is try to take our guns away from us. I also think that the situation is so desperate between the Democrats and the Republicans jockeying for power that we could see another coup d'etat like we had in the sixties."

"We had a coup d'etat in the sixties?" Hansen asked with arched eyebrows.

"Hell yeah, we did! Johnson killed off Kennedy and took control of the nation!"

Hansen just nodded his head a couple of times before exhaling, "Well, oooookay. Listen, Johnny, I appreciate you dropping by, but I got things I just have to get done before dark."

"All right, Burl, but let me say this. You can see by what I've said how close we are to real disaster in this country. And now we have a nig...well, a black man in the white house. That's the reason I take my vote so seriously. Also, that's the reason I believe we as American citizens have to protect our rights to keep our firearms because when this all goes to hell in a hand-basket, it will be up to the citizens to protect our way of life."

Hansen exhaled in relief as Bottoms finally crawled back into the cab of his truck. Both men waved as the big wrecker backed down the drive. Johnny Bottoms was still a nice guy. Screwy as hell, but nice all the same.

Hansen got into bed just as the phone started ringing. Vicki picked it up in the kitchen. In a few seconds Hansen could hear her laughing. When she hollered to announce Chuck Turner on the line, Hansen wasn't surprised. No one could make Vicki laugh as quickly and often as Turner.

Hansen picked up the phone on the nightstand. "Flirting with my wife again?"

"Sometimes I seriously consider taking that woman from you," Turner responded.

"Sometimes," Hansen deadpanned, "I wouldn't stand

in your way. Now, what are you bothering me about this late at night?"

"I'm feeling guilty," Turner said as his tone grew serious. Chuck Turner seldom grew serious. "I hope you're not mad at me for getting in between you and Myers."

"I didn't like it at the time, but you probably did me a favor. One of us was about to get hurt. Come to think of it, who was that stranger Myers decked?"

"His name's Avery…Tom Avery. He just moved here from Texas. Says he's going to put in a motorcycle repair shop. He's about a half-ass outlaw biker, I think, but I ran him and there aren't any warrants."

"What did you do with him?"

"Helped him to his feet, and sent him on his way. Nothing else I could do with him. All he was guilty of doing was popping off to the wrong ol' boy. You can't put a man in jail for stupidity."

"Isn't that a pity? Maybe we ought to get that law changed," Hansen chuckled.

"Wouldn't that be sweet? Well, anyway I just wanted to make sure you weren't pissed off at me."

"I'm not pissed. By the way, your hunting and fishing buddy paid me a visit. He dropped by to apologize on behalf of his cousin."

"Isn't Johnny a hell of a nice guy?"

Hansen laughed before responding, "He's a nut."

"How so? What are you talking about?" Turner asked, sounding slightly defensive.

"Chuck, you have got to know that the man is a conspiracy theorist, a right-wing fanatic and paranoid as hell!"

"Oh, that? That's just Johnny. Besides, some things he believes...they could happen. I mean, he's got me reading some shit that's kind of scary. For example, did you know that George Bush senior had secretly promoted a one-world government?"

"Whatever," Hansen yawned. He simply felt too tired to be bullshitted by the master bullshitter. "Hey, Chuck, you know those sleepers Johnny talks about?"

"Yeah?"

"I'm about to be one of them. Goodnight."

Chapter Five

Rose Swiretynsky plucked prancing and dancing words from her mind and imprisoned them onto her computer screen. She'd never been one to think she created characters in her mind. She chose to believe instead that they were simply souls who chose her heart to call home. Long ago, Rose carved out an intimate niche from within the cavernous rooms of their grand mansion in which to practice her art. Fragrant candles burned here in this refuge of clutter. Her husband never understood why she preferred to work in a tiny place with poor lighting and such prosaic furnishings. He preferred his magnificent study on the floor above her. She'd never been able to adequately explain to Joseph Swiretynsky that her inspiration came from what occupied her rather than what enveloped her.

Rose's fingers merrily tapped away at her keyboard until the sound of footsteps and the turning of a doorknob set her heart to thumping.

"Hello, Mother."

The voice behind Rose Swiretynsky instinctively brought a smile to her lips. In an instant, she swirled around from her desk with arms wide open.

"My Jacob!" the middle-aged mother beamed, proudly nodding a head covered with thick dark hair streaked with dignified traces of gray. As it had been since her son's first day of kindergarten, his returning home at the end of the day prompted Rose to celebrate.

The celebration always commenced with a hug. Rose could remember a time when Jacob would run to fling himself into her arms. In those days he would squeal joyfully and even hug her in return. Now she watched the portly boy of fourteen amble reluctantly toward her, and still she considered herself lucky. She considered it nothing less than a gift from God that adolescence took no greater toll on Jacob's compassionate and sweet spirit. Rose knew most boys his age would not only refuse to hug back, but would probably not even passively endure her daily embrace.

"And how was school?" The question served as part of the litany that accompanied the celebration along with the act of her arms first wrapping and then squeezing tightly around the boy.

Jacob tolerated the motherly affection in accordance with tradition. "School was fine."

Before Rose could proceed beyond the preliminaries, Jacob squirmed out of her arms and made an obvious attempt to read the words displayed on her monitor. "How is your novel coming, Mother?"

Thousands of fans cherished the romantic novels Rose wrote under the name of Savanna Mills, but her son wasn't one of them. His interest in her literary endeavors could only mean one thing.

"You want something. What is it, Jacob?" Rose smiled knowingly.

"I want to play football."

"Oooooh, isn't that dangerous?"

"Mother, riding in a car is dangerous."

"Good point. Okay. Play football," she said as she turned back to her monitor.

"I would have to attend a public school," Jacob announced in a softer tone.

Rose quickly turned back to her son, "That is not good. I do not think your father would allow it."

"You could talk him into it," Jacob pleaded with both words and a hopeful look in his eyes.

Truthfully, in most instances the good Dr. Swiretynsky warmed like putty in Rose's hands. Few issues existed in the Swiretynsky home over which Rose didn't wield tremendous influence. Jacob's education, however, did not count among those issues.

"Oh, Jacob, couldn't you be satisfied playing one of the sports offered at your school? What about tennis or golf?"

"Mother, can you picture me bouncing across a tennis court with racket in hand? I'd resemble a circus bear swatting at flies with a spatula. And I find golf severely boring. I want excitement, Mother. I just seem to have this need for something daring and physical. Something different."

Although she had no doubt as to how serious her son perceived the matter, Rose could not help but chuckle at his last words. It brought to mind a personal joke mother and son had not shared in several years. "That's the wild Indian coming out in you!" she giggled.

Jacob struggled to keep a straight face, but ended up smiling anyway. Evidently her son thought back to his childhood and the questions he'd repeatedly asked about his biological parents. Rose knew and shared abundant information with Jacob about his birth mother, but she knew absolutely nothing about the boy who impregnated Vicki Templin. To amuse the small child Rose told Jacob stories about the role Native Americans played in Oklahoma's history. She would always interject possibilities of his blood father being a descendent of one of the proud and colorful tribes that were exiled to Jacob's birth state.

"Mother," Jacob emphasized with a patient tone, "I am truly committed to doing this. I'm reading every book and magazine I can find on football, and I watch all the football programs on the Classic Sports Channel. I have thoroughly studied the fundamentals of the game and the professionals of today and yesterday. Please, Mother, talk to Dad."

"Jacob, I have to believe your dreams of following in your father's footsteps to Harvard Medical School will be best served by remaining at the Blakemore Academy."

"I believe I possess the intelligence and drive to get into Harvard no matter where I attend school. Besides, Mother, how often have you told me, and I quote, 'The most beneficial education comes when one grasps special opportunities to sample truly unique experiences.' Those words have never been more applicable to a matter in my life, Mother."

Although it thrilled Rose that Jacob had her dearest philosophy committed to memory, it also trapped her. To uphold what she touted to be true, Rose had no choice but to confront her husband with the issue and try to make her son's wishes come true. As always it came down to this — what Jacob wanted, Rose felt compelled to provide.

Hansen pulled up in front of the shack Max Bemo called home and killed his engine. The time had come for the sheriff to confront the big Indian for trashing Joe Buck's place. Hansen would do what Deputy Meeks passed on the night Bemo whipped the two white men in Buck's Cafe and Convenience store.

Hounds of every variety crawled from beneath the house and out of two wrecked cars adorning the garbage littered yard. The emaciated dogs announced Hansen's presence with mournful baying. When none of them seemed motivated to do more, Hansen climbed out of his car. He made it around most of the dogs, engine parts, and discarded remnants of furniture when the shack's front door swung open with an ominous creak. A huge, bare-chested Indian with long braids draped over the front of each broad shoulder stood in the doorway and glared at Hansen.

"If you come to arrest me for fighting, you should go back and get some help," Max Bemo announced in guttural and choppy English.

Hansen grinned and nodded a greeting at Bemo. "Max, it seems to me you did enough fighting Sunday night to satisfy you for at least a week, but here you are making noises like you want to fight me."

Bemo studied Hansen for a second or two before shifting his weight to a less combative stance. "I did not start that fight. I am not going to jail," he mumbled with less venom.

Hansen's next breath came easier as he concentrated on maintaining the confident, relaxed demeanor serving to keep Bemo in check. Hansen was not accustomed to losing fist fights, but then neither was Bemo. Hansen feared if the two of them ever came to blows, one of them would not live to tell about it, and the other would be left in no shape to brag about it.

"Well, for now, Max, seems like you're in luck. Neither one of the two men you fought wants to press charges, but they could always change their minds. Then there's the matter with Joe Buck's place." Hansen chuckled as he stepped up on the rickety porch to look Bemo level in the eyes. "You three dudes tore the hell out of his cafe and store. I'm sure he'll want some kind of compensation."

"That was not my fault," Bemo said as he held his gaze steady with Hansen's.

"That's why I'm here, Max. I came to get your side of the story. It very well could be that you have nothing to worry about."

Bemo averted his nearly black eyes to one of the dogs that plopped down beside the porch to lick itself. The Choctaw Indian's eyes narrowed as he stared at the dog. "I was minding my own business. They was smart asses. Thought they was bad. Started calling me names…"

If Hansen didn't know better, the look on Bemo's badly pock-marked face would have him believe it was the dog Bemo despised.

"…I told them I didn't want no shit, and I tried to walk around them. Then the one with the beard pulled out a knife and said he was going to cut off one of my braids and keep it as a souvenir. I took the knife away from him…"

Hansen had visited the other two men in the hospital before driving out to see Bemo. The men, Mike Rider and Jerry Glass, were from Rattan, a small town fifteen miles east of Antlers. Neither said anything about a knife. However, Rider, the man with the beard, was right-handed and nearly every bone in that hand had been crushed. The surgeon said it looked like it had been run over by a truck.

"...Then the fat man jumped on my back and had me around the neck. He weighed a lot. I had to back into something to get him off..."

The fat man was Glass. He told Hansen that Bemo smashed him repeatedly into a glass front soft drink cooler. His back had been badly lacerated. Looking at Bemo, Hansen could clearly see the claw marks around his thick neck and across the upper half of his muscular chest. It looked as if someone had been hanging on for dear life.

"...While I was trying to get fatso off my back, the other guy came at me with a bottle of beer in his good hand. I hit him a couple of times in the face with my fists. He went down and didn't get back up..."

Mike Rider also had a mild concussion, and it had been difficult for Hansen to understand what he said because his broken jaw bones were wired shut.

"...Fat-ass finally let go, but he did not go down. So I kicked him in the nuts a couple of times. Then he went down."

"Yeah," Hansen grinned, "He's pretty sore today. His balls are about the size of his head."

For a moment Hansen thought Bemo might actually smile, but he didn't. "Okay, Max. That'll do for now. Here in a little bit I'll be dropping in on Joe Buck. If he insists on pressing charges against you boys, I'll be out in a day or two with a warrant."

Bemo stared silently at Hansen for several long seconds. As he did so the bitterness in his dark eyes slowly subsided and what appeared to be a deep sadness took its place. "You will be back," Bemo grunted, "and you, and me, and everyone you bring to help you will be badly hurt. I know this to be true."

"How do you know that to be true, Max?" Hansen asked evenly.

"The Alekchi, Billy Harjo, told me a bad time is coming for Indians in these parts. He says he has seen the trees beginning to walk and shoot fire from their branches."

Having been raised in Choctaw country Hansen knew several Choctaw words and Alekchi happened to be one of them. It meant medicine man. Hansen never met the old Choctaw holy man, Billy Harjo, but he'd heard plenty about him. Knowing how strongly the Choctaws in the area believed in Harjo and his powers, Hansen fought hard to keep skepticism from showing on his face.

"What does that mean?" He asked Bemo.

"I don't know," Bemo responded solemnly, "Before I could ask, the Alekchi turned into a hawk and flew away."

"What?" Hansen blurted incredulously.

"Not really," Bemo smiled just so lightly. "I just like to watch the expression on white people's faces when I say shit like that."

Hansen took a minute to laugh at himself, then he asked, "Did he really say that about the trees?"

"He really said that. But Billy told me he does not know what it means when the trees start to walk and shoot fire from their branches. He is very old, you know. He does not interpret signs and wonders as well as he used to. But he knows this sign is a bad one." Then with an ornery grin, Bemo said, "Maybe you ought to go and see what Billy will tell you about his vision."

Hansen smiled, winked, and nodded his head knowingly as he turned and stepped off the porch. Billy Harjo supposedly took a vow as a young man to never speak the white man's language, and reportedly hadn't done so in the past seventy years.

"No, Max, maybe you ought to go talk to him again," Hansen called over his shoulder as he made his way to the cruiser. Before cramming his huge frame into the comparatively small driver's compartment, he added, "Maybe you should ask the Alekchi for the wisdom to go peacefully when and if I have to come back and arrest you."

"Maybe I should ask the old medicine man to turn me into a hawk, and I will fly away," Bemo responded.

The Choctaw's expression had again turned solemn. This time he didn't smile.

Joe Swiretynsky took a second to remind himself that many, many years earlier it had been Rose's liberal attitudes and independent way of thinking that first attracted him. Back in the early seventies, so-called "liberated" women were just enough of an oddity to be considered chic. For reasons

Joe could no longer remember, back then Jewish women who did not act Jewish had been a real turn-on for him.

"Rose, Rose, Rose," he muttered while pacing in front of the grandiose fireplace in his mahogany-paneled study. "How can you suggest such a detriment to our only child's future, and then just sit there so calmly?"

From her relaxed position in a nearby overstuffed chair, Rose nonchalantly displayed her hands in the air and responded, "Because quite frankly, Joseph, I do not consider it detrimental for Jacob to attend a public school."

Going with his initial response, Joe grabbed his head in both hands and moaned long and loud. "How, my dear wife, could it be anything but detrimental to pluck such a sensitive boy from one of the world's finest Jewish prep schools and subject him to the horrors of public education?"

"Now, you know, Joseph, that I have never liked the fact that we are preparing our son for a life in an anti-Semitic society by educating him in a Jewish school. I continually worry about how well Jacob will adapt to integration after his many years of segregation. Our son, Joseph, needs this experience," Rose said with great conviction.

Joe stopped pacing, spun to face his wife and assaulted the air above his head with a pointed index finger. "Our son needs the experience of being Jewish. He needs to continue to learn our ways and our history. What our son needs is to spend more time in the presence of his people, more time being required to study the Torah and the Talmud. What our son needs is…"

Rose interrupted with a wagging index finger, "Joseph, you're sounding Orthodox again!"

Joe struggled to keep his voice calm. Shouting at Rose was something he just did not do. "I am not sounding Orthodox. I'm sounding like one who conforms to the teachings and tenets of Reformed Judaism."

"I don't know." Rose again wagged her finger. "Sounds Orthodox to me."

Mimicking her sing-song rhythm, Joe asked, "How would you know?" With a mocking wag of his finger, he continued, "You don't know enough about our religion to know the difference!"

"Oh, Joseph," Rose said in a loving tone intended to shame. "Must we turn this into a forum on what little time I spend attending Synagogue?"

Rose made a good point, and Joe knew better than to venture into her worship habits and beliefs. Having been there too many times in the past, he knew it would only add to his frustration. His efforts would be better spent trying to get his point across.

"We brought that child into a Jewish home," Joe sighed with all the patience he could muster. "He has accepted our faith as his own. We owe it to him to provide the most suitable environment for learning what it is to be Jewish."

Rose smiled the smile she'd used for years to tug at Joe's heartstrings. "And with that I agree, but I believe there is no better place for him to learn than in this home.

And there can be no better teacher than his devoted, loving father."

"Your attempts to sway me will not work this time, Rose," Joe said just as the phone on the nearby desk rang. "At stake is something far too precious…" Joe began, then stopped in mid-sentence as Rose walked over to the phone. She looked relieved at the opportunity to do so.

"Hello," Rose answered sweetly while flashing one of her "you-can't-win-so-don't-even-try" smiles at Joe.

"This is she," Rose said into the receiver with the smile still intact.

The smile vanished, and Joe interpreted her new expression as sudden shock.

Rose reached for Joe with a trembling hand, and he moved closer to grasp it. For long seconds she silently held the receiver to her ear, staring wide-eyed at her husband's face. Her normally pink cheeks turned ashen pale as she uncharacteristically stammered her next response.

"Well, uh, yes, I, uh, am sure we'll ah, ah…be here. But why…why now?"

Then again she just listened as her grip on Joe's hand tightened.

"All right," she eventually murmured, "We'll talk then."

Rose hung up the phone without a good-bye. Where their son would attend school no longer burned as an issue with Joe.

Rose did not immediately respond to her husband's questions. She couldn't. First, she had to sit down. Then she had to take several long, deep breaths.

"That was Vicki Templin," she finally managed to speak.

Vicki's maiden name registered just as immediately with Joe as it had Rose.

"Oh, no," he groaned before plopping down in a chair beside her.

"She wants to meet him, Joe," she said in a voice sounding too weak and scared to be her own. "She's coming here next week. She wants to speak to us about Jacob spending the summer in Oklahoma."

"That will not happen," Joe bellowed as he shot out of his chair. "We will not allow this!"

Fighting off the instinct to stand defiantly with her husband, Rose sighed, "You and I have no right to disallow this," she capitulated.

"What are you saying?" He had an edge to his voice she seldom heard.

"He is fourteen," Rose said with her voice starting to break. "The decision to meet his biological parents…to spend the summer with them…must be made by Jacob."

She sat silently for a moment before starting to sob. Joe pulled her up and into an embrace she desperately needed.

Hansen had no particular reason for disliking Joe Buck.

He just did. So before stepping into the man's store and cafe, Hansen forced an attitude check. After all, no matter how Hansen felt about Buck, he was a respected business owner and constituent.

Every time Hansen entered the store he found Buck perched on a stool behind the checkout counter. The same held true today.

"Hi'ya, Burl," Buck offered in a friendly enough tone.

"Buck," Hansen muttered with a nod of his head.

"Did you come to tell me you got that big drunk Indian in jail?"

"Nope. No one has filed charges against him."

"Well, goddamn man, I'll file charges against the asshole," Buck snorted.

"For what?"

"For tearing this fucking place up." Buck's cheeks suddenly glowed red.

"Are you going to file charges against the other two men as well?"

"Hell, no. They can't help it if that blanket-ass was slinging them around like a wrecking ball."

"Do you know who started the fight?" Hansen asked while trying to keep an attitude from sounding in his voice. Buck really tended to piss him off.

"Nope. I don't have any idea," Buck said as he shook his pasty, fat face." But it don't make a damn to me who started it. It was that gut-eater that was doing the damage."

"You'll sign charges and appear in court?"

"You damned straight I will." Buck slammed his hand on the counter.

"Okay," Hansen said as he turned and started out the door. "I'll send a deputy out with the paperwork."

"Hey, Hansen," Buck panted before the sheriff could make his exit. "Why do I get the feeling that you're taking up for that asshole?"

Hansen took a deep, cleansing breath before responding. "I just hate to see the man go to jail if what he did was in self-defense."

Buck slid off his stool and waddled around the corner. "Hell, what difference does it make if he's in jail? He'll still draw his welfare check and own his free land that our taxes paid for."

"That's neither here nor there, Buck," Hansen grumbled.

"The hell it ain't. I'm just like about every other good ol' boy in these parts, Hansen. I'm tired of this bullshit attitude of our niggers and Indians, that just because I'm white and middle-class that I owe them something. I don't owe them a damned thing. I never owned a slave and I didn't whip the red man's ass and throw him off his land. I'm tired of being wrong just because of the color of my skin!"

Hansen shrugged his shoulders. He'd heard it all before. Probably well over half the white males in his county shared Buck's sentiments. And there were times Hansen couldn't disagree with them.

"Well, I'm getting paid by your taxes, too. I better get out there and get busy or you'll be after my ass!"

Buck followed Hansen out the door. "I'm serious, Sheriff. I remember a time when the niggers and Indians in these parts acted right. They didn't play this affirmative action you-owe-me bullshit. But, hell, that's all changing." He continued on his soapbox, "I remember a time we didn't have any foreigners. Now we got Mexicans working all over the county and practically every doctor we have is Asian. All we need now to round out our little melting pot is a few fucking Muslims and a couple of goddamned Jews!"

Hansen crawled into his car without a word. Now he had his reason to dislike Buck.

Max Bemo kept eight hounds that barked and howled at nearly everything that moved. Sometimes they just barked to be barking, but sometimes they meant business. Bemo knew the difference between their barks and howls.

At a little past three in the morning after the big sheriff's visit, the hounds started raising hell. Bemo could not mistake their message. Through an alcoholic haze he struggled off his bare mattress and stumbled toward the front door of his shack. Before reaching it, a couple of the dogs' howls changed to blood-curdling yelps of pain.

Bemo practically took the door off its already shoddy

hinges. His momentum carried him off the porch and into his small and cluttered front yard. The light from a full moon allowed him to watch his dogs scattering in all directions — their tails tucked tightly between their legs. They weren't running from Bemo. He never gave them any reason to fear him.

Before he could determine what spooked them, something landed on his shoulders and immediately attacked his neck. Bemo grabbed desperately at the thing around his throat, his fingers landing on strands of a heavy rope.

Bemo clawed at the noose, but was jerked from his feet. He quickly sobered enough to realize the other end of the rope was tied to a bumper or maybe even a trailer hitch. For several yards he felt every rock and bump on the rough ground beneath him. And then Max Bemo felt nothing at all.

Chapter Six

Hansen walked into Flodell's Diner to find Chuck Turner already seated in a booth. Trisha Bottoms stood next to the booth and leaned in close to Turner. As they often did, the chief of police and waitress talked in hushed tones. Hansen knew some folks around town suspected the two of having an affair, but Hansen considered the suspicions ridiculous. Turner and Trisha's husband, Johnny Bottoms, were simply too good of friends. Turner had his faults, but disloyalty and a lack of integrity didn't number among them. The only thing Turner and Trisha Bottoms had going on was a mutual passion for hearing and passing gossip.

When Hansen reached the booth, the conversation between Trisha and Turner ended abruptly. The gorgeous blonde stepped aside to allow Hansen to wedge himself into the tight space across from Turner. Hansen thought nothing of the private discussions; they were common occurrences between the two. Besides gossiping, Trisha liked to confide in Turner. He had a reputation of a man who could keep a secret.

"I got this one's order," Trisha said as she cut sparkling blue eyes at Turner. "What are you having, Burl?"

Hansen squirmed in his seat to get comfortable and fought for knee space with Turner. The town cop wasn't as big as Hansen, but big enough to make sitting across from him in a booth somewhat of a challenge. The two of them alone filled the booth made for four. "Bring me a couple of those deluxe hamburgers, some fries and coffee."

Turner chuckled, shook his bald head, and said, "Why don't you have her just slap a couple pieces of bread around an entire cow for you?"

"Can you do that?" Hansen winked at Trisha.

"Well, if I could do it for anyone, honey, you'd be the one I'd do it for," Trisha winked back before sashaying away to turn in the orders.

"What have you been up to?" Turner asked as he dug a pack of cigarettes out of a pocket of his uniform.

"I've been working on getting a warrant for Max Bemo. I can't believe that asshole Joe Buck wants to pursue this."

"His store got the shit torn out of it, Burl. What do you expect him to do?"

"File against his insurance," Hansen grunted. "Having Bemo thrown in jail isn't going to earn him a single penny of reimbursement."

"That's true," Turner said as he lit the cigarette dangling from his lips. "But do you think Bemo should get off without punishment?"

"I don't think Bemo's to blame. I think he was just defending himself. At the very least, the other two guys ought to be going to jail, too."

"They're not going to jail?" Turner asked after blowing a plume of smoke up toward the ceiling.

"No. Buck didn't file charges on them. He believes Bemo is to blame for all the damage. Buck's just a bigot!" Hansen then shared Joe Buck's sentiments on those outside the white race.

When Hansen finished, Turner took one last drag off the cigarette, stubbed it out in the tray and exclaimed with a puff of smoke, "I can't totally disagree with Buck."

"You're shitting me!" Hansen huffed.

"No. I'm not shitting you. I can kind of relate to his point," Turner said with the ever-present twinkle dancing in his pale blue eyes. "Hell, Burl, every time me or one of my men arrest a black person or an Indian…and it don't matter what they've done…they say we are arresting them just because we're prejudiced. Now, you tell me that don't happen to you and your deputies."

Hansen knew he might come up with an exception if he thought long enough, but couldn't immediately recall a time when that very thing had not occurred.

"Another thing Burl, I'm sorry, but I'm just pretty damned tired of their bitching and moaning about wanting equality. From where I sit, it looks like they got their equality and are insisting on superiority. Now, does what I think and feel make me a bigot as well?"

Hansen couldn't count the times he'd witnessed Turner interacting with minorities. If he had prejudices, he did one fine job concealing the fact. "Hell no, you're not a bigot," Hansen conceded.

Turner lit up another cigarette and posed a question bracketed in smoke. "Burl, how many blacks do you have working for you?"

"Same amount you do. None."

"Okay. Why don't you have any black employees?"

"I've never had any apply for a job."

"Same here. Now tell me this," Turner said before pausing to inhale deeply on the cigarette, "if you had an opening and a black man applied, and he was the best qualified for the job, would you hire him over a lesser qualified white man?"

"Chuck, what do you think? I've been a jock all my life. I've probably had fewer white team members than black. Subsequently, I've had dozens of black friends."

"So you would hire the best qualified person, regardless of color?"

"Well, of course I would. I don't make decisions about people based on the shade of their skin."

"I don't think I do either, and I'd hire the better qualified black man, too. All right, let's say you have an opening and a black man applies and he's not the best qualified, so, you hire a white man instead. Let's say this black man raises all kinds of hell…contacts the N double A-C-P, the ACLU, and every black politician in the state, and because of some Affirmative Action laws or policies, you have to hire the black man. Now, first of all, could this happen?"

"Could it? Probably," Hansen admitted.

"Probably my ass! It happens all the time. Secondly, if it did happen, would it piss you off?"

"Yeah, it would," Hansen nodded reluctantly.

"Would that make you a bigot?"

"I don't want to discuss this shit anymore," Hansen said, shaking his head.

Turner laughed out loud. "It can get complicated, can't it?"

"Yeah, it sure can."

Hansen felt a sense of relief when Trisha showed up with their food. Both men remained silent as the waitress leaned over to deliver their food. Both men eyed the cleavage always visible when Trisha leaned. The silent observance had become a ritual between the two old friends.

After Trisha had once again swayed away, Turner cut into his chicken-fried steak and said, "You know, what's really tragic is that when a better qualified white man loses an opportunity to a lesser qualified black man because of Affirmative Action, the white man has only one recourse…to hate. That's pretty damned sad."

Hansen nodded his head. He'd filled his mouth too

full of hamburger to do any more.

Hansen worked at devouring his second burger when Turner guided the conversation back to Bemo's impending arrest.

"So anyway, did you get the warrant for Bemo?"

"Yeah, I got it."

"Do you still have that stupid notion of serving it by yourself?"

"Yup, still got it."

"You know, you are past the age where macho shit like that should appeal to you. It would serve you right if that big Indian was to stomp your ass," Turner half teased, half warned.

"Going after him by myself has nothing to do with being macho. It's a matter of principle. Bemo would lose all respect for me if I was to show up with help."

"So what? Who gives a shit if that mean bastard respects you or not?"

"I give a shit. And so does every Choctaw Indian in the county. You and the other whites around here might not think much of Bemo, but he's held in high esteem by the tribe. Besides, I think if I was to show up with help, he'd feel obliged to resist. And on top of that, you don't think he can stomp my ass anyway!"

Then as an afterthought Hansen added, "Do you?"

"I don't know," Turner grinned, "but that would be one hell of a fight to watch."

"Aw, hell," Hansen emphasized with a wave of his hand, "there won't be a fight. He'll come peacefully."

As Hansen washed down his last French fry with a swig of coffee, Turner started telling about the time Bemo whipped three of his best officers. Hansen had heard it before and was paying little attention when he noticed Teddy Hallum entering the restaurant. The old black man looked weary, like any grandfather would who had a grandson missing without plausible explanation.

Hallum made his way to Hansen's booth with the careful gait of a man too old to risk a fall. Turner had his back to the door and didn't see Hallum until he ambled up alongside the booth. Turner reached the part of the story where Bemo finished up with the third officer, but he stopped in mid-sentence.

"Well, hello, Teddy." Turner smiled politely as he scooted over to make room for the elderly gentleman. "Have a seat."

"I'd rather stand, Mr. Turner," Hallum replied coolly. Then to Hansen he said without a smile, "Hello, Sheriff."

Hansen returned the greeting and noticed Turner stiffen at Hallum's abruptness.

"Teddy here is upset with me, Burl," Turner said wearily.

"My grandson didn't run away, Mr. Turner," Hallum said with a shake of his ancient head. "I keep telling you that, but you won't listen to me. I keep telling you that that boy cared too much for his future to throw it away on some girl. He loved football too much for that. He ain't the kind of boy to just up and run away. Darrell wouldn't do that to me and his grandma."

"I know you keep telling me all that, Teddy," Turner replied patiently. "And I've listened to you, but the truth is I've done all there is to do."

Hallum straightened as much as possible a back bent by too many years of hard work. "You'd do more if he was some white boy."

Hansen noticed Turner bristle, but the chief replied calmly, "Teddy, he ran away with a *white girl*, so why am I doing no more to find her than I am your grandson? That doesn't make sense."

"It makes all kind of sense, Mr. Turner, because in the eyes of the whites, when that poor girl decided to take up with a black boy, she made herself as worthless as any nigger in the county."

"Now, Teddy, there is no need to…"

Hallum held up a shaky palm and interrupted. "I'm going to Senator Bristow about this, Mr. Turner. I'm going to see if he can't get something done."

Marcus Bristow was Oklahoma's only black United States Congressman.

"Well, Teddy, a man has to do what a man has to do," Turner said without malice. "I wish you all the luck in the world."

As the old man hobbled away, Hansen sympathized with his pain and frustration, but he had to side with Turner. The chief had no reason to treat the Baker and Rafell case as any more than a runaway. He had, in fact, done all that could be done. Additionally, Hansen could understand a part of the tragedy that the old man couldn't. Hansen knew what it was to be a young man with great athletic skills and a bright future afforded by those skills. He also knew what it was to be very young and very much in love. Hansen could distinctively remember how serious he had been about giving up his dreams for a life with Vicki and their baby. It appeared more than possible that Darrel Baker had done exactly that for Shelly Rafell.

"I have a confession to make," Turner said, rousing Hansen from his thoughts. "At this very moment, I'm thinking things only a raging bigot would be thinking."

Hansen offered his best friend a grin and a wink before offering a tidbit of contemporary wisdom. "Don't be hatin'!"

Jacob sensed something wrong long before being called into his father's study. For the past two days his parents simply had not been themselves. Something weighed heavily on their minds, and by all indications, he feared it to be something of great significance. Being called into the grand room of marble, mahogany and leather only confirmed Jacob's suspicions of something awry.

Access to the study had never been given easily to Jacob. The room truly functioned as the sanctum sanctorum of the Swiretynsky mansion, and Joseph Swiretynsky served as the high priest. Here the doctor retreated after long hours at the hospital. Here he spent time with his favorite books and did his thinking and rejuvenating. Even Rose Swiretynsky spent little time in the room. Jacob always thought that maybe she, too, felt unwelcome there, but she often described the study as too formal and masculine for her tastes.

Jacob normally was summoned into the cavernous chamber when his father's expectations had not been met. The last time had been for making a "B+" instead of the mandatory "A" on a biology test. Once in a great while, a trip to the study resulted in something good for him, but Jacob couldn't remember the last time that had happened. On most occasions, the trip netted only bad. In the study, Jacob had learned his mother would undergo a mastectomy. In the study, he'd been informed that Daniel Swiretynsky, his grandfather, had died.

Many times Jacob at least had an idea why he was wanted in the study. This time he didn't have a clue. However, the moment he walked through the two floor to ceiling doors, he knew he wasn't in trouble. His parents were smiling. Not being in trouble, however, brought Jacob little relief. The smiles they wore were not at all natural. They were obviously smiling to take the edge off some terrible news.

His father occupied his seat behind the massive desk. His mother stood beside him with her arms folded across her chest. She hugged herself as if cold.

"Please come in and sit down, son," Joe sighed as he motioned to one of the two wingback chairs sitting across from the desk.

His father tended to sigh when worried. Jacob chose the chair on the right and inhaled deeply. Then he blurted, "Something bad has happened."

"No. Nothing bad has happened," Joe said, unconvincingly. "Something has developed, however, that causes your mother and me a great deal of concern."

"But!" Rose blurted as she moved away from her husband and toward Jacob. "We do not intend for our concerns to impact negatively on this development."

"I would have added that, dear," Joe said only somewhat patiently.

"Of course you would have, darling," Rose forcibly responded as she rounded the corner of the desk. Her tone of voice made it apparent to Jacob that she had taken charge of explaining the "development."

Sitting down on the very edge of the chair next to Jacob, Rose turned to face him and then reached out and took his hand. "Your biological mother wishes to meet you, Jacob."

Within an instant, a host of feelings laid siege to Jacob's heart and mind, the most dominant of which was confusion. He had no memory of a time when he did not know he'd been adopted. His parents raised him with the fact. Memories of some of his earliest conversations with his "adopted" mother were about his "biological" mother. The possibility of one day meeting the woman who gave birth to him, had always been discussed as very likely and had always been portrayed as a good thing. But right now, this did not seem to be the case.

"I've always expressed a desire to meet her," Jacob responded cautiously.

"And I always thought you should," Rose agreed. "But this is somewhat different. She wants you to spend the summer in Oklahoma with her. She wants you to meet the rest of..." Rose paused to clear her throat, "...the rest of your family."

Jacob's head reeled at the thought of spending the summer far from home in the company of total..."The rest of my family?" The entire message penetrated the sudden mind-fog and left him feeling numb.

"Yes, Jacob. You have a younger brother and sister," Rose smiled weakly.

"Half," Jacob clarified automatically. "They would be my half brother and sister."

"As it turns out, sweetheart, your birth mother," Rose said as she squeezed his hand, "is married to your biological father. Their children are your true siblings."

Jacob pulled his hand free from his mother's and worked it in concert with his other hand to rub his throbbing temples. He knew his birth mother's age, the color of her eyes and hair, and even her height and weight at the time he'd been born. With Rose, he had spent hours discussing what she might be like, and hundreds of hours just thinking about her. He felt he practically knew Vicki Templin, yet he always expected extreme anxiety would accompany their first meeting.

About his blood father, Jacob knew absolutely nothing. And although he often wondered what the man might be like, Jacob never expected to meet him. Furthermore, he never even dreamed of having a brother or a sister.

The thought of meeting just one long-lost blood relative felt daunting enough. The possibility that not just one person, but four, might be disappointed with his appearance or find fault with his mannerisms, simply seemed too threatening for him to consider.

While contemplating all that needed contemplation, Jacob stared into his lap and studied his pudgy, soft hands. Finally, he thought out loud, "Oklahoma is terribly far away...and an entire summer is a very long time."

In unison, his parents exhaled what could have only been sighs of relief.

Hansen parked next to the '74 Ford Maverick resting on rims and rusting away in Max Bemo's front yard. The door to the dilapidated house stood wide open but it didn't surprise him. Bemo lived no differently than most of the whites residing in the hills of Pushmataha County. The open door allowed gentle spring breezes to enter and the hounds to come and go as they pleased. It was simply a backwoods practicality.

The sheriff got out of his car and took a few steps around the assortment of junk Bemo considered landscaping. After propping his left boot up on a discarded engine block and leaning forward to rest a forearm on a knee, he shouted, "Hey, Max, you have company!"

A few howls sounded from beneath the front porch, and a skinny Blue Tick hound hobbled out of the house and high-tailed it away from Hansen. But Bemo offered no response in return.

Hansen scanned the outbuildings still standing on the old farm place but spotted no sign of the owner. "Hey! Bemo!" He shouted louder. "Are you in there?"

Bemo did not respond. Hansen strode to the house and stepped up on the rickety porch, careful to stand to one side of the open door. This time he didn't expect an answer but once again called the Choctaw's name as his mind processed possibilities.

Bemo could still be sleeping off last night's alcohol. He could have left without bothering to close his door. Or, he might be lurking inside, awake, intending to resist arrest. Hansen grimaced at the thought — he might soon wish he had brought help.

Hansen unsnapped his holster strap and rested his right hand on the grips of his .357. He then crept to and crouched against the wall to the right of the doorway. For a fraction of a second he felt protected by the wall of thin material but then realized that any bullet that could be blocked by such a meager barrier probably couldn't take him down anyway. Along with the realization came the hard, cold truth. If Bemo stood inside with a gun and intended to use it, Hansen would already be dead.

"Bemo, if you're in there…here I come!"

He walked up-right though the doorway with his weapon holstered, only to fall blind until his eyes adjusted to the dark. For those terrible long seconds, brutal images of what could happen assaulted his imagination. Finally, when could see, he didn't see Bemo — not in the small living room, not in the kitchen and not in the single bedroom. But some things in the bedroom did catch his eye.

A kitchen chair sat next to the bed. A pair of jeans was draped over the back of the chair, and a pair of boots lay on the gritty linoleum floor between the chair and bed. The window next to the bed had been raised high enough that even a man Bemo's size could have crawled through it.

Hansen bent low to peer out the window. Just twenty or so yards away from the house grew a tree line with dense undergrowth. He could practically feel Bemo staring back at him from the tangled brush. Knowing he could be out there was one thing. Doing something about it was entirely another. Any white man with a lick of sense didn't chase into the woods after a Choctaw Indian. Hansen would just have to come back later. If Bemo wanted to play these kinds of games, Hansen planned to be a lot sneakier next time.

Chapter Seven

Her children's shrill laughter coaxed Vicki out of the house. She plopped into the closest lawn chair on the covered patio and inhaled a breath of early spring air as she settled in to watch the activity producing the wonderful laughter.

Her husband lumbered from the grain silo to the corral, which contained his prized cutting horse — a giant sorrel named Hercules. Burl's arms stretched taut against the sides of his body as he carried two ten gallon buckets of feed toward Hercules' trough. On each broad shoulder, Vicki's husband bore a child. Sandy straddled his left shoulder, and Bret his right. The brother and sister faced each other and hung on for dear life with hands full of their father's hair and ears. Burl seemed oblivious to their weight and gleeful shrieks.

He was a wonderful husband and father, gentle and kind with the ones he loved. For that, Vicki often gave thanks. She knew how ferocious he'd been on the football field and she'd heard tales of how he sometimes carried out his law enforcement duties with law-breaking combatants. Therefore, Vicki considered the side of him he shared with his family a wonderful gift from God.

Burl dumped the feed into the trough and headed back to the silo with the children still bouncing on his shoulders. He smiled broadly, saying something to his kids. The father greatly enjoyed time spent with his son and daughter. The three of them were a pretty tight-knit group. The smile on Vicki's lips faded away as she considered that fact. Could the three of them find room for one more?

As of yet, Sandy and Bret knew nothing about Jacob spending the summer. For that matter, they didn't even know Jacob existed. They didn't know they had a brother, and Vicki didn't know how to tell them. This counted as just one of the many aspects of the venture she needed to talk about with Burl, but Burl hadn't been very talkative about it. When she brought up the topic of Jacob, Burl would listen thoughtfully, but he seldom responded with more than nods, grunts, and one syllable words. It wasn't that he acted negatively about Jacob, he simply didn't act at all. Vicki didn't have a clue what he truly thought or felt about having a second son for the summer. In that she would depart for Boston next week, a lot had to be said and little time remained to say it.

Hansen completed most of his chores before stopping at the patio and pulling a chair up close to Vicki. He sat down before noticing how deep in thought she seemed to be. If he'd made the observation two seconds earlier, he would've kept right on going past the patio.

"I go to Boston next Thursday," she sighed.

Hansen adjusted his weight in the chair he didn't quite trust to hold him. To keep from looking at his wife, he let his gaze fall upon his son's frenzied activity. One of the cats living in the big, red barn had dropped a litter of seven kittens two months earlier. Bret now chased one of them around the barnyard.

"That boy is about to get scratched all to hell again," Burl sighed. "It looks like he'd eventually learn that those kittens don't particularly care for him." Hansen actually didn't ignore Vicki's statement. He just side-stepped it.

"Burl, we have to discuss Jacob spending the summer with us."

Damn. Ever since the woman revealed her intentions, she'd been talking about the summer as if it were a done deal. Hansen admired her optimism, but it was getting tedious. After some strained moments ending in a long sigh, he decided to humor her. After all, no adoptive parent in his right mind would ever agree to what his wife proposed.

"Okay. I'm listening," he smiled.

"You're always listening, but you don't say anything in return. That isn't discussing, and discussing is what we need to do."

"All right," he moaned in a Bret-type fashion. "I'll discuss. Where do you want to start?"

"How and when do we tell them?" Vicki asked while pointing a finger in the direction of the barn.

This is an easy one, Hansen thought while fighting back the urge to smile. "We don't tell them anything until we know for sure what's going to happen. So we'll talk to them when you get back from Boston next week."

"I know for sure what's going to happen, Burl," Vicki said sharply. "I've prayed about this too much not to know that God's going to let it happen. Jacob will be right here with us in less than two months time."

Hansen knew that tone of voice too well to waste time arguing with it. "How is it going to affect the kids knowing…what we did…what happened…that we have another child?"

"At the ages they are now, they'll probably just think it's *cool* that they have an older brother they've never met. I don't think it will scar them for life if that's what you're worried about."

Hansen smirked at his wife but didn't say anything. After all, she could be right. Although he believed they wouldn't have the boy for the summer, Sandy and Bret would have to find out about him sooner or later. Probably best to make it sooner.

"Okay. Tell them."

"How?"

"Start at the beginning and end at the ending."

The answer seemed to satisfy Vicki.

Both children did indeed find the entire situation "cool." When Hansen came into the house after finishing his work to find his wife and children still discussing all the fun things they could do over the summer with their *new* brother, he decided it would be a good time to try to catch Max Bemo at home. Hansen had stayed away for two days to let Bemo think he might not be coming back. Now, just after dark, it should be at least an hour or two before Bemo would head for the bars.

This time the sheriff didn't pull his car into the front yard. Instead, he parked a quarter of a mile away and worked his way through the woods so as to approach the back of the shack. When he reached the clearing just behind the house, it both surprised and disappointed Hansen to find the place dark and quiet. The hounds weren't even baying and they should have picked up his scent long before now.

He crouched and carefully made his way across the small clearing to the window outside Bemo's bedroom. Just enough moonlight existed to see the window again stood open, and still no dogs barked. Hansen came to rest on his knees below the window and listened carefully for noises inside the house but heard nothing. Several long minutes of silence convinced Hansen he'd missed Bemo and he decided to take a peek into the bedroom.

He brought his large metal flashlight with him but had not yet turned it on. Now he raised it high above his head, pointed it into the open window and turned it on. After no apparent response to the sudden and bright beam of light, Hansen cautiously rose and peered into the window only to find the pair of jeans he'd seen two days earlier still draped across the chair by the bed. He aimed the beam downward to find the same pair of boots lying on the linoleum floor. Hansen started for the front of the house, convinced he would not find Bemo inside. The front door stood wide open — the way Hansen last left it. Still, not a single dog made an appearance. Hansen felt a foreboding twinge in the pit of his gut.

As best as Hansen could tell, nothing had been changed or disturbed in the house since the last time he came looking for Bemo. He picked up the pair of jeans from the chair and found Bemo's wallet in the back pocket. The big Indian hadn't just stepped out for a while. He was gone. The perplexing fact caused Hansen to recall the last words Bemo spoke to him.

"Maybe I should ask the old medicine man to turn me into a hawk, and I will fly away."

He'd certainly disappeared, but Hansen dreaded nothing as benign as glorious wings carrying him away.

"I'm still not convinced he's going to talk to us," Hansen mumbled as he turned onto the dirt road leading to the Alekchi's house.

"He will talk to us, goddammit!" Chuck Turner asserted from the passenger's seat with vigorous nods of his head.

"I know you've been saying that all morning, but they claim he hasn't talked to a white man in over seventy years."

"If by *they* you are talking about the Choctaws," Turner grinned, "*they* also claim he turns himself into wolves and bears and eagles and shit like that."

Earlier at breakfast Hansen explained to Turner what he'd found at Bemo's place the night before. Since Bemo mentioned having recent contact with Billy Harjo, the chief of police suggested they pay the old medicine man a visit.

"I know some really bright and educated Indians who believe he actually can do all that," Hansen said without taking his eyes off the winding road.

"Well, if he has that kind of power, it should be easy for him to tell us what happened to Bemo," Turner mumbled before lighting up a cigarette.

Turner had agreed it was highly unlikely Max Bemo would go anywhere without his wallet, or that he'd leave barefooted — both men betting Bemo didn't own another pair of shoes. Like Hansen, Turner expressed a gut feeling that Bemo probably wasn't going to turn up alive. The two old friends figured Bemo probably met up once again with the two men he'd badly beaten in Joe Buck's Cafe and Convenience Store.

The old man sat on the front porch in a stained and ragged recliner. He turned his head toward Hansen and Turner as they approached and rotated firm and unflinching eyes from one man to the other.

Both lawmen walked up to the edge of the small porch and stopped.

"Hello, Mr. Harjo. I'm Burl Hansen and this is the chief of police at Antlers, Chuck Turner," Hansen said with his right hand extended.

Harjo moved his gaze to the outstretched hand, held it there for a second or two before straightening his head to look away from Hansen and Turner. The sheriff dropped his hand back to his side. He didn't sense animosity, just indifference.

"Mr. Harjo, we are here to ask you some questions about Max Bemo," Hansen began. "He's disappeared, and we're concerned about his welfare. Have you by any chance seen or heard from him in the past couple of days?"

The drawn face of countless and deep wrinkles that crisscrossed like roadways on a map registered no emotion. In fact, Harjo responded only by bringing his thin arms up and crossing them over his chest.

"Listen, Billy," Turner interjected, "We believe you might have been one of the last people to see Bemo. He could be in deep shit. You might be the only one able to help him."

Harjo feebly raised one hand to swat a fly away from his face but remained silent. Hansen viewed the action as symbolic of what the old man felt about the officers. The fly settled on one of two long braids that still held some black in them but had turned mostly a dingy-looking gray.

"Even if Bemo's all right," Turner continued, but this time with an edge to his voice, "we've got a warrant for his arrest and unless you want an interfering charge slapped on your ass, you best get to talking."

The squeak of an opening screen door caused Hansen and Turner to jerk their heads in that direction. A lean and fit looking Choctaw who appeared to be in his late twenties stepped out of the house. The man wasn't very tall, but stood erect. He wore coal black hair neatly cut into a flat-top.

"He hasn't talked to a white man in many years," the young man offered in a voice void of an Indian or Okie accent.

"So I've heard," Turner grumbled. "Who are you?"

"I'm Mike Walker. Billy's my grandfather. I've been staying here with him for the past week and a half, and Max Bemo hasn't been here."

When the young man finished, the old man started. His words were to his grandson, were not English, and seemed to go on forever. Although Harjo's voice seemed weak, the language he spoke sounded forceful. Mike Walker appeared to listen carefully until Harjo finished speaking, then responded with a simple, "Yes, sir."

"My grandfather wants you to know that it is not hate that prevents him from talking to white people. As a young man, he was told in a vision not to use white man's words. He doesn't know why, but says it's not good to go against a vision. He believes all people should try to live in peace and help each other whenever they can. He wants you to know that he will gladly talk to a white man…if he ever meets one that speaks the Choctaw language.

"Finally, he says he can't help you find Max Bemo, but that he had a dream two nights ago that he was talking to Max, but that Max could not talk back. My grandfather says this is a very bad sign, and he wants me to show you something he thinks you should see."

As Hansen turned to follow Mike Walker, Turner leaned over and gently placed a hand on Harjo's bony shoulder. "We might need to talk to you some more in a little while," he said with a playful smile, "So, don't you be flying off anywhere!"

The revered medicine man continued to look straight ahead, yet to Hansen's surprise, Harjo's thin, pursed lips moved to form a smile — one that could only be described as cocky.

Hansen and Turner followed Mike Walker behind and down below Harjo's house to an old barn. When they reached the backside of the barn, Walker didn't have to point out what he wanted them to see.

A crudely animated head roughly five feet in diameter was painted in black midway up the back wall. A headband with a single feather, braids, and a large crooked nose left nothing to the imagination about what the artist had intended to depict. The entire wall stood riddled with at least a hundred small holes.

"Bullet holes," Turner observed.

"Five-point-five-six millimeter," Walker confirmed. "Follow me and I'll show you the casings."

The three men walked out of the small pasture and into a copse of trees. Walker stopped just inside the cover of the trees and started pointing out the brass shells lying scattered on the ground.

Hansen picked one up. "You're right, Mr. Walker. They're definitely five-point-five-six."

"Yes sir," Walker responded. "And they were fired on full automatic from what I'd bet were M16 rifles."

"Full auto M16 rifles? That's bullshit," Turner snarled.

Turner's agitated response surprised Hansen. He turned around and looked at his notoriously easy-going friend. Turner's frown and furrowed brow surprised Hansen even more. When the two men's eyes met, Turner evidently detected the surprise. His troubled expression quickly changed to one of embarrassment.

"Okay. I'll bite, Walker," Turner said with just slightly more civility as he turned away from Hansen. "What makes you think this was done by automatic weapons?"

"First of all, Grandfather was out in his backyard when this happened. He said it sounded like a single clap of terribly loud thunder. For as many rounds as we can prove were fired, it would take a long time to put that many bullets down-range with bolt-action or semi-automatic rifles.

"Secondly, it's only twenty-five meters from here to the barn. The rounds are scattered all over the wall, and I've found other holes in trees and outbuildings both to the left and the right of the intended target. Even the worst marksmen firing single-action would have put more rounds on the target. However, even expert riflemen would have difficulty controlling an M16 on full auto.

"Finally, if you'll study the pattern in which these casings were discharged, you'll see…"

"Just who in the hell and what the hell are you?" Turner suddenly huffed.

"I'm Captain Mike Walker, U.S. Army Special Forces. I'm a weapons expert, sir."

"Why in the fuck didn't you tell us that in the first place?" Turner growled.

Turner's highly uncharacteristic agitation perplexed Hansen. "Hey, uh, Chuck? What the hell, man?"

Turner mumbled something and turned aside, shaking his head. Hansen stepped up into his place, "How many shooters do you think there were, Captain?"

"Six. You can tell by the groupings of the casings and the boot prints left in a muddy creek bed about a hundred meters south of us."

"Damn," Hansen exhaled before mumbling his jumbled thoughts, "I have no idea who would do something like this…or why."

"There's one more thing, Sheriff," Walker said as he bent and scooped up a handful of the brass. "When Grandfather saw the men leaving to the south, he cut across to intersect their path in order to get a closer look. They crossed within feet of where he was hiding and he…"

"You mean to tell me…" Turner said as stepped back closer to Walker, "…that that feeble old man was able to make it through these woods fast enough to get that close?"

"Grandfather is still very good in the woods," Walker said matter-of-factly to Turner. He then looked back to Hansen. "My grandfather has a flair for theatrics, so in his words, he described what he saw as walking trees. From what I can get from him, they were wearing camouflaged trousers, shirts, and hats. They'd even gone as far as to camouflage their faces and hands."

At this, Turner emitted an exasperated sigh, turned on his heels and stomped off into the woods.

Hansen stared after his friend for a moment before turning again to Walker. "I suppose you're on leave?"

"Yes, sir. I'll be here for another two weeks. Longer if anything else like this happens."

"Good. We'll go back up to the house and I'll make out a report. Maybe with a little nosing around I can come up with…"

The exploding roar of a gunshot set Hansen to jerking frantically at the .357 strapped into his holster. Captain Walker hit the ground hard and fast. The single shot came from the direction Turner had gone. With a shout of his friend's name, Hansen bound into the woods with his gun in hand.

Hansen found Turner just yards away standing in a shooter's crouch with both hands gripping his nine millimeter. He intently scanned the woods in front of him with his finger tensed on the trigger.

"What is it?" Hansen shouted as he came breathlessly alongside Turner.

"It was a goddamned timber wolf!" Turner shouted back.

"A timber wolf?" Hansen gasped incredulously before dropping his gun down along his side.

"That's what I said, a goddamned timber wolf! It was standing right the fuck there," Turner exclaimed as he pointed just a few feet to his front with the barrel of his pistol. "The son of bitch growled at me. It was fucking huge. I thought it was going to attack me!"

"You must be mistaken, sir," Walker said from behind them.

Hansen and Turner wheeled around at the sound of the soldier's calm voice. The man could move like a whisper in the woods. Hansen would have guessed he was still back hugging the ground.

"No, sir," Captain Mike Walker grinned broadly, "There hasn't been timber wolves in Oklahoma for the last hundred or so years."

Turner waited in the car while Hansen wrote out a report. The chief had gone straight from the woods to the car and hadn't said another word to Harjo or his grandson.

Turner still sat brooding when Hansen climbed into the cruiser. The sheriff waited until they were turning out of the drive before asking a burning question. "What in the hell got twisted into your panties back there?"

"I'm telling you, Burl, I saw what I fuckin' saw!"

"I'm not talking about that. I'm talking about how you treated Walker. He wasn't doing a damned thing but telling us what happened, and you were getting all up in his ass."

Turner averted his eyes from Hansen and turned to look out the passenger window. For long seconds he remained quiet, and Hansen didn't push him.

"What do the shrinks call it when a person knows what's really happening, but doesn't want to believe it?"

Turner finally spoke, but he didn't turn back to look at Hansen.

"Denial?" Hansen answered.

"Yeah, that's it. Denial...I was in denial, Burl," Turner said, shooting Hansen a pained glance. "Plus, I guess I did a little of that shooting the messenger shit. I mean, hell, I kind of believed what he was saying. I just didn't want to. Jeez, man, we've got a bunch of nuts running around all camo'ed up and committing hate crimes with full automatic weapons? That just bothers the hell out of me. Don't it you?"

It did, and Turner's very unusual behavior suddenly made sense. "Yeah, it's damn sure scary," Hansen concluded as he reached for the microphone to his police radio.

"County One to dispatch," he said into the mike.

"Go ahead to dispatch, Sheriff," dispatcher Edna Flowers replied in her nasal twang.

"We're finished out here at Harjo's, Edna. We're headed back in."

"Ten four," Edna acknowledged. Then after a slight pause, she came back on the air, "Hey, Sheriff, we just got the report back from the OSBI on that stolen Ford Deputy Meeks recovered up around Albion. Since you have the chief with you, ya'll might be interested in hearing what they come up with."

"And what would that be, Edna?"

"Well, first Sheriff, they didn't get any good prints.

They think the car had been wiped down. But they did come up with a blood type and some hair. This is the kicker, Sheriff, they found a bunch of short black hair that they believe came from the head of an African-American."

It took Turner only seconds to make the connection. "Oh shit," he grumbled.

Hansen acknowledged the transmission, signed off, and stole a glance at his passenger. "It won't be Darrell Baker's hair. I still believe he ran off with the girl. Don't you?"

"I'm the one who saw the fucking timber wolf, Burl," Turner responded dryly. "So right this minute, I don't know what the hell to believe."

Chapter Eight

Hansen had already finished his breakfast and was sipping his third cup of coffee when Turner scooted into the booth across from him.

"Old man Hallum finally found some of his grandson's medical records in Chicago. The blood type matches," Turner grimaced.

"It is not his blood in that damned car," Hansen insisted.

"I would really like to believe for once that you actually know what you're talking about."

"Chuck, the blood in the car was A positive and Darrell Baker is A positive. So the hell what? A positive is one of the most common blood types. And nothing else fits either. How in the hell do you tie a car stolen in Durant and recovered in Albion to an alleged abduction in Antlers? And if Darrell is dead, where is Shelly Rafell? Where's her car? I'm telling you, Chuck, the kids are together and they'll surface before too long."

"That's easy for you to say, Burl. Teddy Hallum isn't feeding you a daily diet of I-told-you-so sandwiches dipped in shit!"

"Well, we all have our cross to bear," Hansen admitted just as Trisha Bottoms walked up with a pot of coffee.

"What'll it be for you this morning, sweetheart?" Trisha cooed to Turner as she bent to fill his cup and then refill Hansen's.

As she did so, Hansen absently picked at a few of the many ranch-work related scabs on his hands.

"Bring me a short stack, good lookin'," Turner winked. After Trisha swayed out of earshot he said to Hansen, "You didn't even sneak a peek at her tits."

"Damn, Chuck, her old man is a good friend of yours."

"So what? He knows she has great tits, and besides, you stare at them every other day. Man, you are in some kind of funky mood. What's wrong with you this morning?"

"Vicki's on her way to Oklahoma City. She's flying to Boston today."

"Oh...today's the day."

"Yeah, today is the day."

"So you've been saying the parents won't go along with it. Are you starting to think otherwise?"

"Not really, I mean if you'd adopted the kid and raised him and he was only fourteen would you allow him to go and stay three months with his biological parents?"

"Probably not."

"Me either."

"Well, there you have it. It's not going to happen."

"Right. But what's eating at me today…what if she pulls this off? As remote as the chances are…what if she pulls it off?"

"Well, then you're going to have Jacob for the summer. Would that really be so bad?"

"Yes, I think it would. I believe things are better off left just the way they are right now," Hansen sighed.

"Why do you feel that way?"

Hansen looked Turner in the eye for a second before waving him off with both palms and saying simply, "Awwwwwww, bullshit!"

"It was getting a little too touchy-feely for you wasn't it, big guy?" Turner ribbed. "Yup, big tough Burl Hansen can't be sharing his true feelings with his best friend in the entire world.

"You know, seriously, Burl, you need to learn to open up and talk about the things that are bothering you. You just need to learn to communicate. Hell, it would help you in all your relationships."

"Oh, you mean be more like you?" Hansen scoffed.

"Hell, yes. That's exactly what I mean."

"And how many wives have you had?"

"Four…but they were all non-communicative bitches!"

"Yeah. Whatever," Hansen concluded as Trisha approached with Turner's pancakes.

"More coffee, Burl?" she asked after setting the plate in front of Turner.

"No, thanks, Trish. I got to get to work here in a few minutes."

"So when will Vicki get back?" Turner asked when the waitress left.

"She's meeting with the boy and his parents today. She'll fly back first thing in the morning."

"I guess she'll give you a call tonight and let you know how it went?"

"She didn't say she would. Knowing her, she'll want to save the dollar or two the long distance call would cost."

"Damn, I'd be wanting to know immediately if he was coming or not."

"Like I've said, I'm sure he's not coming. The only reason I'd want to talk to her tonight would be to console her. I know she'll be hurting after they tell her no."

"Jeez," Turner smirked while shaking his head, "Console her? Poor woman. I can't imagine being consoled by someone as communicative and tender as an armadillo."

Vicki took a cab from the airport to Boston's Beth Israel Hospital. After getting initial directions from a receptionist at the desk, she still approached two additional employees to help her find the way to the hospital's cafeteria. She selected a table that offered an unobstructed view of the entrance, took a seat, and looked at her watch. She felt some comfort in being an hour early — about the only comfort she did feel. She could use the time to gather her wits and spend yet more time in prayer.

Rose Swiretynsky suggested meeting in the cafeteria. Joseph Swiretynsky was the chief cardiologist at Beth Israel. Considering the time of their meeting and the doctor's hectic schedule, Rose selected the cafeteria for the sake of convenience. Vicki knew there were certainly more neutral grounds on which they could meet but at least this would be better than meeting at the Swiretynsky home. Besides, she didn't need more neutral ground — she had Jesus.

Vicki got only thirty minutes to calm her nerves before Rose stepped into the cafeteria. Vicki recognized her immediately. With the exception of a few more pounds and a different way of wearing her thick, black hair, Rose looked as she had fourteen years earlier. Vicki struggled to her feet as Rose scanned the crowded dining room. Rose's large, dark eyes quickly locked on Vicki as the very dignified woman made her way to the table.

Vicki had carefully planned her first words, but she expected the three of them to make their appearance together. Now she didn't know what to say and developed an even worse case of the jitters. Why did Rose come alone? Had they decided to keep Jacob from her? Had he refused to come? Vicki bounced the questions around in her head and still struggled for initial words as Rose came to a stop in front of her.

For a fraction of a second Vicki believed the exquisitely dressed woman standing before her had no words either, but then Rose took Vicki into her arms.

"Dear sweet Vicki," Rose said into her ear as she hugged tightly, "the woman who afforded me the greatest joy of my life."

Vicki hugged back. Words still eluded her, but tears came to her eyes. When they pulled apart, she felt a sense of relief when she saw the older lady had tears in her eyes too.

Rose sat and motioned for Vicki to do the same. Somehow Vicki managed to do so without collapsing.

"We love him dearly," Rose began with a voice cracking from emotion. "Jacob is our life."

A beautifully manicured hand adorned with fine jewelry reached across the table and took hold of one of Vicki's much plainer versions. "Vicki, what are your intentions?"

"I just want to meet him. I've never, ever stopped thinking about him. I just want to spend the summer with him," Vicki managed as she dabbed the tears with her free hand. "We want to get to know him, and for him to get to know us…and…" Oh, how Vicki now wanted to stop and not tell the rest, but doing so would be nothing short of denying the very source of her being there. Stopping now would be a blatant form of rejecting the only hope she had for making her dream come true. "…and I want him to know about Jesus Christ."

With the words came a relief and power that washed

over Vicki like warm, soothing water. And to her surprise, Rose did not jerk her hand from Vicki's.

"Do you mean to convert Jacob?" Rose asked, eyes widening, but her voice remaining calm.

"I mean to show him a living example of Christianity," Vicki responded with newfound confidence. "I will tell him about Jesus and his teachings and I will encourage him to attend church with me and the kids. Nothing will be crammed down his throat or forced upon him."

"I could not help but pick up on something you said," Rose said soothingly, "Does your husband not attend church?"

Vicki wanted to avert her eyes from Rose's but she didn't. "My husband is a very good man, and I'm sure he believes in God. He just doesn't have much use for church."

The reply seemed to relieve Rose. After patting Vicki's hand quickly a time or two, she pulled hers back. "Let me be honest with you, Vicki," she said with a smile stitched with sadness. "If I had my way, I wouldn't want to give Jacob up for the summer. But I believe the decision to go or to stay belongs to him."

Vicki could not help but smile broadly, and Rose's response came quickly, but gently.

"It is his decision, but I think he has already decided to stay here."

"Will I get to talk to him?" Vicki blurted.

"Of course. He's looking forward to meeting you. At this

moment he is waiting anxiously in his father's office. You will get to talk to him, and," Rose paused ominously, "You will get to talk to my husband. Who, at this time, is finishing up an emergency surgery. He should be here any moment."

"Thank you for being so kind," Vicki said. This time she reached across the table to take Rose's hand.

"I owe you a lot, Vicki. So much so, in fact, that I feel obligated to warn you that Joseph will not be this gracious. He and I have completely different ways of looking at life and the world. And by the way, when you are talking to him, leave out any reference to Jesus. That will *not* go over well."

The man approaching the table didn't look like the Joseph Swiretynsky Vicki remembered, but it had to be him. This man locked eyes with her the second he stepped into the cafeteria and he maintained the terribly cold stare for the length of the dining room. The young Doctor Swiretynsky of Vicki's memory had a full head of hair and was clean shaven. The man approaching looked nearly bald on top and wore a full and well-kept beard of gray. This Joseph Swiretynsky looked sterner and intensely more intelligent than the one of fourteen years earlier — both of which served to make him more intimidating. Vicki promptly reminded herself that Jesus cleared the way with Rose and would do the same with her husband.

Joseph did not use a hug with his greeting or even a handshake. Instead it consisted of merely two icy words and a nod of his head. "Mrs. Hansen."

"Hello, Dr. Swiretynsky," Vicki replied with as much confidence as she could muster.

Joe then simply stood and stared intently at Vicki for a number of long seconds. If the man had any sympathy for the reasons she'd come, it didn't show in his eyes or mannerisms. The piercing gaze served to completely unnerve Vicki. When Rose finally spoke, Vicki breathed a sigh of relief.

"Won't you please join us, dear?" Rose delivered the question in the form of a demand as she jabbed a finger at the chair she intended her husband to take.

To Vicki's surprise Joseph went immediately to the chair.

"In your absence, Joseph, Vicki and I cleared the air on the matter at hand. I have explained that although we would rather Jacob not leave us for the summer, the decision is his to make."

"And did you emphasize" Joseph said to Rose while practically snarling at Vicki, "that we consider her presence here as no less than a merciless foray into our hearts and lives?"

"No, darling, I saved that sentiment for you to express," Rose smiled facetiously.

Joseph appeared undaunted. "And did you inform her that Jacob has no desire to spend the summer in Oklahoma?"

"She did," Vicki spoke up. "But I'm hoping I might say

something to make him feel better about my proposition."

Now Joseph addressed Vicki directly. "Words do not exist, Mrs. Hansen, which could persuade me that any good can come from your cruel and ridiculous notion."

"Oh, but good can come from this," Vicki emphasized with emotion, "If nothing else, Jacob will know that there are others…like you…that love him dearly."

"You love him? You don't even know him," Joseph scoffed.

"She brought him into this world," Rose interjected abruptly. "Do not even try, Joseph, to understand a woman's love for her children."

"All right. What about your husband and children? Do they love him?" Joseph mocked.

"If given the opportunity, they will grow to love him, and he will grow to love them," Vicki insisted. "And, Dr. Swiretynsky, my desire to spend just a few months with Jacob is not cruel. If I thought for a minute that this could harm you and your relationship with Jacob, I wouldn't be here."

"Joseph," Rose inserted pointedly, "I have quizzed Vicki on her intentions and motives and I found them to be honorable. Besides, this conversation may be all for naught. I believe it is time to introduce Vicki to a very special young man."

The declaration that caused Joseph to cringe sent Vicki's heartbeat into a frenzy.

Jacob brought a book to read but he couldn't concentrate on it. He turned on the television in his father's office but found nothing that could occupy his attention. Having a need to do something, he paced. Back and forth he tread for what seemed like hours. And all the while his heart and mind raced. Parts of him wanted to be here, and parts of him did not. His pants legs were starting to get damp from where he continually wiped his sweaty palms. When the knob to the office door finally started to turn, Jacob's knees all but buckled.

His mother and father came through the door first and both embraced him, blocking his view of the door.

"Follow your heart," his mother whispered.

His father just sighed one of his sighs and squeezed him tightly.

When they stepped away from him his eyes fell on the woman in the doorway. She, too, appeared to be standing on weakened legs and her eyes welled with tears. Jacob expected Vicki to be younger and not nearly as pretty.

"May I hug you?" were her first words to him. They were faint and quivering.

Jacob tried for yes but emitted only a prepubescent squeak. So, he nodded his permission. An instant later Jacob was in his birth mother's arms.

He anticipated the hug and expected it to be awkward at best, yet the emotions that seemed to radiate from the woman's embrace left no room for awkwardness. Contrary to what he'd both expected and dreaded, it did not feel like a hug from a total stranger. It felt like the embrace of someone who loved him very much. While in Vicki's arms his nervousness subsided because the love made it apparent that this woman would not think him too fat or too freckled or anything less than perfect. It made it easy for Jacob to hug her in return. When he did, Vicki started to sob. Then she gently pulled away.

"Oh, I'm sorry," she moaned through her tears while digging for something in her purse. "I'd promised myself I wouldn't do this." Pulling tissues from the purse and dabbing her eyes and nose, Vicki continued. "It's just that I've dreamed about this moment for so long."

Fighting hard to hold back his own tears, Jacob cleared his throat and said, "I know. I've heard about you all my life and I've always looked forward to one day meeting you."

Vicki turned to Rose and Joseph with a look of surprise. "He's always known about me?"

"We never wanted his adoption to be a surprise. He has, indeed, known about you for his entire life," Rose responded.

The revelation seemed to please Vicki very much. Smiling radiantly, she took another step back and simply studied Jacob for several very long seconds.

"Oh, Jacob," she sighed happily, "you're such a good looking young man. As a matter of fact, you look just like your real father did when he was your age."

Before Jacob could respond, the elder Swiretynsky

spoke for him. "We prefer to use the word *biological* when referring to you or your spouse. I'm his *real* father."

"Of course," Vicki nodded as her face flushed red, "I'm sorry. I didn't mean to be offensive."

"It's okay," Jacob quickly insisted while joining Rose in turning disapproving eyes upon the *real* father. Looking back at Vicki, he said, "Tell me about him. I know absolutely nothing."

"We never met the man," Joseph offered in a voice that sounded duly reprimanded if not apologetic. "There was nothing we could tell him."

"Well, his name is Burl and he's the sheriff of the county where we live," Vicki started, but then paused to giggle. "An Oklahoma sheriff with such a country name as *Burl* Hansen must strike you as so stereotypical!"

It most definitely struck Jacob, but for an entirely different reason. Surely it could not be, but he just had to ask. "Not *the* Burl Hansen?" he exhaled.

"*The* Burl Hansen? Who is *the* Burl Hansen?" Joseph asked.

"He was a linebacker for the Chicago Bears. One of the best to ever play the game," Jacob said out the corner of his mouth without taking his eyes off Vicki. "Is he one and the same?" he gasped.

"He is," she laughed, "one and the same!"

Jacob suddenly fell powerless to stand still. In a series of jumps, skips, and hops he ended up with his arms around Rose. "Can you believe this, Mother? I have the blood of Burl Hansen surging through my veins!"

Without giving his mother time to respond he practically bounced to his father. "Can you believe this? Can you believe this?" He clasped onto his father's shoulders.

"No…I can't," Joseph mumbled before sighing the mother of all sighs.

In the next instant he bounded back in front of Vicki. "You said I look like he did when he was fourteen? Was he built like this?" Jacob asked while patting his significant belly.

"Exactly like that," Vicki chuckled.

Jacob threw his hands in the air and joyfully cackled, but when he wheeled to share his delight with his parents, his laughter caught in his throat and died there. Both were trying hard to hide it, but he could tell. His joy broke their hearts.

Chapter Nine

"What d'ya want, Burl?"

Hansen looked up from his desk to see Herman Grambs standing in the doorway. "Get in here, Herman, and push that door closed behind you."

"What'd I do now?" the trustee scowled.

Hansen pushed back his chair and propped his boots up on the desk top. "Just sit down, Herman. We need to talk about a few things."

"Now, Burl, I been doing my duties as trustee as best I can," Grambs piped in as he eased into the lone chair in front of Hansen's desk. "I've been doing all my sweeping and cleaning real damn good, I'm here to tell you. I mean, hell, Burl, you just pay me three dollars a day, but I been bustin' my ass to do you proud. There ain't no son of a bitch that can..."

"Herman!" Hansen boomed, "Shut the hell up!"

"Okay," Grambs mumbled.

"You've been doing all right, Herman. There's just a

few things you need to do different. First of all, quit spitting your tobacco juice in the trash cans around here."

"What for?"

"Because when we have to dig something out of a trash can we end up getting that gross shit all over our fingers."

"Well, it don't make no sense to me why you'd be digging around in a trash can anyhow. If'n you've throwed something away, you ought to make sure it's something that needed to be throwed away in the first damned place."

"I can't argue with that logic, Herman. So, let me just say this, stop spitting in the trash cans or I am going to stick your face into one of them."

"Okay."

"And when you clean up the dispatch room, just clean it up and get out of there. Edna says you have been flirting with her and it makes her uncomfortable."

"Flirting with her?" Grambs flared. "Why, hell, Burl, I ain't flirting with that ugly old thing! Shit, even if I wanted to, she looks at me like I'm some kind of pervert!"

"You are some kind of pervert, Herman," Hansen returned dryly. "That's why you're here."

"That ain't been proved in a court of law," Grambs mumbled with a shake of his shaggy head. "Not this time, anyway."

"Are you listening to me, Herman?" Hansen growled.

"Yeah, I'm listening to you," Grambs growled back.

"Good. Now, some of the other inmates and all the

deputies are complaining about your personal hygiene."

"My personal what?"

"Your ass, Herman. Your stinking ass. I have told you once and I will not tell you again to wash your dirty, smelly ass! I want you to start taking a shower everyday. Hell, I can smell you clear over here."

"Okay."

"One more thing. Do you have any good information for me yet?"

"Nope. Ain't got none."

"You do remember that's part of the deal, don't you? It's a privilege being a trustee, and privileges don't come free."

"I know, Burl, and I've been listening for stuff, but I ain't heard about no drug labs, or anyone dealing in stolen cars, or anything like that," he shrugged.

"Here's the deal, Herman. You have another month until you go to trial. Since you can't post bond, you're here to stay. Staying is easy as a trustee. But if I'm going to scratch your back, then you are going to scratch mine."

"Okay."

Herman was practically out of the door when a final thought struck Hansen. "Hey, Herman."

"What?"

"Do you know anybody in this county that owns or deals in automatic weapons?"

"Can't think of nobody." He shook his head as he reached into his orange coveralls for a pouch of chewing tobacco.

"Are any of our new prisoners saying anything about

the missing boy and girl?"

"Just that pretty little thing ran away with a jigaboo. Hell if I'd known she was that desperate, I'd let her be my girl," he said as he stuffed a cheek with the black leaves.

"She is only sixteen, Herman," Hansen moaned with a sad shake of his head.

"So? My mama was only thirteen when she married my old man. I always say if they're old enough to…"

"Herman?" Hansen interrupted with a wave of his hand.

"Yeah?"

"Get the hell out of here."

"Okay."

Hansen went out shortly after lunch to run some errands. He returned to his office to find his wife at the window with her back to the door. Vicki stood still and quiet and appeared to be staring at the buildings across the street.

Hansen took a deep breath as he removed his cap and hung it on the hat tree just inside the door. Vicki made it back from her trip earlier than he'd expected.

"How's it going, Baby?" he asked gently.

Vicki didn't respond for several seconds, and Hansen held his breath until she did. Vicki was obviously hurting.

"I saw Herman Grambs out working in the flower

beds," she said evenly. "He said my ass looks as good as it did twenty years ago."

"Well," Hansen said before clearing his throat, "You do still have a nice ass, but twenty years ago you were only ten."

Vicki didn't laugh, but at least she wasn't crying. "So… how did it go?"

Vicki turned from the window to face him. Hansen felt ambushed by the radiant glow and beaming smile.

"Jacob will be here June the third!" she squealed.

Of all the words that rushed his mind, Hansen settled on, "Really?"

"Really!" She sprinted the length of the office and sprung into his arms. Numb from the mind down, he held her tightly. He listened in a near daze as she thanked him, thanked God, gave details of her trip, and description after description of what the boy looked like and how he acted.

Hansen listened and occasionally he nodded or responded with either a single word or small groupings of words. Mostly, however, he concentrated on keeping his true thoughts and feelings from pissing all over Vicki's parade.

Normally he finished up outside before dark. On the evening of his wife's return, however, Hansen moped around in his tool shed until Vicki shouted for him at a little before nine.

"Burl! Come on in the house. The kids want you to kiss them goodnight!"

Vicki met him at the back door with a hug and then took him by the hand and led him back to Bret and Sandy's bedrooms.

Both children were still ecstatic over the news their mother brought home to them. Bret seemed content with just expressing his glee to his father, but as usual, declarations weren't enough for the ever curious Sandy.

"How come you're not acting happy, Daddy? Don't you want to meet our big brother?"

Hansen put on a fake smile and cut his eyes to look at Vicki, who flashed a sly grin and arched her eyebrows. "Well, uh, sure, honey. Of course, I want to meet him. And I am happy. I'm just too fat to turn cartwheels and too old to giggle."

Surprisingly, Sandy accepted the response without further questions and hugged and kissed her father goodnight. Hansen stopped at the door of her bedroom and glanced back at his baby girl. Small hands formed into loose fists were rubbing vigorously at closed eyes. He would have to remember to put on a better show for the kids tomorrow.

Vicki followed him down the hall leading from their bedrooms but didn't say a word until they reached the kitchen.

"Do you think you will be all right with this by the time he gets here? She asked softly.

For simplicity's sake Hansen avoided making eye contact and quickly replied, "Sure."

"I wish we could talk about whatever it is bothering you about Jacob coming here," Vicki sighed.

Hansen did too, but he wasn't sure words existed to adequately explain exactly what bothered him. At the very least he certainly didn't know the words that would make Vicki understand why it bothered him. Then again, as had often been his way in dealing with deep feelings, Hansen thought it might be best just to keep it all locked safely out of everyone's reach but his own.

"You want a beer?" he asked, retrieving one from the refrigerator for himself.

Vicki declined the offer just as a knock sounded at the front door. They seldom had uninvited visitors, especially at nine o'clock in the evening. Hansen had a gut feeling that the caller was there on business. Confirmation came when he opened the door to find fifteen-year-old Randy Myers bleeding from the mouth and nose. The winded teen apparently had sprinted the mile from his home to the Arrowhead Ranch.

"Oh, Lord, son," Hansen winced as he held the door open and motioned for the boy to come inside.

Randy stayed glued in place. "It's Daddy," he moaned through busted lips, gasping to catch his breath. "He's bad drunk, Sheriff. I'm afraid he's going to kill Mama!"

Vicki rushed out of the house and started doing what she could to help the boy.

"Keep him here," Hansen said as he flew down the porch steps. The kid had seen enough violence for one night.

Hansen turned his headlights off before pulling down the long drive leading to the Myers' home. To keep from being heard he idled his car up to the house and across the yard. He parked the cruiser parallel to and not more than twenty feet in front of the porch.

He crawled out of the car, removed the pump shotgun from the trunk and laid it across the hood of his car. With the car and shotgun between him and the front door, Hansen took a step back and dropped his arms to his side. He could hear Suzy Myers crying as things crashed around inside the house.

"Butch Myers!" he shouted at the front door. "This is Burl Hansen. Get your ass out here!"

The crashing and breaking instantly stopped, but Suzy cried louder than ever. It took only seconds for Butch Myers to jerk open his front door and stomp out onto the porch.

"Ain't nobody called the fucking law," he bellowed at Hansen.

Seeing that Myers's hands were empty, Hansen left the

shotgun on the hood and walked around in front of the cruiser. "Your son ran down to my place," Hansen said without raising his voice.

Myers looked back over his shoulder at the door and shouted, "Randy! Come on out of the house, boy!"

"He's not in the house, Myers. I told you, he's at my place."

It took a few seconds for the truth to soak in. "Well, I guess I'll be taking that up with him," Myers hissed.

Hansen fought to keep from picturing the boy's frightened and battered face. If at all possible he wanted to do what he had to do without going into a rage. "It looks to me as if you've taken up enough with him already. That's why I'm here…and that's why you're going to jail."

"Get off my property!" Myers spat through gritted teeth.

"Butch Myers, you are under arrest for assault and battery on a minor. Now, you can make it easy on yourself… or you can make it a whole lot of fun for me!"

"I'll give you some fun, you sorry mother fucker!" Myers roared as he stormed down the porch steps.

Hansen resisted the urge to meet his opponent halfway. Instead he braced himself and positioned his fists defensively in front of his face. Myers' hands were also clinched but both were down at his sides. When the one-time contender took the step that put him within striking distance, his right fist shot upward.

Hansen moved his hands in an attempt to block the

uppercut, but it did no good. With blinding speed and uncanny accuracy Myers brought the fist up from his waist, through Hansen's posed fists, and crash landed it beneath the sheriff's chin. The force of the blow rocked Hansen's head back but didn't move him out of his stance. But the left hook — that Hansen didn't see coming — set him stumbling back a couple of steps.

Another quick right followed the left. All too suddenly Hansen felt like a man swatting at a swarm of stinging wasps. The pain of the blows landing on his face and head preceded the sickening realization that he was in trouble. He wouldn't be able to take much more of the punishment without going down. The thought of going to the ground did something to Hansen that few things did — it frightened him. Myers was tanked on liquor and hate. That combination often kept a man inflicting damage long after his opponent crumbled.

Hansen desperately began to strike out, but every time he swung, he hit nothing. His air punches were countered with brutal combinations to his face. Hansen started to taste blood as his vision blurred. Three words suddenly and involuntarily came to his mind and he mouthed them through battered lips. "Help me, God!"

At that very instant Myers moved in close and started working on Hansen's midsection. It took only seconds of the onslaught before Hansen had to concentrate what little fight he had left on just staying upright. Soon the plea of those three words began to bounce frantically through his mind over and over like a mantra…Help me God… help me God…help me God. Without a miracle, Hansen was going down. When he did, he knew Myers would kick him and stomp him until no signs of life remained.

A few blows later, all of Hansen's hopes for divine intervention perished when his knees buckled. He toppled forward and reached out with both hands. Myers then made his first and only mistake in the encounter. He didn't move clear of Hansen's grasp.

At first Hansen clutched only clothing but he used the grip on Myers' shirt to pull the boxer into his chest. From there Hansen managed to work his arms around Myers' arms and midsection to establish what he'd always heard called a "bear hug." For the first few seconds he just held on and worked to catch his breath and clear his mind. Myers squirmed and cursed as he struggled to break the hold.

Before he could, Hansen started to squeeze with everything he could muster, and Myers began to scream. Hansen straightened his back and lifted Myers inches off the ground. Myers stopped screaming and began gasping for air. Hansen had to loosen his grip, but only long enough to adjust his hold and fill his own lungs with air. With a loud and angry growl through gritted teeth and busted lips, he jerked his arms together even harder than before and squeezed until he felt Myers go limp.

Because he hurt like hell, because he couldn't keep from picturing Randy Myers' bleeding face, and because he didn't want to fight Myers again this night, Hansen repositioned the still form in his arms until he looked like a groom carrying his bride. With a grunt and mighty heave, he hoisted Myers as high as he could and then slammed him to the ground. When Myers didn't bounce quite high enough to satisfy Hansen, he picked him up and slammed him down again.

Hansen stumbled the few feet to his patrol car to get his handcuffs and then used them to secure Myers' dangerous hands. He grabbed his prisoner by the ankles and dragged him to the car. He crammed Myers into the back seat before nearly collapsing into the front. When he knew he could talk without gasping, he picked up the microphone to his radio.

"County One to dispatch."

"Go ahead, County One," Mark Rogers, the evening dispatcher, responded.

"I'm out at Butch Myers' residence and I have him in custody. I'll be in route to the jail here in a few minutes."

"Ten-four, Sheriff, I'll log it in. Do you need any assistance out there?"

"No," Hansen sighed wearily. "Butch is pretty calm right now."

Hansen couldn't rest as long as he wanted. He had to make sure Suzy was all right. After grunting and groaning to get out of the car, he took just a few more seconds to lean back against it. His eyes scanned the starry sky. After a few moments of contemplation, he whispered,

"Thanks." He then hobbled off to check on Suzy.

He dropped the wrench and stepped back from the old Harley he'd tinkered with. Antlers' newest businessman turned his entire attention to the police scanner. He always kept the scanner on when alone in his shop. A prerequisite for being in his line of business demanded keeping up with what the cops were doing. Excited over what he'd just heard, the tattooed man hurried to his phone and dialed the number he knew by heart.

He responded to the voice that answered, "This is Tom Avery…" He had to get used to using the name again. He hadn't been Tom Avery since leaving California. Before that, in Florida, he'd used another name.

"…you know that bastard that kicked my ass right after I got in town? That old boxer?" Avery hissed into the receiver. "Well, he's on his way to the county jail. You need to get down here. There's a little bar on Highway Three just a few miles east of the county line called the 'Getaway.' Hurry your ass over there. I'll be waiting."

Chapter Ten

Hansen stepped out of the Myers' house to find his prisoner sitting upright in the back seat. He situated himself behind the steering wheel and looked back over his shoulder.

"Suzy signed complaints, so listen up. I'm going to read you your rights."

"I know my fucking rights," Myers wheezed.

Hansen read them anyway and asked if he understood them. Myers just grunted and then moaned. He didn't say a word all the way to the county jail.

"I'm going to get you out of the car in a few seconds, Myers. Are you going to give me any more trouble?" Hansen said, breaking the silence he'd found refreshing.

Myers didn't answer for several seconds. When he did, his words came haltingly. "I think you busted my goddamned ribs."

Hansen turned on the dome light and adjusted his rear-view mirror so he could look at himself. His right eye was nearly swollen shut, both lips were busted, and his cheeks looked puffy and were already bruising. He glanced back at Myers. "My heart bleeds for you, asshole!"

It did not surprise Hansen to find his undersheriff milling around in front of the booking desk. Pete Marsh had no family and practically wed himself to the department.

"My God," Marsh said with a shake of his head as Hansen all but carried Myers into the holding area. "He doesn't look so good…and neither do you Burl. What the hell happened out there?"

Hansen helped Myers into a chair in front of the booking desk. "Ol' Butch was feeling a little mean tonight. He whipped his wife and whipped his son and then whipped me pretty good too."

"It doesn't look like Butch faired too well either," Marsh grimaced.

Myers slumped in his chair with his arms wrapped around and hugging his torso. "He got lucky," Myers gasped.

"That is pretty much the way I see it, too," Hansen agreed, feeling no need to deny it. All that really mattered is that he'd been the last man standing.

"Damn," Marsh said with another vigorous shake of his head, "Burl Hansen and Butch Myers going toe-to-toe. I would have paid to see that fight."

"Well, you'll not get another chance," Hansen smirked. "If it ever happens again, I'll just shoot Butch right between the eyes."

Marsh laughed. "You've had a tough night, but I have some good news for you."

Hansen looked up from the booking slip he filled out on Myers. "What?"

"Jerry Glass was booked an hour ago for DUI."

Hansen's head pounded and his face hurt like hell but neither kept him from smiling. Two of his deputies recently tried to locate Mike Rider and Jerry Glass, and both were reportedly working offshore in the Gulf of Mexico. Hansen had been anxious to question the men on the disappearance of Max Bemo. Because of the fight at Joe Buck's, they seemed the most likely suspects.

"Hey, Webb," Hansen shouted to the evening shift jailor, "come over here and book Mr. Myers for me." Then he turned back to Marsh, "Pete, go get Glass and bring him into the interview room. I'd like to have a word or two with him."

The small and stark interview room's single chair sat menacingly in the center of the room and faced the door. Hansen leaned against the wall behind the chair with his arms folded across his chest. He didn't move a muscle when Marsh escorted the squat and round Jerry Glass into the room.

"Sit down," the sheriff barked at the prisoner.

Glass looked uncomfortable with the surroundings. Although disheveled, he proved sober enough to move steadily to the chair without difficulty. He hesitantly turned his back to Hansen and squeezed into the chair.

"Glass, you have the right to remain silent…" While Glass craned his neck to look over his shoulder, Hansen grumbled the rest of it from memory. "…Do you understand your rights?" Hansen concluded.

"I understand them," Glass said after clearing his throat, "but I don't understand why you're telling them to me."

"You don't know why you're here?" Hansen responded.

"I know why I'm in jail, but I don't know what I'm doing in this room."

Seconds of silence followed as Hansen considered a strategy. Glass turned sideways in his chair and spent the seconds looking nervously back and forth between Hansen and Marsh. The undersheriff had taken a position on the wall opposite his boss.

Opting for a shock effect, Hansen broke the silence with a threatening shout. "Max Bemo is missing. We think he's dead and we think you killed him."

The tactic brought the response Hansen hoped for. Glass all but came out of the chair. "Whoa, now, Sheriff! I ain't seen that man since the night me and Rider got into it with him in that store."

"Where is Rider?" Hansen fired back.

"I guess he's on the drilling platform out in the Gulf of Mexico. That's where I've been and would still be there if I hadn't got fired."

"Why'd you get fired?"

"The foreman said I was drunk on the job. I had a few drinks all right, but I was a hell of a long ways from being drunk."

"What day did you and Rider leave for the Gulf?"

"Let's see," Glass said as he brought his shaky hand up to rub at bloodshot eyes. "It was the day after we got released from the hospital. They let us both out that afternoon after you talked to us. I think that was on a Tuesday. We left early the next morning. That would have been Wednesday."

Bemo disappeared between the time of Hansen's visit on Tuesday and the attempt to arrest him on Thursday. Glass had still been in the county for part of that time. The corresponding periods were circumstantial at best, but encouraged Hansen to push harder.

He walked up and stood directly behind Glass's chair. "Was it you or Rider that actually did the killing?" he growled.

"Now, I done told you, Sheriff. I ain't done no…"

"Where'd you boys hide the body?"

"I want a damned lawyer!" Glass practically screamed.

"Only guilty people need lawyers, Glass! Is this your way of telling me it was your idea to kill Bemo? That it was you who did the killing and you that got rid of the body?"

"I ain't saying another goddamned thing, man!" Glass bellowed.

"Let me tell you something, Glass. We have enough on you boys to get a warrant for Rider," Hansen lied. "When we drag his ass back to Oklahoma and put some heat on it, what's he gonna say? There's a better than average chance that he'll give your ass up to save his own. That's how it always happens. Don't you watch TV, Glass?"

The prisoner didn't respond and Hansen leaned in and shouted the question directly into his ear this time. "Do you watch TV, Glass?!"

"Yeah, sure. I watch TV," his voice trembled.

"Then you know that's how it happens. We split you two up, we offer him a deal, and he gives you up. He gets the sweet deal and you get drugs pumped into your veins until you're dead." Hansen softened his tone, "But you know, Glass, you could be the one getting a deal." He placed a hand on the prisoner's shoulder, "You want to make a deal, Glass?"

"I didn't do anything. I don't need no deals. I just need a fucking lawyer!" The man looked to be on the verge of tears.

Hansen turned and walked to the door. "Mr. Glass, you're a dumb ass. I don't waste a lot of time on dumb asses. Pete, stuff this dumb ass back in a cell. Maybe with some time to think, he might grow a little smarter."

Hansen went from the interview room to his office.

Marsh joined him there five minutes later.

"Burl, I think they killed Bemo."

"Oh, I do, too. I just don't know how to prove it."

"We need a body," Marsh said with a nod of his head.

"A body or a confession, and I don't think we're going to get one out of Glass. He lawyered up too quickly. He knows how the game is played. Tomorrow I want to try to find out when and if Rider is coming back to Oklahoma. Maybe we'll have better luck with him."

"I'll get all I can on him, Burl. Now, why don't you head home and get some rest?"

Hansen thought that sounded wonderful, but before he could pry his weary bulk from the chair, dispatcher Mark Rogers popped into the office.

"Sheriff, we got a call on a fight at the Getaway Club. You guys be willing to respond?"

"I'm game," Marsh piped.

Hansen couldn't match his subordinate's enthusiasm, but got up and moved toward the door. "It's on my way home. I'll back you, Pete."

Hansen and Marsh pulled into the Getaway's parking lot, one right behind the other. They parked their cars a safe distance from the lone man standing and bleeding just outside the front door.

"Do you know him?" Hansen asked Marsh as they got out of their cruisers.

"Never seen him before," Marsh responded.

Neither had Hansen. "Well, let's go meet the gentleman," he sighed.

They were still several yards away when the short and slender man hailed them. "I'm the one who called the cops."

Neither officer offered an immediate response, waiting until they were face to face to open the dialogue. "How bad you hurt?" Hansen asked. Even up close it proved impossible to determine if the blood covering the man's face and soaking his t-shirt came from one or multiple wounds.

"I know the son of a bitch busted my nose and lips, and he might have knocked a couple of teeth loose, too. I want that asshole put in jail!"

"Who is this 'asshole'?" Marsh asked.

"I don't know his name. Some biker-looking bastard. You can't miss him. He's the only one in there with tattoos all over his arms and a nasty dew rag on his head."

"Sounds like Tom Avery," Marsh said to Hansen.

"Yeah, it does," he agreed before saying to the wounded man, "Tell us what happened."

"Man, I'm sitting at the bar when this dude walks in. He sits down next to me, but we don't talk. He's talking to the bartender and pretty much acts as if I don't exist, which is okay with me because he don't look like my kind of people anyway.

"So, we're sitting there and all of a sudden I accidentally knock my beer over and it splatters on his leather vest. Then he just backhands me clear off my barstool. He just fucking slaps me backwards without a single word!"

"Did you fight back?" Marsh questioned.

"Hell, no! That fucker has arms as big as…" the man paused to look around for a point of reference. His eyes fell on Hansen. "…hell, nearly as big as yours. He did all this damage with just one blow," he exclaimed, pointing to his face. "I didn't want or need any more of that shit!" The man seemed to notice for the first time the condition of Hansen's face. "Damn, what happened to you?"

"Pretty much the same thing that happened to you," Hansen drawled. "What's your name?"

"Danny Todd."

"Do you live around here, Mr. Todd?"

"No. I live up in Ada. I was just passing through. I've been down visiting my sister in Hugo and just stopped for a few beers."

"You do want to press charges?" Marsh insured.

"I damned sure do. He had no right to slap the hell out of me over an accident. And it isn't as if a little beer could hurt that filthy vest of his. I hear those bikers shit and piss on each other's vests as some kind of initiation. Hell, beer could only do it good!"

Marsh chuckled and Hansen would have too if his face hadn't been throbbing. Danny Todd and his story seemed legit enough. "Let's go in and get this law breaker,"

Hansen said to Marsh.

"Ten-four," Marsh agreed.

The tattooed man in the damp leather vest and skull cap was in fact Tom Avery and he'd moved from the bar to the single pool table. Avery looked directly at the two lawmen when they entered the musty dump of a tavern. He acknowledged their presence with a smirk and then put the six ball in a corner pocket.

Hansen and Marsh went directly to the bar. Marsh kept an eye on Avery while Hansen got a reluctant confirmation of Todd's story from the Getaway's bartender and owner, Vic Rutley. With all they needed, the cops headed toward Avery.

The biker laid his pool stick across the table as Hansen and Marsh approached. He leaned back against the wall and crossed one heavily muscled and inked arm over the other. He eyed the officers like a kid eyes cauliflower, but didn't say anything.

Hansen didn't like the look on his face and let it show in his tone of voice. "Didn't your mama ever tell you it isn't nice to pick on people smaller than you?"

Avery considered the comment a long moment before bringing up a finger and pointing at the sheriff's damaged face, "Looks as if you *need* to be picking on people smaller than you!" he growled. "And about my mama, all she ever told me worth a damned was don't talk to strangers or fucking cops!"

Before Hansen could think of a pithy come-back, Marsh interceded on his behalf. "You better watch your tongue, Avery. The sheriff took on Butch Myers tonight and nearly killed the poor son of a bitch. If memory serves me right, Myers kicked your ass like a stepchild."

Avery looked from Marsh to Hansen and then back to Marsh. After a slight pause, he grinned broadly, shook his head, and brought his hands up to communicate the universal sign of surrender. "Point well taken, Deputy." Avery turned a smiling face to Hansen. "I guess I'm going to jail."

"You guessed right," Hansen nodded.

Avery slowly turned away from the officers and criss-crossed his hands in the small of his back. With the smile still in place, he looked over his shoulder and said to Hansen, "You don't strike me as the type to beat a hand-cuffed man. Why don't you go ahead and slap those babies on me."

"Damn," Hansen replied with mock sadness as he granted the request. "Your mama might not have taught you any manners, but she didn't raise no fool."

"My mama was a fine woman, Sheriff," Avery nodded good-naturedly. "I got a naked tattoo of her across my ass. Wanna see it?"

With Avery tucked away in the back seat of Marsh's cruiser and Danny Todd on his way back to Ada, Hansen and his deputy leaned back against the sheriff's car and studied their prisoner.

"I thought for a second or two in there that he was going to get froggy and jump," Hansen commented.

"No. He didn't want any part of you from the very get-go. He just had to save a little face. He's just your everyday run-of-the-mill maggot," Marsh observed.

"Yeah, he is. But you know," Hansen smiled, "If I wasn't real careful, I think I could grow to like the guy."

"Yes, sir," Marsh nodded thoughtfully. "He's somewhat personable…for a maggot."

Hansen pushed off his car and turned for the driver's door while wiping sweat from his brow. "Damn it sure is hot for a March night."

"You did enough to work up a sweat tonight, boss. You sure you don't want to stick around and see what else we can stir up?" Marsh grinned.

"Don't think so. I think I'm going to let you get our illustrated man to jail while I'll get myself home and to bed." As an afterthought he added, "Pete, why don't you put him in a cell next to Herman Grambs. We might just get some inside info on the man."

"Good idea," Marsh agreed, then chuckled, "When I last seen Grambs he was telling Butch Myers how Butch had fucked up by not going from boxing to championship wrestling. He was coming up with all kind of dumb-assed names that Butch could have used."

"Ole, Herman," Hansen laughed in turn, "gotta love him!"

Between his sixth and seventh birthday, many decades now past, Billy Harjo learned he lived in a world much different from other people. Until then he didn't know he could see things and hear things they couldn't. No one, not even his parents, were like him. None of his brothers or his sisters knew the things he did because they didn't have a special relationship with the wind and the rain. Animals didn't treat any of them as one of their own.

The day Billy became aware of his special medicine still burned in his mind as if it happened only yesterday instead of back when his people didn't have indoor plumbing and still plowed their fields with mules. He'd been on the back side of his family's barn talking to an old man he didn't know when his mother suddenly rounded the corner and let out a scream. She scrambled forward as if to protect him, and the old man Billy thought he saw with his eyes instead of his spirit, hurried away. His mother acted frantic, gasping as she gathered her young son in her stout arms.

"The old man meant me no harm," Billy offered in his defense.

"Old man, Billy?" His mother gasped. "That was no

human, Billy. You were talking to a bear!"

Billy chuckled at her response. "Mama, bears don't have names, but men do. He told me his name was Charlie With Three Eyes."

His mother pulled him even closer and let out a gasp. "Did he have a terrible scar, Billy? Did it run the length of his right jaw?"

"He did, Mama. He said a horse kicked him."

Billy's mother dropped her arms and began to chant in a mournful wail.

This time Billy grabbed her. "What upsets you so, Mama?"

His mother seemed to struggle with her words. "Charlie With Three Eyes was your grandfather, Billy. He died many years before you were born. They called him Three Eyes because he saw what others could not. I fear he has passed his medicine on to you."

"Do you fear it because it's bad medicine, Mama?"

"Billy, people see enough evil in this world with just two eyes," she replied somberly.

Billy's special talents did many times throughout his long life prove to be more of a curse than a blessing, as they did now in the still darkness of the early morning hours. Presently, the frightened voice of a young boy babbled outside the walls of Billy's shack. Billy's old bones ached and he did not cherish the idea of struggling from his bed to see what horror tortured the youth. He'd hoped the boy would slink off into the darkness to leave him in peace, and worried if he did not, that Billy could do him no good. As of lately, his powers had diminished. When finally convinced the boy wouldn't or couldn't leave, Billy forced himself out of bed and painfully hobbled out his front door.

A chubby white boy — *Na hullo vlla nakni nia* — stood quaking in Billy's front yard. He didn't know the Na hullo vlla nakni nia but did know the man standing next to him. The big man's head hung low and his once strong arms dangled uselessly at his sides.

"Max Bemo," Billy called out, "For what reasons do you torment this boy?"

Bemo offered no response. Even Billy Harjo could not always get the dead to talk. In years past, a more powerful Alekchi might have easily deciphered the meaning of the vision. For now, Billy only knew for sure that Bemo came from the past, and the Na hullo vlla nakni nia came from the future and unless mighty spirits intervened, both man and boy would spend eternity together in anguish.

Chapter Eleven

From where Hansen sat, he could see out the plate glass window at the front of Flodell's Diner. March, April and May had been unseasonably dry, but the first two days of June brought dark, brewing clouds and heavy rains. Hansen stared out the window at the downpour and though lost in his thoughts, he kept an ear tuned to Chuck Turner.

"What are you looking at?" Turner finally asked as he turned in his seat to follow Hansen's gaze.

"Just the rain."

"You're staring at the rain and your mind is a thousand miles away. I can't blame you though. I'm sure you're damned nervous about this week," Turner grunted as he turned back to face Hansen.

Hansen shifted his gaze from the shower to his friend. "Yup...The boy gets here."

"Yes, he does. And I think maybe it's about time you start referring to him as 'Jacob,' or 'my son.' You know, that's just a little warmer… has a more positive feeling than, 'the boy.'"

Hansen grunted, nodded, and quickly changed the subject to something less personal on his mind. "You know Herman Grambs is pleading out in front of Judge Shelton today?"

"Yup. Douglas Shelton is a fine man, but a tough judge. I fear that poor hillbilly is on the way to the big house," Turner said.

"I believe you're right. And I can't help but feel sorry for the ignorant bastard. He's never spent any hard time, and he's scared shitless."

"I would be, too," Turner observed gloomily, but then arched his eyebrows and spouted enthusiastically, "Hey, I know something that would lift your spirits."

"Yeah? What's that?"

"A Harley."

"A Harley-Davidson?" Hansen winced.

"You got it. I'm thinking about buying one off Tom Avery."

The name momentarily took Hansen back to the night almost three months ago when he'd put Avery and Butch Myers in jail. It was ironic that when both cases got down to the nitty-gritty, Danny Todd and Suzy Myers dropped their charges, and Randy Myers changed his story, insisting that a bad fall and not his father caused the damage to his face. Of course, Butch Myers still awaited trial for the assault on Hansen, but for their crimes that March night, both Avery and Myers spent only a day and a half in the county jail.

"I don't know about that Avery," Hansen said after his few seconds of recollection. "He's a likeable enough guy, but I have a feeling that he's just as crooked as they come."

"Well, I haven't caught him dirty on anything yet. Other than the run-in with Myers and that incident at the Getaway, he's been a model citizen. Since I don't know of any laws he's broken, if he wants to offer me a good enough deal on a Harley, I plan on doing some business with him," Turner declared.

Hansen took his last sip of coffee and then pointed at Turner's huge abdominal overhang. "What model you getting...a Fat Boy?"

Turner opened his mouth in defense, but a sudden and roaring burst of thunder covered his words. Hansen turned back to the window in time to catch sight of a blinding flash of lightning that brought him back from his moment of levity. With everything else weighing on his mind, it was now officially storm season in Oklahoma — a time notorious for death and destruction.

His mother insisted he keep his eyes shut while she led him by the hand into his bedroom.

"You can open them now," Rose Swiretynsky said, her

voice brimming with excitement.

Jacob did and found himself standing before his bed, which was covered with a cascading line of brightly colored long-sleeved shirts. Each was adorned with pearl snap buttons and ornate stitching of lassos, broncos, six-shooters, cacti, spurs and other things considered predominately western.

"Aren't they adorable?" Rose exclaimed happily.

Jacob closed his gaping mouth, swallowed hard and let his mouth gape again. Four pairs of denim jeans lay in display below the shirts.

"Those are Wranglers, darling. Levi's simply are not the jeans of choice for Oklahoma buckaroos!"

"Buckaroos," Jacob repeated under his breath as he examined a leather belt beside the jeans. It had the letters J-A-C-O-B engraved across the portion intended for the small of the back and a silver buckle the size of a coffee saucer that bore a gold-plated man mounted on the back of a gold-plated…"cow," Jacob mumbled out loud.

"What was that dear?" Rose beamed proudly.

He was helplessly dazed from sensory overload. "A man on a cow," he mumbled barely above a whisper.

"Not just any man," Rose trilled, "It's a cowboy, and that's no simple cow, darling, that's a rambunctious bull! And look at these," she said as she reached to retrieve a pair of high-topped footwear with eyelets, a tongue, necessarily long shoestrings, and toes slightly less round than those of a penny loafer. Leather tassels were attached across the tops of the toes.

"What are those...*things*?" Jacob grimaced.

"Oh, my precious, these are lace-up ropers. They are extremely chic in the western states...the preferred boot for the most fashion conscious wranglers!"

"According to whom, Mother?"

"According to the salesman at Morgan's Western Emporium, Jacob."

"I would think one should be somewhat skeptical of a Bostonian's knowledge of acceptable western wear, Mother."

"Oh, Jacob, you don't like your new ensemble," Rose pouted, clearly hurt.

Jacob gladly turned from the articles of clothing to face his mother. He tried to be gentle, "I do appreciate the thought, but this *stuff* is simply not my style."

"Jacob, you cannot do cowboy things without cowboy clothing."

"I do not intend to do cowboy things."

"You are spending the summer at a ranch, darling. Of course you'll be doing cowboy kinds of things. Besides, I'm sure these are the exact styles Burl Hansen wears."

"You think?" Jacob said as he turned back to give the hideous items a second chance.

"Of course, he's a rural county sheriff and a rancher. He certainly doesn't wear blazers, pleated slacks, brogans, and Ferragamo ties!" Rose laughed.

Jacob felt not the least bit apprehensive about spending

the summer with Vicki. She had already expressed love and acceptance. He still had that bridge to cross with Burl. "Do you think he might like me wearing these sorts of things?" he winced.

"Jacob, I really don't think he will care what you wear, but the clothes might serve as a sign of your willingness to experience the things he is part of and that are a part of him."

"The least I can do is try them on," Jacob said as he picked up one of the shirts that did not look nearly as ridiculous as it had only minutes earlier.

Vicki left no room for compromise. The entire family would spend the night in Oklahoma City so they could all meet the boy at the airport the following day. They would have dinner at one of the city's finest restaurants, and Burl would make the necessary adjustments to his schedule. As a result, Hansen spent the Monday before Jacob's arrival trying to stuff two days of work into one. He sat at his desk doing so when the knock sounded at his door.

"What is it Paul?" he asked without bothering to look up. He knew the half-hearted knock of his head jailer.

"Herman Grambs is throwing a ring-tailed fit to talk to you."

Hansen looked up into the perpetually frowning face. "He's already back?"

"He's been back two hours," Paul Winters nodded.

Hansen glanced at his watch. Where had the afternoon gone?

"Yeah," Winters said with the closest thing to a smile Hansen had ever seen on him, "just like we expected, Judge Shelton hung it in his ass. He's out of here!"

"Where is he right now?" Hansen always made a conscious effort of keeping his dislike for the jailer from sounding in his voice.

"He's locked down."

"Locked down? What the hell for?" Hansen barked.

"He's now a convicted felon, Burl. That's our policy."

Hansen absolutely hated it when Winters was right about anything. "Well, I'm overriding policy," he boomed, suddenly not caring what sounded in his voice. "Go get him."

"You're the boss," Winters moaned as he turned to go.

Hansen took a deep breath and swallowed back the words burning like acid on the tip of his tongue. If he could ever confirm his suspicions about Winters, the jailer would see just how much of a boss he could be.

Slimy little Grambs normally slithered. This time, however, he slinked into the sheriff's office. His frantically blinking eyelids accentuated a wide-eyed jittery look of terror. When Hansen offered him a seat, he said he preferred to stand and asked if he could close the door so they could talk in private.

"Why sure, Herman," Hansen replied to the strange request. When Grambs had something to say, he normally spewed it to the world.

Grambs closed the door, turned back to Hansen and squeaked, "I'm going to prison, Burl."

When right words didn't come quickly, Hansen sighed and nodded his head.

"You know, Burl, there's been a bunch of boys through here the past few months that have been in the pen. I've done been told some awful things by them boys. I been told that those convicts are gonna take me as some kind of child molester. Now, I ain't never laid a hand on a child, Burl. I've just...well...showed my...you know...to younger girls. I didn't touch any of them and I didn't harm any of them, and I don't deserve to have done to me what I've been told they'll do to me. I don't want to be hurt in them ways, Burl. I don't want to go to the pen."

Hansen had seen things since becoming the sheriff he wished he'd never had to see — things that disturbed him. He could now add to this list the sight of tears tumbling down Grambs' leathery cheeks. After a long, deep breath, he ran a hand through his hair and replied, "Herman, you waived your right to a trial to make a plea. Did you honestly not think you'd be doing some time in prison?"

"I hoped he might have mercy on me," Grambs sighed.

Hansen just shook his head, "I, uh...I'm sorry, but I

don't know what else to say."

With a quick and anxious look over his shoulder at the closed door, Grambs shuffled up close to Hansen's desk and all but whispered, "I got some information Burl. It's really big stuff. If I tell you, could you get it fixed so that I could do my time here in your jail?"

"Herman, it's just too late for any kind of deals," Hansen said softly.

"Not for what I know Burl. Not for what I know. It's damn big stuff. It's not too late if I know stuff and that stuff can keep me from going to a place where they are going to beat me and...stick things up my you-know-what."

Hansen did not appreciate the misdirected guilt he experienced and started feeling aggravated at Herman for misdirecting it. "If it's all that big, Herman," he said evenly, "then why didn't you let me know about it before now?"

"Because I don't want to die Burl."

Hansen could tell by the look in Grambs' eyes, the expression on his face, and the tremble in his voice that he was serious — dead serious.

"What have you got, Herman?" Hansen asked, leaning forward in his chair.

"I can't tell you all I know Burl. I can only tell you parts, but they'll be important parts. If I tell you all I know, I'll be dead for sure. You see, Burl, I'm between one of them there rocks and a hard place. I know some stuff that can get me dead, and if I don't trade some of it, then I'm going to a place that will probably kill me anyway. You got to help me Burl."

"Herman, I don't know that I can do anything, but you have my word that I'll do what I can."

Grambs didn't say another word until he leaned close enough to whisper into Hansen's ear.

Vicki put the last touches on the guest bedroom as she heard a car coming up the gravel drive. A glance at her watch revealed it was much too early for Burl to be home. When a peek out the window revealed her husband was in fact home, she hurried to meet him at the front door. There were things she'd asked him to do in preparation for Jacob's arrival and stay. It was very sweet of Burl to actually take off early to do the things. He deserved to be greeted with an enthusiastic hug and kiss.

The moment Vicki threw open the door and came face to face with Burl, she knew he'd not come home early to do sweet things. Written all over his face was the expression men carried with them from boyhood that signified a mother or wife wouldn't like what they had done…or planned to do.

"What?" Vicki asked pointedly.

"Chuck and I have to go to Seminole," he said as he brushed past her and started in the direction of their bedroom.

"You'll be back late tonight?" she asked, dreading the answer she already knew and wondering what business he had in a town over a hundred miles away.

When he stopped and turned to face her, the apologetic look on his face confirmed her anxiety. "I don't know when we'll be back, but it won't be tonight."

She had only enough time to scowl and move her hands to her hips before he continued.

"We think that's where we can find Darrel Baker and Shelly Rafell…we're going there to look for their bodies."

The revelation dissolved Vicki's objections. "Oh, no," she gasped while following her husband to their bedroom.

"Herman Grambs gave up the information," Hansen said as he started throwing things in an overnight bag, "but he wouldn't tell me how he knows. He's afraid whoever killed the kids is going to kill him too if they find out he told."

Vicki felt like collapsing on the bed. Instead, she stepped in and started taking the items of clothing and toiletries from her husband and placing them neatly in the bag.

"Do you have any idea who it is?"

"I have lots of ideas, but that's all I've got. We haven't checked the booking records yet, but I'm guessing Herman has had contact with at least fifty different prisoners over the past three months."

In the next instance Burl grabbed the bag and started out of the bedroom with Vicki following close on his heels.

"Is there anything I can do?" she asked.

Burl stopped in the kitchen, laid his bag on the table and opened up his arms. "You can give me a hug."

Vicki moved into his arms and wrapped her own tightly around his waist. "I'll be praying for you."

Hansen nodded and said, "Tell the boy I'm sorry I couldn't meet him at the airport."

Vicki sighed, shrugged, and watched her man walk out the door.

Chapter Twelve

Hansen tried to calm his nerves by turning from the lake to study the countryside. The sparsely wooded land of scrub oaks and bois d'arcs lay basically flat with just a few rolling hills. It wasn't ugly country, but it paled badly in comparison to the dense forests of tall pines and the mountains in Pushmataha County. His mind strayed less than a minute from the work at hand before a voice carried up from the water.

"Looks like they've found something!"

Hansen turned abruptly and hurried down toward the bank where Chuck Turner stood with Seminole County Sheriff Marty Burgess. The three men had made arrangements the night before to have divers at Seminole's Sportsman Lake by nine this morning. The four divers had been in the murky water for close to six hours now. They concentrated their search on the deep waters below the low bluffs on the east side of the lake. If someone intended to sink a car, it would be the most likely place to do it.

Burgess and Turner watched the lone man in the large bass boat serving as the dive platform. Hansen noted that two of the divers had come topside and were hanging on to the side of the boat.

"It's a car all right," the man in the boat shouted to the men on the bank. "It's down about thirty feet. Go ahead and call for that wrecker."

"Don't get your hopes up, boys," Sheriff Burgess said as he walked to his patrol car to radio for the wrecker. "We pull two or three stolen cars a year out of this lake. This one might not be the one you're looking for."

"I hope it's not our car," Turner mumbled under his breath. "I hope it really ain't down there."

Hansen nodded his head and looked at his watch. In fifteen minutes the Southwest plane from Dallas would be landing in Oklahoma City. He figured it would land about the same time the wrecker reached the lake.

At the airport in Boston, Jacob had felt like a one-man Wild West show. Although he wore the least obnoxious of his new shirts, he'd seemed to attract every eye in the terminal. When he changed planes in Dallas, he felt slightly less conspicuous because there were numerous men milling about who appeared to be cowboys. Only they weren't of the rhinestone variety. His jeans were so newly stiff and tight on his heavy thighs that he squeaked when he walked. When he'd stopped to buy a soft drink, the woman behind the counter found great humor in the young "urban cowboy" with the Bostonian accent.

Later the pilot announced they were making the final approach into Oklahoma City's Will Rogers World Airport, and Jacob's thinking turned from his apparel to the world awaiting him. Just how different would it be? His father insisted it would be a culture shock. His mother countered that basically only the scenery would change — that Oklahomans might dress and talk differently than he was accustomed to, but when you got below the layers of different customs, people were the same no matter where they lived. His father scoffed at that sentiment much like he had Jacob's new clothing.

Joe Swiretynsky opposed the summer trip right up to the bitter end. Only moments before Jacob boarded the plane did he cease fire and take his son in his arms to tearfully wish him a wonderful time. He didn't let go of Jacob before reminding him how much he loved him. The feelings between the father and son had always run deep and neither ever had problems verbalizing them.

As soon as the wheels of the plane reached to touch Oklahoma soil, Jacob made a wish that it could be much the same between Burl Hansen and himself. Along with the thought of his blood father came the lightning-like surge of emotions that always struck when he said or thought the famous name. This time the effect felt even more breath-taking than usual because Jacob was only minutes away from meeting him.

The divers came up to signal a successful attachment of the two-ton wrecker's heavy cable to the submerged car's frame. It could not be pulled up from the direction it entered the lake because of the bluff. It would be coming out from a different angle, front-end first. The divers had already identified the car as a Camaro. Hansen now waited anxiously to confirm that it was *their* Camaro.

Turner moaned loudly when the first few feet of the car broke the surface of the still lake. Three months under water took its toll on the paint job, but the red finish was intact. The wrecker operator disengaged the screeching winch the moment all four of the Camaro's tires were on dry land. He crawled up into the big truck and dragged the car about a hundred feet from the water's edge. When he killed the noisy engine the sudden hush seemed practically abusive.

At first no one moved. All stood silently by and watched and waited for the water to drain from the vehicle's compartments. Turner walked up to the rear of the car once the water stopped gushing and wiped away the algae covering the tag. He blocked Hansen's view of the tag, but when his friend groaned an obscenity, Hansen knew they'd found Shelly Rafell's Camaro. They now knew that at least half of what Herman Grambs revealed had proven to be true. Hansen stood on suddenly weakened legs, taking quick shallow breaths while contemplating the measures necessary to determine the accuracy of the second half of Grambs' allegations. The wrecker driver approached with a cordless drill and assortment of other tools.

"You might as well get to it," Hansen said, his voice breaking.

Turner stepped aside as the man with the drill walked up to the rear of the Camaro and started to work on the trunk lock. The two sheriffs and chief of police lined up several feet behind the man and watched silently as he worked. Short minutes later, he straightened and turned to face the lawmen.

"I've punched the lock and tripped the latch. It must be rusted shut," he winced while simultaneously extending a small pry bar toward the officers. "I don't really care to be the one that opens it."

When the other two men offered no immediate response, Hansen reached out and took the tool while wondering why in the hell he had done so. Why had he always felt required to do the things that no one else could stomach? He reluctantly forced his legs to move him up to the car. He took and held a deep breath as he applied the business end of the bar under the lip of the trunk lid and pushed downward. It popped open without much force but only about three inches. Hansen knew any hesitation would only compound his dread. He grabbed the trunk lid and hoisted it upward. The condition of the two bodies sent him stumbling backwards.

The roof of the county courthouse became Herman Grambs' favorite place in the world he'd lived in since March. From on top of the four-story structure he could see the world he came from — and the one to which he so desperately wished to return. From the roof he could see the Kiamichi Mountains.

The only thing Herman wanted out of life now was to go back to the peaks rimming the north and east horizons. He wanted to hunt coons at night and deer early in the mornings. He wanted to spend his afternoons lounging on the riverbanks while fishing for catfish. He wanted to hear his hounds bay and his rooster crowing at dawn. And he didn't want to be around any people, because lately, people meant nothing to him but trouble and a whole lot of potential harm.

Today Herman didn't have much time to spend on the roof. That asshole Paul Winters had really loaded him down with work, and Herman intended to get it done fast and get it done good. A man needing big favors had to do everything just right. Although he didn't have much time, he didn't need it. Just mere moments of glancing at his mountains could make him feel better. A simple glimpse of the Kiamichis seemed to instill hope that Burl Hansen would do something to keep him from going to prison.

With a few minutes remaining, Herman stepped right up to the edge of the building. He knew it only put him inches closer, but inches closer to the mountains was still inches closer to home. Herman gave the range one more longing glance before being startled by the crunching sound of footsteps on the brittle portions of the asphalt roof. Too much had been said and far too much done for Herman to be anything but jumpy. He spun so abruptly he lost his balance and for a split second Herman thought he might go over the edge, but he regained his footing.

"Damn, it's just you," Herman grinned sheepishly to the lean man walking up behind him. "I thought it might be...well, I though it might be somebody else."

Since being elected, Hansen had seen more than a few dead bodies. Some were mangled in car wrecks and one died of a self-inflicted gunshot to the head. The rest died of natural causes — mostly old age. The two hideous forms in the trunk were his first "decomps." Turner tried to make him feel better about tossing his lunch, but it didn't help. Hansen couldn't be fooled. Vomiting mere feet away from bloated bodies the color of the night sky just proved him unsuited for a career in law enforcement.

Sheriff Burgess walked to his car to radio for agents from the Oklahoma State Bureau of Investigation. Hansen and Turner moved thirty or so yards upwind of the bodies and his puke. Both stared silently at the car while Hansen spit every few seconds. Regurgitated tacos had a way of staying with a man.

"I guess there's no doubt about that being Darrell and Sally," Hansen said, breaking the silence and nodding toward the car.

"Not enough doubt to keep me from having to notify the next of kin," Turner said gloomily.

Hansen selfishly felt relieved that the Hallums and Marlene Rafell lived in the city limits, and he didn't volunteer to accompany Turner. He'd done his dirty work for the day by opening the trunk.

"Who could have done such a thing…and why?" Turner wondered out loud.

"Herman knows who did it," Hansen said. After a few seconds of considering what few pieces he held of this puzzle, it hit him — like a bolt of lightning.

"And I know who did it, too!" he said, turning to face his friend.

"Huh?" Turner blurted as he wheeled from the car to stare at Hansen.

"It was Jerry Glass and Mike Rider." Hansen suddenly felt energized.

"What in the hell makes you think that?"

"First off, they're on the run," Hansen reasoned. "Rider hasn't come back from Mexico since Bemo went missing, and Glass hauled ass back down there the minute he got out of jail on that DUI. As a matter of fact, he failed to show for his court date the other day. Those boys aren't coming back and now I know why."

"All right," Turner said with a thoughtful nod of his head, "I can buy that they're good for whatever happened to Bemo, but how are you tying them to our dead kids?"

"Think about it. What was the motive for killing that boy and girl and stuffing them in the trunk?"

"Hell, I have no idea," Turner frowned.

"It was obviously racially motivated. It was a hate crime. So, our suspects have to be big-time bigots. Glass and Rider had their initial run-in with Bemo because he was an Indian. I think they're the bigots that killed Darrell and Shelly."

Turner shook his head no. "The only thing you can prove that those men ever did to Bemo was call him names and push him into a fight. There's too big of a gap between that and what happened to Baker and Rafell. I'm sorry, old buddy, but you're just grasping for straws. You have absolutely nothing that can link those assholes with that dead boy and girl."

"That's where you're wrong," Hansen proclaimed. "Herman Grambs is our link. We just have to convince him that we can protect him from Glass and Rider."

Jacob walked out of the skyway and straight into the

arms of Vicki Hansen. After embracing him, kissing both his cheeks, and gushing her joy in a flood of greetings and welcomes, she stepped to the side and held out a hand in presentation of the two small forms standing behind her.

"Jacob, this is Sandy and Bret. Sandy and Bret, this is your big brother, Jacob."

Sandy stepped right up, raised her arms and opened them wide, "Hi, Jacob," she beamed with a smile that lacked the two bottom front teeth. "I'm glad you've come to stay with us."

Jacob bent low and hugged the pretty little girl with the long brownish-red hair. Before he could say anything though, she bounced back and looked at her other brother.

"Don't just stand there, Bret," she quipped with hands on hips, "Give our big brother a hug!"

The little boy looked back at Sandy and snarled, "Brothers don't hug each other." Bret had at least as many freckles as Jacob and the same sandy-blonde hair, only his was cut short in a flat-top. When he looked back to Jacob, the snarl dissolved into an expression of curiosity. "Nobody told me you was a cowboy."

"Actually, I'm not a cowboy. I'm simply disguised as one." Jacob smiled at the boy clad in shorts, t-shirt and high-tops.

"Nobody told me you talked funny either."

"Bret!" His mother and sister chorused.

"Well, you people ought to tell me these things. Anyway, he does talk funny," the boy snarled once again.

While Vicki made motherly corrections and Sandy echoed her, Jacob looked around in anticipation of locating Burl Hansen. Maybe he'd parked the car or awaited them in the baggage claim area. The next thing he knew both of his hands were in both of Vicki's.

"Oh, honey," she said apologetically, "You must be looking for Burl."

Before Jacob's heart hit the floor, she quickly added, "He wanted to be here so badly, but something just terrible has happened at home."

"He's looking for two big kids that are murdered," Bret blurted loudly.

"Lower your voice, Bret, and stop interrupting," Vicki sighed.

"Well, he is! And he's looking for who murdered them, too!"

Vicki hooked her arm in Jacob's and started him down the terminal. "It's probably the worst crime ever committed in our county. I'll tell you all about it on the way home, but please don't be upset that Burl's not here."

His blood father, the great Chicago Bear defensive lineman, could not make it to the airport because he had to track down the perpetrator of a double homicide. Jacob wondered what kind of fourteen-year-old son could be upset over something so amazingly cool.

Undersheriff Marsh had tried five times in the last hour to raise Hansen on his cell phone. When not dialing, Marsh paced. Before calling a sixth time a very obvious alternative came to mind — he could get a message to his boss through the Seminole County Sheriff's Office. That he or no one else thought of the simple solution earlier just pointed to how distraught they all were over the news needing passed to their sheriff.

Marsh asked his dispatcher to call Seminole County. He'd instructed Edna to just tell their dispatcher to have Hansen call his office. In less than ten minutes, Edna informed Marsh she had Burl on the line. Marsh told the dispatcher he'd take the call in Hansen's office. Although everyone present knew what had happened, he stepped into the private office and shut the door behind him.

"Hi, Burl," Marsh said weakly.

"Hey, Pete. I'm sorry I didn't call earlier it's just, well, Herman had it right, Pete…the kids are in the trunk."

Hansen obviously thought Marsh called for an update, and although the news about the *runaway* juveniles didn't shock Marsh, Hansen would expect it to. "Damn, Burl. I was hoping that would all be bullshit."

"It's not bullshit, Pete."

Marsh detected the stress in Hansen's voice and he sincerely hated to add to it, but some things could not be helped. "Burl, we have bad news on this end, too. Herman Grambs has committed suicide."

After a long pause, an uncharacteristically emotional

voice whined, "Oh fuck, Pete, tell me you're just pulling my leg. Tell me this is just a really bad joke."

"I'm sorry, Burl. I knew you'd take it hard. I wanted to tell you in person, but I knew you would want to know about it as soon as possible."

"This is blowing my mind, Pete. Hell, I'm right now less than thirty yards from two dead bodies he told me about. And he told me about these bodies because he was afraid of going to prison and being killed. And he wouldn't tell me who murdered the boy and girl because he was afraid that person would kill him as well. Now you're telling me, Pete, that this guy that was so afraid of dying has killed himself?"

"He jumped off the courthouse, Burl. He was found lying in the alley."

"That just does not add up, Pete."

"I don't know what to tell you boss…except he's dead, and every indication we have is that he jumped to his death from the fourth floor of our building."

Marsh gave Hansen several seconds to respond. When he didn't, the subordinate added, "Listen Burl, I know you really cared for Herman, and I'm sorry I had to break this to you."

"Yeah, Pete," Hansen exhaled, sounding more tired than Marsh ever heard him sound. "I appreciate you letting me know. We can discuss it more in detail when I get back there. And, uh, I hope you're okay. I know you had grown fond of him as well."

Burl wasn't wrong. Marsh grew to like the little bastard all right. As a matter of fact, pushing him off the edge of the building had been one of the hardest things he'd ever done. But, there it was again — some things could not be helped.

Chapter Thirteen

"Me and Daddy caught them catfish ourselves down at the river," Bret boasted.

Jacob looked from the boy back to the heaping platter Vicki placed in the middle of the table. "What…exactly… is a catfish?" Jacob asked diplomatically. The steaming and breaded hunks of golden-brown didn't look unappetizing, just unfamiliar.

"Oh, good," Vicki said as she stepped from the kitchen into the dining room with another platter of different steaming brown stuff. "I was hoping you'd never had fried catfish. I wanted your first meal here to be typically Oklahoman. Besides the fish, we're having home fries, slaw, and my special made-from-scratch biscuits."

Bret grabbed a chair and bellied up to the table. "Daddy says catfish are bottom feeders. He calls them river pigs 'cause they'll eat just anything. He says he don't know how something that eats, shi…uh…crap, can taste so good!"

"Did you wash your hands, Bret?" Vicki scowled.

"Yes, ma'am."

"I can tell from here that you didn't wash them well enough. Get back in there and scrub them good."

Bret stomped away from the table with a drawn out, "Awwwwwww, Mom!"

"If you haven't noticed," Vicki chuckled to Jacob, "that is one of his favorite expressions."

Jacob certainly noticed. Upon Vicki's invitation, he took a seat at the table and breathed deeply, absorbing the combination of wonderful smells. He'd never been a finicky eater. If the fish tasted half as wonderful as it looked and smelled, then it wouldn't matter to him what it ate while alive.

Vicki called out for Sandy and then took a seat across from Jacob. When the young ones were seated Vicki bowed her head, and the children followed her lead.

"Thank you, dear Heavenly Father, for this food. Bless it to the nourishment of our bodies. In Jesus name we pray, Amen."

Jacob raised his head to find his younger brother staring curiously at him. He quite obviously expected Jacob to react to the prayer's ending.

"Bret," Vicki said sharply, "I suggest you fill your mouth with food."

Jacob greatly appreciated the timely intervention. It was much too early in the visit to tackle the inevitable.

"How about another piece of pie?" Vicki beamed. The boy most definitely inherited his father's appetite.

"I would most assuredly burst," Jacob smiled as he pushed his chair back from the table with a groan.

"Give me another one!" Bret piped.

"You've had enough," Vicki answered.

"I only had one piece. He had two." The smaller boy said with a thumb hitched toward the bigger boy.

"Jacob got twice the amount of pie because he is twice as big as you are," Vicki said, smiling at Jacob again.

Bret studied his older brother a second or two before nodding his head in agreement. "He's a big 'un all right!"

"Yes, he is, and you two little ones have chores to do," Vicki said as she got up from the table.

Sandy left the dining room without a word. Not so with Bret. He mumbled and grumbled his way through the house and out the back door.

Jacob laughed and it pleased Vicki that the little exhibition amused him.

Anyone sharing living space with Bret Hansen had to have a sense of humor. When Vicki started gathering plates, Jacob stood up.

"I'll help you," he politely offered.

His statement spawned an observation and Vicki stopped what she was doing. "You haven't called me anything," she said softly with a smile.

"I beg your pardon?" Jacob responded with arched eyebrows.

"You haven't called me anything. I mean, you haven't, you know, used any names to address me. Do you know what I mean?" she asked, biting her lip.

She could tell by the look on his face that he knew exactly what she meant.

"I didn't know how to refer to you…what to call you," he said sheepishly.

"What would you be most comfortable calling me?"

Jacob averted his eyes to the cluttered table and after a long pause finally cleared his throat and said, "Probably… Vicki…It just wouldn't feel…I mean…I have always…"

Jacob's discomfort was practically tangible, and Vicki rushed in to take him off the hot seat. "Then 'Vicki' it is!" She beamed with a fabricated smile. With time, she hoped, he might choose to call her something different, but for now she would be most pleased with him just being comfortable in his new surroundings.

"I just want you to know, Jacob, that for weeks now I've wondered about little things like this. Like, what do you want to call me? What kind of things do you like? What do you dislike? And…and would you even like me? I guess that was my biggest concern."

"I know," Jacob nodded earnestly. "I worried that you might think I'm too fat, or that I have too many freckles," he blushed.

"We have so little time to be together," Vicki said as she moved closer to her son, "that I don't think we can hesitate to speak our minds, to clarify for each other what we think and feel." Vicki brushed the back of her fingers lightly against Jacob's freckled cheek. "And for the record, I think you are a very handsome young man."

Jacob smiled shyly, "Thank you." Then he quickly changed the subject. "Will Burl be comfortable with me calling him Burl?"

Vicki faked yet another smile. "I think that will be just fine with him." Actually, she feared Burl would not be comfortable with Jacob calling him anything other than his given name.

"Speaking of whom," Jacob inserted, "does he normally work this late?"

She sensed something bothersome behind the boy's sweet smile. Vicki worried that he might be thinking what she too had suspected — Burl was making no special efforts to get home quickly.

Taking her son by the hand and turning him from the table, Vicki responded, "Get used to it. Your birth father is a workaholic…but I'm sure he's very anxious to get here and see you." Vicki chose her last words carefully. She wouldn't lie to her children.

"While we are waiting," she added, leading Jacob from the dining room, "there's something I want to show you."

Jacob followed Vicki through the living room to a set

of closed French doors. She positioned him in front of them and told him to close his eyes. A sucker for surprises — when they weren't comprised of garishly decorated buckaroo clothes — Jacob carried out the order.

Vicki opened the doors before taking hold of his hands. "Now, don't peek," she laughed playfully.

She pulled Jacob several steps forward. "You can look now," Vicki exclaimed.

He opened his eyes and his mouth dropped open.

"Burl calls this his study," she giggled. "I call it his shrine."

Bookshelves lined the walls. Books were separated in some places by trophies, others by football photographs, sports articles, or game balls. On the wall adjacent to the doors, hung a display case full of sensational championship rings, all arranged to show deference to a most spectacular ring in the center of the case.

"Is the one in the middle…" Jacob paused to swallow hard, "…the Super Bowl ring?"

"His one and only," Vicki smiled. "I'm sure you know he was traded to Indianapolis the last year he played pro ball. Don't tell him I told you so, but it kind of bugs him that he played all those splendid years in Chicago and then got his only Super Bowl ring as a Colt. The rest of the rings are from high school, college, and division championships. Did you see this?"

Jacob pried his eyes from the rings to see Vicki hitching a thumb over her shoulder to the wall behind them. Covering the entire portion was a life-size poster of Burl Hansen ferociously sacking Payton Manning.

"Oh...my...goodness!" Jacob stammered.

"Pretty scary, huh? I think that was in 2005. He had no idea that Payton would be his teammate two years later," Vicki said with a shake of her head.

"It is incredible," Jacob said before turning his head to slowly scan the room. "I'm simply astonished."

"I thought you might be," Vicki grinned. "Tell you what, why don't you stay in here and browse while I clean the kitchen?"

She closed the doors behind her, and Jacob quickly lost himself in his *real* father's glorious past.

Peter Marsh felt like kicking himself. His normally exceptional ability of judging character most certainly failed him this time. Butch Myers had proven once again to be ignorant and irresponsible as well as habitually late. The longer Marsh waited in the abandoned old school building, the angrier he became. Finally at nine-thirty, headlights lit up the dark interior of the ancient rock structure. Marsh recognized the rumble of Myers' old Ford pickup. He was thirty minutes late.

The big subordinate entered the building muttering one of his lame excuses. Marsh loudly cut him off, "Shut the fuck up!"

"Hey, who the hell do you think you are talking to me

that way?" Myers roared in his well-polished tough man brogue.

Marsh remained silent just long enough to create the effect he wanted and he made sure his tone rang ominous when he did speak. "Poor Butch. How quickly you forget. I guess you need a reminder."

Myers cleared his throat. "Damn…Pete…what are you all pissed off about?" The bravado was gone. "Hey, uh Pete, why don't you step out of those shadows so I can see you? You know this place gives me the creeps. The way you're standing there…I can't see you…it's spooky. I don't like this goddamned place."

Marsh remained in the shadows. He didn't want Myers to see the gun in his hand. "By now you know what happened at the jail today," he said calmly.

"I know Grambs committed suicide…heard he jumped off the building. Is that why we're here? Is that why you're so pissed?" Myers' words held a nervous edge.

Marsh pulled the trigger and the .357 thundered in the confined quarters. The bullet hit exactly where Marsh intended, and Myers went to his knees with a scream. Dust and chips of rock pelted the head Marsh intentionally missed by mere inches.

Marsh darted out of the shadows before Myers could gather his wits and pressed the big revolver between a set of wide and quivering eyes.

"He didn't jump off the building, Butch. I pushed him off the building. And you know why I was forced to take such drastic action, don't you?"

"What the fuck's gotten into you, Pete? What the fuck are you talking about?"

Marsh pushed harder on the pistol, pulling back the hammer. The sound of the revolver being cocked echoed off the rock walls and big, bad Butch Myers began to sob.

"Why did you tell him, you ignorant son of a bitch?" Marsh asked in an ice-cold whisper.

"I was drunk, Pete! Goddamn, man, you know how drunk I was the night Hansen put me in jail. Please, Pete, I don't want to go like this. Don't kill me in this fucking place!" Myers begged between great, shaking sobs.

"I can't trust you anymore, Butch."

"Pete…it wasn't like I told an outsider…Grambs was one of us, for God's sake!"

"He wasn't one of the Inner Circle, you fuck!" Marsh thundered. "I hand-pick everyone in the Inner Circle just like I hand-picked you!"

"Give me another chance, Pete! Oh, God, please just give me one more chance...I didn't tell him about the big Indian. I just told him about the kids. I didn't say shit about Bemo…see Pete? You can trust me. I didn't tell him *everything*!"

"So you didn't tell him about this place?"

"No! No! I swear to God I didn't!"

"So, no one but our little groups knows about the cellar that's right down below our feet, Butch?"

"If anyone else knows...I wasn't the one to tell them," Myers gasped as he swayed back and forth on his knees.

"You know, Butch, old Bemo is probably really ripe by now. I bet that body is looking just awful. You want a chance to see it, Butch? Up close and personal? There's always room down there for one more!"

When Myers collapsed the rest of the way to the floor in a heap of hysterical cries, Marsh holstered his weapon.

"You got one more chance, Butch. But I promise you, you don't want to fuck up again."

"Oh, God, Pete, I won't. I'll never let you down again. I swear, Pete...I swear on my mama's grave that I won't. I'll make this up to you, too, Pete. You can trust me, man. From this point forward, you can trust me, Pete!"

Marsh would never trust the man again — but he still had a need for him. "Okay, Butch, one more chance. And there won't be another. You can bet your life on that. It'll be you and Bemo...together for eternity!"

Myers babbled words Marsh could not make out, but his animated gestures — like the redeemed reaching upward for Christ — expressed his gratitude.

"Get your ass off the floor, Butch. We have work to do...the commander wants us to interview a possible candidate."

Jacob carefully lifted the ball from its wooden cradle.

According to the little gold plate on the cradle this football had seen service in the Super Bowl. Jacob rotated it in his hands gently, as if it was made from the finest porcelain instead of the hide of a barnyard animal. Moments of close examination revealed scuffs and scrapes on the football. Still, Jacob held it like one might a small baby. The battle scars made the ball even more deserving of care and respect. From behind Jacob, a gruff male voice expressed a different opinion.

"You can't hurt it, you know. It's just a football."

Jacob spun around to find standing in the doorway the man to whom the wonderful room paid tribute — the one, the only, the legendary Burl Hansen of Chicago, Indianapolis, and Super Bowl fame. He was the first real celebrity — the only famous person — with whom Jacob had ever come face to face. The football fell from his hands and bounced away.

By virtue of his hopelessly shy nature, Jacob in normal circumstances would have contained his excitement and merely gawked from a distance. But this was no normal circumstance, no chance meeting, and not just any great person. His own flesh and blood filled the doorway and Jacob responded accordingly. He bound across the room with arms open wide and threw himself at the father he'd never met.

Jacob's arms wrapped as he hugged and he expected the same in return, but Burl did not hug back. Jacob hung on for ten seconds. He suddenly felt very embarrassed by the prospect of backing away from an unreturned embrace. Of all the things he did not understand at that moment, one thing seemed clear: the longer he held on, the harder letting go would be.

Jacob's arms fell slack like those of the giant towering over him. He backed away while dropping his chin to his chest and letting his gaze fall to the floor at his feet. Only one explanation for the awkward introduction seemed possible — Burl did not want Jacob here. Only one thing remained uncertain for Jacob — did *here* only apply to the man's study or his world in general?

Hansen could sense the boy's pain but he felt absolutely incapable of doing or saying anything to alleviate it. Upon first entering the study, he'd watched the boy for several long minutes before forming his first words. After fourteen years of feeling the loss, his first exchange with a son he'd never seen had been about a stupid football.

Hansen felt like a man wrapped tightly in a choking web of his own emotions so thickly woven he couldn't reach out. He couldn't even hug back.

The mere sight of the boy touched him deeply. So much, in fact, he came close to bursting through the barriers holding him back. Vicki had been right. Looking at Jacob was like looking back in time at himself. He came close to hugging back, but not close enough. It just felt wrong.

It felt wrong to bring the boy into their lives for such a short period of time. He would be here and then he would be gone. Nothing good could come from growing close only to give him up once again. Hansen simply could not bring himself to play daddy for just a few short months.

His concerns did not end there. From the depths of his heart Burl feared it could be a very bad time for this boy to be in Antlers, Oklahoma. What if it hadn't been Glass and Rider who murdered the two kids and engineered Bemo's disappearance? What if someone else killed simply because of racial differences? People who would kill over colors of skin would as well strike out at those of different creeds. No, it was not a good time for a Jewish boy to be in Pushmataha County.

But here he stood dejectedly in front of Hansen. When he couldn't do anything else, the father extended his right hand, and the boy accepted it.

"I'm sorry I'm so late getting here," he said, trying hard to make it sound like the truth.

The boy didn't look as though he bought it, but responded pleasantly, "I understand."

Burl hoped he didn't. "Hey, it's, uh, just been a really bad day and I'm really exhausted. After a good night's sleep, maybe we can sit down in the morning and, uh, well, get acquainted."

Jacob nodded his head and smiled feebly. Hansen returned the same before backing out of the study and retreating to his bedroom.

At well past midnight, Tom Avery's hotrod pickup sat parked in front of his shop. Marsh pounded on the locked door until a light came on inside. When Avery opened the door, he did not seem surprised to find Marsh and Butch Myers.

"I hope this is a social call," Avery grinned as he squinted sleep-matted eyes.

"I intend for it to be," Marsh responded.

"Then come on in," Avery said as he stepped aside and motioned the two men inside.

Marsh stepped into the cluttered and oily little shop and came right to the point. "For several months now you've been nosing about and asking a lot of questions about what we thought was a tightly held little secret."

"I've heard things," Avery shrugged.

"From who?" Marsh questioned.

Tom Avery hesitated then shrugged again. "I was in the army with the dude that sold you the M16s. He won't talk to nobody else, but he'll talk to me. We're tight."

Marsh tucked the tidbit of information away. They would have to find another dealer. From what he knew about Avery, no real harm had been done, but they couldn't take any chances in the future.

"Well, we've been doing our own nosing about," Marsh

nodded. "It seems that you're an okay kind of guy."

"I'm your kind of people," Avery grinned.

Butch Myers grunted his suspicion, and Marsh cut his eyes at him. He'd instructed the idiot to keep his mouth shut.

"Oh, yeah?" Marsh responded to Avery, "How's that?"

"I believe in the same things you do."

"We believe in the United States of America, Avery. A proud and strong United States. Nothing more, nothing less."

"I can dig it," Avery chuckled.

"That's good," Marsh responded harshly. "You be here and ready to go at five Saturday morning. I'll pick you up. Do you know how to dress like a turkey hunter?"

"I'm a hell of a turkey hunter, Deputy."

"Let's hope so," Marsh said as he nudged Myers toward the door.

Chapter Fourteen

Jacob leisurely awoke to the noise and aroma wafting up from downstairs. He lay still for a moment trying to process his surroundings but once fully lucid, he could not remain in bed a moment longer. He pulled on jeans, shirt and boots to the accompaniment of the lively sounds coming from below, most of which were being generated by the shrill voices of his brother and sister.

The aroma smelled of breakfast. Vicki expressed relief the night before that the Swiretynsky's did not "eat kosher" because it would prevent her from preparing many of her favorite foods. Jacob always felt fortunate his family did not observe the laws of kashrut, but more so now than ever. He absolutely never tasted anything as delightful as last night's dinner, and now, the smell of bacon and eggs filled the air.

The prospect of eating another of Vicki's meals certainly didn't slow Jacob down, but it wasn't the true reason he rushed to get downstairs. He wanted to see Burl. Jacob felt dejected and embarrassed after their initial and brief encounter in the study, until Vicki intervened.

She had knocked on the door to Jacob's new bedroom moments after he'd crawled beneath the sheets. With a distraught look on her face, she explained, "I didn't even know he was home until I went into our room to get ready for bed." She clumsily skipped over whatever she knew about the first meeting between father and son by saying, "He's had just a terrible day."

Vicki went on to repeat what Burl off-loaded onto her — about the two bodies in the trunk. What they looked like. The terrible odor. About how Burl knew the man, Herman Grambs, since boyhood. How Herman Grambs took his life by jumping four stories onto a concrete sidewalk. And Jacob went to bed feeling awful in one respect, but a lot better in another. After a day of heartache and horror, who could blame a man for not being able to return a hug?

The staircase in the Hansen's rambling old ranch house was not at all like the grand, spacious one in the Swiretynsky mansion. When in a hurry, Jacob could easily descend from the mansion's staircase covering two steps at a time. Here, he slowed considerably for the steep and narrow descent. From the base of the staircase, however, Jacob had the length of a dining room to pick up steam before literally bursting through the door separating the dining room from the kitchen.

With a beaming smile he found Vicki frying bacon at

the stove, Sandy perched at the kitchen table coloring, and Bret on the floor crashing a large metal truck into a line of smaller plastic cars. Burl was nowhere to be seen.

"I assume Burl is out doing ranch...stuff?"

Vicki picked up on the hopeful note in Jacob's words and the doubtful look in his eyes.

She took a deep breath and forced a smile before saying, "Oh, honey, it's almost nine o'clock. Burl's been in his office for nearly two hours by now."

When the boy's head dropped and his shoulders slumped, Vicki laid down her spatula and moved to him. She placed a finger beneath his chin, pulling it up until his eyes met hers. "Don't take his not being here personally, Jacob. A ranching sheriff has to be taking care of his livestock before dawn and his constituents by seven."

Of course, Burl could have made exceptions just this one day, but Vicki wasn't about to point that out to her son. She also didn't want him to know that his father left home even earlier today than usual. She really didn't know what time her husband got up because Burl hadn't bothered to wake her. But there remained one fact Vicki would point out — something she intended to insure. "Don't worry though. He will be home on time this evening. You can bet on it."

Jacob still looked disappointed but no longer devastated.

Vicki gave him a hug and then went back to her stove. "I took a chance on you being ready for breakfast. I'll have bacon, eggs, gravy and biscuits for you in just a minute or two. I hope you're hungry."

"Famished," Jacob nodded. "Has everyone else already eaten?"

Vicki couldn't beat her youngest son to a response.

"Sure did," Bret said with a condescending smirk and shake of his small head. "As Dad would say, 'heck, boy, it's nearly lunch time!'"

It amused Vicki to see Jacob simply ignore Bret. The ability to do so proved necessary for maintaining one's sanity around the Hansen place.

"Tell you what, Mr. Smart Mouth," Vicki said while looking down at Bret, "once your big brother has finished eating, you can give him a tour around the ranch."

"All six hundred acres?" Bret quipped.

"All of it that he cares to see," Vicki quipped back.

"Cool," Bret muttered under his breath.

Yeah, cool, Vicki thought. She didn't want Jacob anywhere near the house when she got the sheriff of Pushmataha County on the phone.

For the first time in his life, Jacob stood in a place where no matter what direction he turned, he couldn't see some type of manmade object. From his vantage point in the small meadow, he could see stands of towering pines, ravines and rock-strewn hilltops, but not apartment buildings, office complexes or malls — not even a house or barn. For several seconds he paused just to breathe deeply of air not containing any smell he recognized.

"What'cha stopping for?" Bret called back to him. "Ya see a rattler or something?"

"A rattler?" Jacob stiffened.

"Yeah, you know, a rattlesnake," Bret said as he trotted back to his older brother.

"There are rattlesnakes here?"

"Sure, there's rattlers, copperheads, and cotton mouths around the ponds. We have snakes out the ass around here!" Then after a slight pause, "Don't tell Mom I said ass!"

Jacob couldn't imagine how it might come up in conversation with Vicki. "I don't intend to."

"Do you cuss?"

It took Jacob a second or two to translate the dialect. "No, Bret. I don't 'cuss.' Nor do I curse."

"Huh?" Bret said with nose and eyebrows scrunched, but quickly let it pass. "Well, I do. I use damn and hell and shit a lot. But I don't use the 'F' or 'GD' word much..." Then with eyebrows arched and eyes squinted the boy uttered, "...I don't think Jesus cares much for those words... do you?"

Jacob fought off the urge to smile at the little guy's attempt at being sly. Instead, he went with a hunch. "Didn't your mother tell you that you shouldn't be trying to discuss Jesus with me?"

"Oh, yeah, I forgot," Bret grinned. "Don't tell her I said anything about him, okay?"

The topic of Jesus would sooner or later most definitely come up in conversation with Vicki. And with all the shocking facts that would surface with such a talk, Bret's indiscretion would rank far too insignificant for even an honorable mention. For on the topic of religion, Jacob held a secret he'd never revealed to anyone. But since he intended his relationship with his birth parents to be based on truth and honesty, he would no longer be able to keep it a secret. He hoped it might be easier explaining to biological parents what he *was* than confessing to his adoptive parents what he'd *become*.

"Okay," he finally gave in.

"And remember, don't tell her I cuss. She wouldn't like that at all."

"I will not tell her."

"Good. You know brothers are supposed to trust each other. So, I trust you. Hey, you want to see my favorite secret hideout?"

"How far away is it?" Jacob's feet were already starting to hurt.

"It ain't but a hop, skip, and a jump."

A hop, skip and a jump it would most definitely be, Jacob thought as he once again trudged after the spry adolescent — especially if they were to cross paths with a "rattler."

Hansen looked up from the report on Grambs' death when Marsh called to him from the outer office.

"Burl, Vicki's on line two."

"Tell her I'm busy...that I'll get back with her later."

Seconds later Marsh stuck his head in Hansen's office. "Hey, uh, boss, Vicki says unless you're on the toilet or in conference with the governor, you better get on the phone. She's adamant."

Hansen knew what she wanted, didn't want to talk about it, and considered just not picking up. That tactic, however, would delay the inevitable for just the twenty minutes it would take Vicki to get into town.

Hansen grumbled an expletive and grabbed the receiver. "What is it, Vicki?"

"I never thought I'd be saying these words to you, Burl, but you are one sorry son of a bitch!"

"I am in no frame of mind for your shit, woman!" Hansen bellowed without regard for those in the outer offices.

"Don't you try to scare or bully me, Burl Hansen! Any man that ducks out of his home in the wee hours of the morning to keep from facing a teenaged boy can't be all that rough and tough! You're not only a sorry son of a bitch, but you're a coward, too!"

"I'm going to hang up on you, Vicki!"

"You do, and you can find some place else to sleep tonight. As a matter of fact, why don't you just go ahead and do that, and make sure it's a place you can stay for the next couple of months while Jacob is here, and if you can stay gone that long, why don't you just plan on staying gone from now on you cowardly and sorry son of a bitch!"

He did not detect as much as a quiver in her voice. If she was bluffing, she did one damn fine job of it. This had already gotten out of hand, and Burl didn't want it to end up slipping out of reach.

"Now, Vicki you don't mean that," Burl said with a much more tender tone.

"The hell I don't!"

When Vicki cursed, she wasn't bluffing. "Baby, you don't understand."

"You're damn right I don't understand. How can I understand when I don't even know what you're thinking or feeling?"

"Vicki, I haven't heard you say this many foul words in five years...that's about how long you've been active in church, I guess."

"Don't you start up that road, Burl!"

"I'm not trying to be ugly, Baby. I promise. I'm just trying to calm you down."

"Well, you don't worry about my cussing. That's between me and my Savior. You just better worry about the harm you're doing to one sweet and innocent kid."

After a long, hard sigh Burl offered the only defense that came to mind. "I just have a lot on my mind. I need some more time to think this visit over and come to terms with it."

"That's a crock, Burl," Vicki shot back without hesitation. "You've had three months to think this visit out. If you haven't done it by now, you're not near as bright as I've always given you credit for.

"And I know you have problems…big problems…" for a second her voice softened, but only for a second. "…but you are a big boy, Burl, and it's time you reached down between your legs, grabbed a handful of balls and started acting like a big boy, Burl!"

Now Hansen really wanted to lash out and say some hurtful things for no other reason than just to continue the fight. But why fight a battle just for the sake of fighting when the war looked to be as good as lost? Vicki had buried the battle-axe of truth right up to the hilt — square up the middle of his ass.

"Okay. Okay," Burl sighed again, "What can I do to make this thing right?"

"For starters you can be home on time this evening."

"Okay."

"Better yet, come home early."

Hansen almost told Vicki not to push it, but then he thought of a better response.

"Okay."

Butch Myers picked up another rock and threw it with a vengeance into the murky waters of the Kiamichi River.

Then he took another healthy swig from the pint bottle of cheap whiskey. He couldn't afford anything but the cheap stuff nowadays, but it hadn't always been that way. When he'd been a by-God contender, he'd drunk some of the finest whiskey in the swankiest joints that the greatest cities had to offer. But back then the world and everyone in it hadn't yet started shitting on Butch Myers.

His manager and promoter had been the first to dump on him. He'd told them both he wasn't up for that fight. Hell, he'd just gotten over the worst bout of the flu he'd ever had in his life. But they wouldn't listen — they thought it too late to go making any changes — told him he could take Oscar Henning by the third round healthy or not. After all, who'd ever heard of Oscar Henning? He was a nobody.

And everybody agreed that the ref shit on him. If he'd just called Henning for the head-butt in the second round or the low blow in the third, things might have turned out differently. Then the fans shit on him, too — started cheering that black bastard on — the whole house turned on Butch. The whole world turned on Butch. They all shit on him.

Now Pete Marsh started doing the same. He'd dumped on him and embarrassed him and humiliated him badly. He made Butch cry like a weak and sniveling coward. Butch never cried in front of another man before — *never.*

Marsh really pissed Butch off, but he really couldn't blame him for what he'd done. Because of Marsh's position in the organization, he had to keep people in line. No, Butch didn't blame Marsh. He blamed Burl Hansen.

If that goddamned Hansen hadn't put him in jail, Butch wouldn't have had the opportunity to talk to that goofy sonofabitchin' Herman Grambs. And if he hadn't talked to Grambs, Grambs wouldn't have blabbed to Hansen. The more cheap whiskey Butch guzzled, the clearer it became that Hansen fell right dab in the center of all his problems. It all kept leading back to the big bastard with the badge — the one person the whole world would never dream of shitting on. But, by God, that could all end. It could end real fast.

Myers found another rock and threw it with all his might into the Kiamichi River. He'd always loved the old river. He'd been miles and miles up and down its winding, sandy banks. Looking north he realized he had no idea where it started. Glancing to the south, he wondered where it ended. It hadn't been too many miles down river from here — no more than twenty — where they'd killed the black kid in a most brutal fashion. That had been Butch's way of getting even with Oscar Henning.

Now, he promised, he'd find a way to get even with Burl Hansen. Butch brought the bottle to his lips and considered the irony of coming to this conclusion while sitting on land belonging to Hansen. The son of a bitch even owned part of the wonderful river. Hansen had every damned thing. He'd never been shit on. Not yet anyway.

"Please, Bret," Jacob huffed breathlessly, "put that thing down!"

"I told you it won't hurt you!"

Maybe not. But the hideous prehistoric looking creature with all its scales, plates of armor and horrible looking claws could certainly make Jacob harm himself. Stumbling backwards the first few feet, Jacob wheeled around and continued to lumber up the steep hill and away from his giggling little monster of a brother. Bret would have no doubt already caught him had he not been struggling to hold on to the squirming captive the size of a large house cat.

"It's just an armadillo!" Bret squealed with laughter.

"I know what it is," Jacob screamed over his shoulder, "I've seen pictures of them in books, but I still do not want it near me!"

"Okay, pussy," Bret called out disappointedly, "I'll let it go."

Jacob turned in time to see the ugly shelled thing scampering across the ground with speed and agility it didn't seem capable of. Jacob fell into a sitting position and waited for Bret to catch up.

"I guess if I find a bull snake you won't want to play with that either," Bret piped.

"I have no desire to handle snakes, Bret."

"What about a mountain boomer?" he asked hopefully.

"What is a mountain boomer?"

"It's a lizard about this long." Bret spread his hands to specify eight to ten inches. "They're mean and they bite, but they don't bite real hard."

"No, Bret, I don't care to play with a mountain boomer or anything else reptilian."

"Rep what?"

"How much farther are we going, Bret?" Jacob exhaled heavily.

"We can see it from the top of the hill here."

Bret climbed on and Jacob struggled to his feet and followed after him. Jacob got to the top of the hill and paused to catch his breath, but the view that stretched below stole it away again. The rocky knoll upon which they stood tumbled steeply down and dissolved into lush grasslands. After several hundred yards the sea of waving green gave way to drifts of brownish but sparkling sand that disappeared beneath a substantial expanse of water. Jacob grew increasingly enthralled with the diverse scenic wonders of his "native state."

"This is absolutely beautiful," he exclaimed.

"Dad says this is some of the richest bottom land in the county. That's the Kiamichi River," Bret pointed with a stubby index finger.

After romping through the waist-high grasses, the boys pulled off their shoes and shuffled their way up stream in the sun-warmed sand. The occasional litter along the bank and aquatic wonders washed ashore occupied their attention and conversation for the longest time. At a sharp bend in the river where ancient willows reached from a high bank to shade the water, Bret grabbed hold of Jacob's arm.

"That's it right there underneath the branches of those weeping willows!" he shrieked joyously. "That's my favorite secret hideout! Come on!"

Bret didn't release the hold on Jacob's arm until they were tucked away beneath the thick overhang of brittle looking limbs. The canopy did in fact provide adequate concealment and the sand beneath, being shielded from the sun, felt cool and seemed softer to the touch. It was in fact a fine favorite secret hideout and Jacob told his brother as much.

Bret stretched out on his back and folded small hands behind his head. "Dad thinks this might have been an Indian camp back in the old days, but we've never found any arrowheads here."

"Have you found them in other places?" Jacob asked as he followed his little brother's lead and settled back into the cool sand.

"Hell, yes! We've found arrowheads all over this ranch."

"That is so amazing. I'd love to find some."

"Yeah, all Indians like arrowheads," Bret emphasized with quick nods of his head.

"What do you mean by that?"

"Well, we're part Indian you know."

Jacob shot upright. "We are?"

"Sure. Dad got us all Indian cards. I bet he'll get you one, too."

"What is an Indian card?"

"It's a card that shows you're an Indian. We're part Choctaw and Cherokee."

The fact thrilled Jacob. "Fabulous!" He would definitely have to learn more about the so-called "Indian cards."

"You know," Bret said as he rolled over and upon an elbow to face Jacob. "You sure say some weird things for a kid. Don't you ever say words like 'wow' and 'cool?'"

"My father…the one in Boston…literally abhors…I mean hates those two words."

"Ain't it a long ways between here and Boston?"

"Well, yes," Jacob responded before falling back in the sand again.

"So relax, big brother. I won't tell him if you say them. Hell, I don't even know the man and probably won't ever see him anyhow."

After a moment of thought, Jacob grinned, "Cool!"

Both boys started laughing. Then something rustled in the branches overhead.

Jacob cut his laugh off in mid chuckle. "What was that?"

"Probably a bird," Bret said through his laughter. "But sometimes snakes like to crawl around up there and fall off into the water!"

Jacob flew out of the favorite secret hideout in a shot. Bret stumbled out after him with both arms wrapped around his heaving rib cage.

"I was just joking," he cackled.

"You are a real funny character," Jacob grinned after

catching his breath. Then he reached out and grabbed Bret by his arms and playfully pushed him backwards into the soft sand. Bret grabbed a handful of the sand and cocked it back behind his head for launching. Jacob laughingly ducked and spun to face the water so that the sand would hit him in the back instead of in the face. When he did, his eyes fell on the lone man standing and watching them from the far bank of the river.

"Look. Who is that?" he asked Bret.

The younger brother stepped up and alongside the older and stared across the expanse of at least a hundred yards. "Dunno. He's too far away."

Bret raised his hand and waved vigorously, and Jacob did the same. The man staring back did not return any form of greetings. After several long seconds he brought what looked like a bottle to his lips and drank from it for the longest time. The man then heaved it forcibly into the river. Although the distance was far too great, Jacob got the impression the man had thrown the bottle at them.

"Maybe we should start back now," he said softly.

"Yeah, probably so," Bret agreed without taking his eyes off the man on the other side of the river.

"Leave me alone. I'm an old man and I'm dying. Let me do it in peace."

You can't die now. You must work your wonders one last time. The Great One has sent me as a messenger.

"You?" Billy Harjo scoffed. "I have spoken to the Spirit of All That Is through bears and mountain lions and the soaring eagle. Why during my last hours would he send such a despicable creature to send me a message?"

He commands us all. He does not see through the eyes of man. To the Great One none are despicable.

Billy leaned forward in his ragged recliner to stare down at the bottle wedged between his bony knees. "Damn this white man named Jack Daniels," he mumbled. "I do not know if it is his medicine or mine that makes you talk."

Whiskey has never spoken to you in the Choctaw tongue.

Billy reluctantly nodded at the truth. He considered throwing the bottle at the antagonist, but too much of the amber colored pain reliever remained in it. "If I could reach my broom I'd send you flying as I have so many of your kind over the years."

Do the bidding of the Great One and your sins against my kin will be forgiven.

Billy broke into laughter and said, "I must surely be drunk." His laughter gave way to a fit of coughing that left him feeling weak and vulnerable.

"What does the Great One require of me?"

Seek the help of those who love you. You must not sit here and die now.

Billy turned his head to the telephone on the table next to his chair. His grandson, the great warrior, insisted that he have it. Billy had yet to use it, but knew the number his grandson took pains to teach him. He used a bent and crooked finger to jab at the numbers stamped on small buttons.

"Hello?"

"Who is this?" Billy grumbled in response to the female greeting.

"This is Angela. Who are you?"

"You do not recognize the voice of your great uncle?"

"Uncle Billy? What are you doing?"

"I'm calling you."

"You don't sound well."

"I'm not well," Billy said with a pathetic shake of his head. "I've been reduced to talking to a rat."

Chapter Fifteen

Hansen opened his cruiser door and started to get in when Chuck Turner's city patrol car pulled into the courthouse parking space beside him. Hansen closed the door and strolled around to the front of the black and white and up to the driver's door while Turner worked at dislodging his great belly from beneath the steering wheel.

"You need a tilt wheel," Hansen grinned.

"I have a tilt wheel…it's tilted."

"Then you need a removable steering wheel."

"Bite me."

"Having a rough day?"

"I got the positive I.D. on the remains a few hours ago from the medical examiner. I just made the death notifications."

"Oh. I see." Hansen didn't bother to ask how it went. As a general rule of thumb death notifications went only one of two ways — shitty, or very shitty.

"Where are you off to?" Turner asked after several moments of reflective silence.

"Home."

"It's three o'clock. Are you feeling sick?"

"Nope. I'm going home early and get acquainted with the…my son."

"Oh, yeah. How did it go last night?"

"After the day we had, how would you have liked going home to a fourteen-year-old son you'd never met?"

"I don't know," Turner shrugged.

Hansen knew. But it'd go better today. He had it figured out. The boy obviously liked football, and Hansen could talk football for hours upon hours to anyone willing to listen. He could reveal all the successes and hopes and philosophies about football and never have to go into more intimate topics or levels of involvement. Hansen had done it hundreds of times with hundreds of strangers. Yes, football would be their common ground. Hansen could let Jacob into the part of himself that loved football while keeping him out of the depths of his heart. The boy would enjoy it, and no one would end up getting hurt. Hansen had it all figured out but was still relieved when Turner changed the topic.

"Did you look into Herman's death?"

"All day long. I damn sure don't understand it, but I can't disagree with Pete's investigation. The poor ignorant bastard committed suicide."

More reflective silence followed. This time Hansen

interrupted it. "Well, guess I better hit the road."

"Yeah, I've got a ton of reports to write on our two dead kids."

And all Hansen had to do was talk a little football.

Myers stumbled out of his pickup and held on to its door to keep from falling. He hadn't drunk too much to be driving. Hell, he never did. And he hadn't nearly fallen because he'd been drinking either. The damned gravel in his driveway tripped him up. It was difficult to walk on, and Myers had done his fair share of falling on the trek from his drive to his front door. He always blamed it on the damned gravel.

Had he not paused to steady himself, Myers would probably not have noticed his son. Randy was in front of the barn, tossing a mostly deflated basketball at a netless and rusty rim barely hanging on to a dilapidated backboard. As usual, the boy hit his shots. At the first of last year's basketball season, Randy's coach told Butch that by the time Randy reached his senior year, every university in the state would be courting him. Butch came home from the conversation with the coach and promised to buy Randy a new ball and build him a dandy of a regulation goal and backboard. He'd just never gotten around to it.

But he would, by God, get around to it. Because no matter what any son of a bitch thought, Myers loved his son. Sure, he'd knocked him around a little bit, but that had always been for Randy's own good. A man who loved his son had the obligation to toughen him up. After all, life wasn't going to treat him with kid gloves. Nobody knew that better than Butch Myers and he didn't want Randy finding out about life the way he had. No, he loved the boy too damn much to let strangers teach him how tough life could be.

Some people didn't understand that — some people like Burl Hansen. If that big, nosey bastard had his way, he'd taken Randy away from Butch and that would have been the last straw. Randy was the last and greatest thing life had yet to take from Myers.

Of course, someone like Hansen wouldn't understand how life and people in it stole things of value — like dreams and hopes of greatness and glory. Hansen never had a thing in his life taken from him. Even that boy he'd given up for adoption had been laid right back in his lap.

The last thought took Myers' mind back to the river and to the two boys playing on the opposite bank. They looked so happy — in a smug sort of way — secure in the fact that just because they were the sons of the all mighty Burl Hansen that life and nothing in it could ever cause them any harm.

Myers used the grip he had on the pickup door to viciously slam it shut. Then he sent first his right fist and then his left crashing into the side of the door. The impulse had been so violently cleansing that Myers cocked his fists to do it again. But then he had a sudden thought — an inspiration — that provided so much more satisfaction than pounding on the already battered old truck. Myers gave the revelation only seconds of consideration before nodding his head and allowing a grin to creep across his lips. After all, it made so much sense. Why should Myers tear up his own truck — and his own flesh — because of a hatred so consuming that nothing too atrocious could be done to alleviate it?

Hansen pulled into the drive to find Bret sitting uncommonly idle on the front porch.

"What are you doing out here?" he asked the small boy as he started up the steps.

"I'm in time-out."

The father figured as much. "What did you do…this time?" Hansen grumbled.

Bret dropped his head and stared at the concrete floor. "I got Jacob cat-scratched."

"What do you mean you got him cat-scratched?"

Bret didn't look up. "You know…how you taught me to. 'Member? I held the cat…like you showed me…and asked Jacob if he wanted to hold it, and when he said yes, I handed it to him with one hand and twisted the stupid thing's tail with my other hand… and it worked just like you said it would."

"I didn't 'teach' you to do that, damn it. I just told you how I used to do that when I was a kid. I specifically remember telling you not to do it."

Bret looked up slyly. "You told me not to be doing it to my sister. You didn't say I couldn't do it to a brother."

Burl fought off the urge to chuckle at the reasoning. "Well, it's a good thing you are already being punished," he said with mock severity. "How bad is he scratched?"

"Pretty good…I mean…pretty bad," Bret nodded with pursed lips. "That cat attacked him like he was a field mouse. Mom's doctoring him up, now."

Burl started into the house, but paused and asked out of curiosity, "How did your mom find out what happened. Did he tell on you?"

"Naw. She was looking out the window. She saw him bleeding."

Burl started again for the door and again curiosity got the best of him. "What do you think about Jacob? Do you like him?"

"Well, he's afraid of snakes and stuff…but I like him a lot. He's pretty cool."

Burl could put stock in that seal of approval. "How long are you in time out?"

"Thirty long ones."

"Are you learning your lesson?"

"I guess."

"You better be," the proud father grinned.

Jacob sat at the kitchen table with Vicki administering

first aid. Bret was right. The scratches were pretty bad. The look Vicki gave Hansen clearly did not express joy.

"I told Bret not to be doing it," Burl shrugged in his own defense.

"You shouldn't have taught him how to do it in the first place," Vicki said pointedly.

"I didn't 'teach' him…" Burl started before deciding any argument would be futile. Looking to Jacob, who seemed embarrassed, Burl concluded with a solemn, "Sorry."

"He didn't intend to harm me. He was only playing," Jacob smiled.

"That is no way to play," Vicki inserted.

Jacob tried to take Bret off the hook and it impressed Hansen. "Say, uh, Jacob, do you…play any football?"

Just the mentioning of *football* by Burl Hansen did what the pain-relieving ointment failed to do. It took the sting out of the nasty scratches on Jacob's hands and forearms. Or, at least, it took his mind off the pain.

"No, sir. I've never played football on an organized team. However, I intend to start next year."

"I guess I was about your age when I started," Burl said in an easy manner as he pulled up a chair. "I wasn't worth a damn at first!"

Burl talked football, and Jacob listened intently, not

failing to realize he was being provided the type of opportunity of which sports enthusiasts across the nation fantasized. Dancing through his mind were the things he could learn, the knowledge and talents he could carry into his first year of football — assuming, of course, that he would be allowed to change schools and try out for the team.

For now Jacob would make the assumption he would play because he'd already allowed too many negative thoughts and worries to practically ruin his first two days in Oklahoma. Now it appeared evident Burl would accept him, and they would develop the relationship Jacob hoped for. His stay from this point forward would do nothing but get better. Jacob could just feel it.

Pete Marsh showed up on time Saturday morning — straight up five o'clock. Tom Avery, doing his best impersonation of a turkey hunter, was ready to go.

When he stepped outside with his automatic twelve gauge, Marsh rolled down his window and barked, "Take that back in. You won't need it."

Avery felt uncomfortable doing so, but reluctantly obeyed. At least he still had the twenty-two pistol hidden away in the top of his boot. There were no greetings exchanged when he got into the truck. Marsh just slammed it into gear and took off.

Through training, Avery developed a good sense of direction and near perfect recall. Even in the dark he kept up with the directions they traveled on the winding, county back roads and committed each turn and every key point along the route to memory. Marsh remained quiet, practically brooding. Avery tried getting acquainted with the deputy but he couldn't get him out of his shell. Marsh seemed to be a man with a burdensome load on his mind. Avery committed that to memory, too.

It was nearly dawn when Marsh pulled off the black-topped county road and drove across a cattle guard onto what wasn't much more than a dirt trail. The deeply rutted path snaked its way through heavy woods and finally dwindled away to nothing just yards away from a dry creek bed. Marsh continued forward, blazing his own trail for a hundred or so yards before the oak and pecan trees and their undergrowth become too thick to allow further intrusion.

Marsh killed the truck, climbed out of the cab and reached in behind the seat to retrieve an M16 rifle. "Come on," he said without even a glance in Avery's direction.

The lawman moved through the dense foliage and rough terrain with the fluid grace of a man trained to do so. Avery matched his pace and ease of movement. Four years in the Army's Special Forces taught Avery how to move through the woods. He wondered what branch of the service trained Marsh — Army or Marines.

Within ten minutes of leaving the truck, the two men

emerged from the thick foliage into a small clearing that Avery judged to be less than fifty yards in diameter. Marsh kept up his pace until reaching the center of the clearing. Then he spun abruptly to face Avery.

All too late, Avery's senses screamed "setup" and he wished that instead of leaving his shotgun at home he'd told Marsh to kiss his ass.

"What the fuck's going on?" Avery hissed.

"Consider it a welcome party," Marsh sneered.

Avery held eye contact with Marsh as his mind went to the twenty-two auto hidden in his right boot. Even if he could get to it quickly enough, the small pistol would do little good against the M16. Still, it looked to be the only chance Avery had as there would be no better time to make a move since the barrel of the rifle was not yet trained on him.

In the next heartbeat Avery spun away, dove for the ground and hit it at a roll. For three complete rotations he struggled desperately to pull his pant leg up over the top of his boot, all along wondering why Marsh did not fire. At the top of the fourth roll, a glimpse of Marsh revealed the M16 slung harmlessly across his shoulder. Avery rolled into a sitting position. Marsh gawked as if looking at some special kind of idiot.

"What in the hell are you doing?" Marsh asked with a curious smirk.

Avery opted for the truth. "I thought you were going to kill me."

"Why would I do that?"

"I don't know. I just got freaked about you leading me into a clearing in the middle of nowhere with nobody else around."

Marsh strolled over to Avery and offered him a hand. After helping him to his feet, Marsh removed the rifle from his shoulder and handed it to Avery.

"This is yours. Take care of it." The undersheriff turned away from Avery, faced the direction they'd been traveling, and scanned the woods in front of him. "And by the way, we're not alone. There is somebody else around."

Marsh took a few steps forward and started waving his arms in wide arcs over his head. Avery looked in the direction Marsh faced.

The meaning of the signal became immediately apparent. The woods in a great semicircle before them suddenly came to life. At least fifty expertly camouflaged men started moving from concealed positions just inside the tree line. Avery was impressed. No undisciplined or ill-trained force of this size could have hidden in such close proximity without him detecting it.

"This is a small element of what we are now referring to as *The Battalion*," Marsh began. "When we first started training barely two years ago, we didn't have enough men to even fill a platoon. That's what we called ourselves back then, The Platoon. In a year's time we were The Company. Right now we have members from a three county area and we're near five-hundred strong. Within another year we want to be The Regiment."

What stood before Avery was a dream come true. All of his work had paid off. Tom Avery could now join The Battalion. "This is too cool," he exhaled.

"We think so," Marsh chuckled. Then more officially, "Okay, next order of business is to introduce you to the commander. We have checked you out well enough to believe you can keep your mouth shut. In a minute you'll understand why that quality is so vital to our operation. Don't violate our trust."

The implied threat rang clear and ominous. "I won't," Avery responded solemnly.

The men who materialized from the woods arranged themselves in small groups about the size, Avery noted, of squads. Marsh led Avery in and around several of the groups and didn't stop until they came to one consisting of only five men. It appeared to be the command group. Two of the men had their backs to Marsh and Avery and he hailed one of the two.

"Hey, Boss, you want to say hello to your new recruit?"

A heavy-set man wheeled around, grinning broadly, "Hey, Tom, welcome aboard!"

Although the voice and features seemed familiar, Avery did not immediately recognize the man through the intricate patterns of the green and black camouflage paint which coated his face. A moment later Avery made the connection and his pulse quickened. The battalion commander was Chuck Turner.

Chapter Sixteen

Vicki walked into the tool shed as Hansen cleaned the chain saw's spark plug.

"What kind of work are you doing this morning?" Her terse question clearly belied her true interest.

The tone implied that no matter what he had planned, she had a different agenda. "I've already got a full slate, Vicki," he informed her emphatically.

"Will you be doing anything Jacob can help with?"

"I thought he was going to Sunday school and church with you."

His response did not answer her question so Vicki did not respond.

Burl dutifully added, "I'm going to clear brush and limbs out of some fence line. It's pretty much a one-man job."

"I've been thinking..." Vicki started. Those words from his wife always made him cringe. "...this is his first Sunday here, and although he was sweet enough to accept my invitation to church, I might be rushing things a little. I don't want him to be uncomfortable or confused about... you know...our beliefs."

The point had crossed Burl's mind as well.

"Well, anyway," she continued, "he hasn't had much time with you...alone."

He cringed again. "We've been doing a lot of talking," he quickly inserted on his own behalf.

"Yes, about football. But I was thinking you two could have some real quality time together. I'm sure he'd love that."

Hansen breathed in deeply. True enough, he'd not once been alone with Jacob. And although the thought of some one-on-one time felt uncomfortable, it did have merit. Jacob very well could not be ready for Baptist teachings. "Yeah, well, I guess he could hang out with me." Much still remained to be said on the topic of football.

"I do want him to go to church with us, but there's plenty of time for that. I think staying here...just this one Sunday...would be a good thing." With her mind made up and her decree issued, Vicki took leave of the tool shed.

Jacob took hold of yet another one of the large limbs Burl cut out of the monstrous oak and started dragging it to the brush pile. Halfway to the pile his feet caught in the branches and he fell backwards, landing on his butt. The high-pitched whine of the chain saw fell silent, and Burl's laughter took its place.

"Bet you wished you'd gone to church now," Burl called out. "But look at it like this…it's a great way to get in shape for football!"

For reasons Jacob did not know, but intended to find out, Burl obviously intervened with Vicki's efforts to take him to church. Could it be, he wondered, that father and son shared common beliefs on the subject of religion? And what better opening could he have for broaching the topic? Jacob delivered his load and trudged back to Burl's side.

"Why don't you attend church?"

Burl glanced down at the idle chain saw in his hands, and Jacob thought for a moment that instead of answering, Burl intended to crank it back to life. But after long seconds of obvious contemplation, he placed the saw on the ground next to the barbed wire fence and leaned back against the tree he'd been mutilating.

"I'm just not the church going type, I guess," he shrugged.

Burl appeared uncomfortable with the topic, but Jacob went for broke. "But you do believe there is a God?"

Burl stiffened, "Well…of course."

Jacob's next words were not spontaneous. Much thought and deliberation went into the decision to reveal his greatest secret. "I don't."

Hansen's first impulse was to grab up his saw, start it up and just keep on sawing until the time arrived for Jacob to go back to Boston. Because of the impossibility of doing such, he instead gawked at Jacob and struggled for a response.

Having no doubt sensed Hansen's loss for words, Jacob filled the void with a rapid fire explanation. "I'm sorry. I know this is shocking. It's just that I could never admit this to my adoptive parents and I just want you and Vicki to know the real me... what I believe...what I feel."

Burl felt as if an ugly, gnarled fingernail tickled its way down the length of his spine. "With all the wonders of life and nature," he finally managed, "how can you not believe in some kind of God?"

"With few exceptions, the wonders of nature can be duplicated in laboratories. Too, I find it easy not to believe because of life and the things that happen in life...like teenagers found dead in trunks of cars."

Hansen winced at the pain the reminder released from deep down inside. At first he tried to blame the searing emotional pain on his mental image of the decaying bodies and the terrible impact Jacob's revelation would have on Vicki. But as he glanced away and stared across the fence line he'd been clearing to the land on the other side, he realized his anguish ran much deeper. The heavily wooded land on the other side of the barbed wire belonged to Butch Myers, and with the thought of that name came a tag to hang on his true feelings. It was a deep and foreboding dread.

In the fight with Myers months earlier — when Hansen feared for his life and had no place else to turn — he'd turned to God. When life and living turned on Jacob, as life and living eventually did to all, where would he turn if he didn't believe there was a God to turn to?

With his eyes back on the boy who looked so much like himself, Hansen addressed a silent prayer to his maker and asked for a miracle of belief for the unbelieving. And for his own part, Hansen understood that the relationship with his son would now have to transcend football.

Myers sprawled in a rickety chaise lounge in his back yard and seethed at the sound of the chain saw. That sorry son of a bitch Hansen always worked around his place — always improving it — always making it look better — always making Butch Myers look worse. It worked as just another way for Hansen to rub his good fortune in Myers' face.

Every few seconds Myers brought a fifth of whiskey up to his lips, took a hearty swig, and thought about just how much he hated Hansen. Every swallow, as it had for days now, served to solidify what Myers intended to do about it. Oh, he'd had his doubts — his moments of thinking he just couldn't do it — but when he'd think of backing down, Myers would just take another drink and think about Darrel Baker…and Sally Rafell… and Max Bemo.

It seemed kind of funny. Not to say that what happened to them was funny. No, that wasn't one bit funny, but it did seem funny that Myers would intentionally think about them. For such a long time he struggled to keep them out of his mind — and his dreams. Especially his dreams. It felt weird that he now needed to think about what happened to them — the role he had played — how they had screamed — how they had bled. He needed to think about all that now because it stood to reason if he could do what he'd done back months ago, he could certainly do what needed doing to right the wrong that life and Hansen and all the people like Hansen had done to screw him.

Myers stared in the direction of the hateful buzzing sound made by Hansen's saw. It came from an area where he'd thought he'd seen Darrell Baker a few nights after the Camaro and the bodies had already been dumped in the lake. The black boy darted from tree to tree, motioning for Myers to come into the woods. Myers contributed what he'd seen to shadows and limbs and wind and the stress constantly hounding him. And even though he'd cussed the thing he saw and threw the bottle from which he'd been drinking at it, he'd known damn good and well that it couldn't be Darrell Baker.

That boy was dead. Trisha Bottoms picked him up on the road after she'd finished her shift at Flodell's Diner. And just like Pete Marsh planned it, she delivered him to a secluded clump of trees next to the Kiamichi.

Myers' first cousin, Johnny Bottoms, reached in the car and grabbed the boy. Johnny hadn't particularly liked that horny nigger with a taste for white women sitting so close to his wife. Baker threw one hell of a fit — screaming and crying. The camouflaged fatigues, shotguns, and black ski masks scared the holy hell out of the bastard.

It took Johnny a while to get the strong buck out of the car, and all the time Myers stood motionless — having second thoughts — wishing he wasn't there. He had a good reason to hate people the color of the boy. It had been his kind who robbed him of his boxing career. But he'd never killed one of them. Hell, he'd never killed anyone.

When Johnny finally got Baker out of the car, Marsh stepped in and tried to help get him under control. The boy kicked and swung his arms wildly. He was a big boy and crazy with fear. Joe Buck had been selected for the mission, too, but the fat slob of a storekeeper just huffed and puffed and generally got in the way. Bottoms and Marsh had their hands full, and Myers did not move an inch.

Not until Marsh bellowed, "Myers you fuck! Get the sonofabitch!"

Moved to action by the reprimand, Myers grabbed Baker from behind and stood him upright. Marsh then drove the butt of a shotgun into his solar plexus…once… twice …three times. Then Myers let him crumble to the ground.

"Shooting is too merciful for the motherfucker!" Marsh screamed as he landed the first heavy combat boot to the kid's head.

Then they all joined in. They kicked and they stomped, and for long seconds the boy cried. Even long after he fell silent, they kicked and stomped some more. It was hard for Myers at first, but it grew easier. It wasn't long before he shoved the others out of the way so that he could get a clearer shot. He kept at it until Marsh and Johnny Bottoms pulled him away. From a distance of only a few feet, Myers stared down at the boy and tried to catch his breath. He'd never seen human brains before.

When it all sunk in, Myers turned and heaved up the contents of his stomach. Joe Buck had already done so.

"The motherfucker got what he deserved," Marsh insisted over and over.

Myers worked to convince himself that it was true. Niggers had no right fucking white girls. It wasn't something they could allow to get started in their little town. And white girls that would fuck a nigger...

Johnny happened to stumble across Sally Rafell later that night. He'd just finished towing a stranded motorist with his wrecker, when he saw her sitting in the Wal-Mart parking lot. He'd pulled over and called to report to Marsh and get his instructions. What Marsh came up with was risky, but they might not have a better chance. Marsh told Johnny to try and give him fifteen minutes so he could pick up Myers from a local bar.

Johnny parked his truck a block away and walked to the Wal-Mart. It was late for small town folk and the streets were pretty much empty. Johnny just walked right up to Shelly's car when he felt certain there were no witnesses. He knew the girl well because he'd dated her mother for years before he'd married Trisha. It didn't take him long to talk her into letting him take the new Camaro for a spin.

Johnny drove Shelly and her car to the place Marsh told him to. Marsh and Myers were already there. Johnny bounced out of the car without explanation, and Shelly bounced out to get one. Pete Marsh pulled what he called a "throw down" pistol and intentionally shot Shelly in the upper thigh. She went to the ground screaming. Marsh thrust the revolver into Myers' hands and told him to put her out of her misery. When Myers hesitated, Marsh got in his face. "You better do your part in this one, motherfucker!"

So Myers did. He reached right down and point blank shot three rounds into Shelly Rafell's pretty face. Her blood splattered on his hands and clothing.

That left Max Bemo. It had been Joe Buck's place that the big welfare Indian tore up, so, it had been Buck that had come up with the way Bemo should pay for the damages. But when they got one end of the rope around Bemo's neck and the other around the bumper on Myers' pickup, fat ass Buck lost his gumption and Marsh ordered Myers to take the wheel and drag Bemo to death over the gravel country road.

The memories weren't sweet, but reliving them now served a purpose. Grimacing at the incessant whine of the chain saw, Myers again brought the bottle to his lips. This time he drank until it was empty.

Jacob had his arms partially filled for yet another trip to the mountainous brush pile when Burl turned off the chain saw.

"How are you holding up?" Burl asked.

The only parts of his body that weren't hurting were those parts that had gone numb long ago. Yet, Jacob fought to keep his discomfort from showing in his voice and expression. "Quite well, thank you!"

The ends of Burl's lips turned slightly upward as he nodded thoughtfully. It seemed Jacob's response pleased him.

This had been the only conversation they shared since the termination of the discussion over the existence of God. Burl had had the last word on the topic when he'd averted his eyes and said haltingly, "I appreciate you being honest with me. I really do. It's something…I needed to know. But with Vicki, well, sometimes with women in general…what they don't know…can't hurt them. I'm not telling you to lie. I'd just like you to wait a while. Don't tell her just yet."

Jacob wasn't sure just exactly why, but it seemed like sound advice.

Now, several hundred feet of fence line later, Burl nodded in the direction of the truck, "Well, I'm not holding up 'quite well.' As they say down in these parts, my ass is dragging. Why don't we save the rest for another day?"

Sensing he had not fooled Burl anyway, Jacob smiled wearily and replied, "Well, if you insist."

Burl chuckled, clapped Jacob on the back and struck out for the truck. Jacob practically had to run to keep up.

Hansen pulled the pickup off the rutted trail leading home and stopped next to his favorite pond. "You feel like wetting a hook?" He asked the weary looking boy sitting next to him.

"I beg your pardon?" Jacob asked, arching his eyebrows.

"That's Okie for 'do you want to try your luck at catching a fat bass?'"

"Do I want to fish?"

"Yeah. Do you want to fish?"

"I've never fished before."

"Well, you are not going to find a better time or place to try your hand at it. Come on."

Hansen pulled his rod and reel and a small tackle box from behind the seat. Jacob trailed him to the bank of the pond and watched attentively as Burl tied a bright colored crank bait to the line. After demonstrating a half dozen times or so how to cast and reel, Hansen handed the fiberglass rod over to Jacob.

Jacob's first attempt to cast sent the lure plopping loudly into the water only a few feet from the bank and well to the right of where he intended it to go. Hansen's laughter and encouragement to try again seemed to put the boy at ease. His second attempt went only a few feet farther out, but straight out in front of him. The third cast was a pretty good one.

"How will I know if I catch one?" Jacob asked as he clumsily worked the reel's action.

"Oh, you'll know," Hansen chuckled.

"Will it jerk the rod from my hands?"

"If you get one big enough to jerk the rod from your hands…I'll be going in after it!"

Hansen gave further tips and instructions and Jacob proved to be a quick study. He soon managed to land the lure pretty much where he wanted.

"See that mossy spot over there?" Hansen pointed. "Lay your lure just to this edge of it."

"What if I get it tangled up?"

"We'll either get it loose, or we'll lose it. Not a big deal. There are plenty more where that one came from… Wal-Mart!"

The last time the lure hit the pond a big mouth bass broke the water to swallow it. And the fight was on.

"Set the hook! Jerk it! Give him some slack! Reel it in! Reel it in!" Hansen shouted directions and fought back the urge to free Jacob of the bowing rod.

And he was glad he did. It took a while, but Jacob landed his fish. Father and son bellowed with delight, stomping the tall grasses along the bank as they danced to celebrate man's victory over the creatures from the deep.

After tucking in the two little ones, Vicki walked into the living room to find Jacob sound asleep on the couch. Burl, who seemed to be studying him from a nearby recliner, promptly abandoned his private thoughts to stare vacantly at the television.

Vicki would have given much more than the proverbial penny for those thoughts, but that wasn't the way it worked with Burl. Matters of the heart had to be cunningly plucked from her man.

"He's had a full day," she whispered with a nod toward her son. On top of his working and fishing, Burl took him into town and gave him a tour of the jail. He made a special point of running down Pete Marsh and Chuck Turner to introduce them to Jacob.

Burl smiled fondly and whispered back, "The boy's not afraid of work."

She knew Burl placed a lot of stock in that virtue. "He loved every minute of it…I could tell," she sighed.

"Caught his first fish," Burl added as an afterthought.

The subtle pride in his voice did not go unnoticed.

"Yes, he did. Thanks for taking the time to make that happen."

Burl didn't respond and didn't need to. After a few seconds he looked back to the sleeping boy. "He's never driven a car or shot a gun or ridden a horse."

Vicki's heart all but melted. Burl, in his own way, let her know that Jacob would do all that and more before summer's end. After long moments more of splendid silence, Vicki said, "I'll wake him and walk him upstairs."

"You go and get ready for bed. I'll take care of him."

Before Vicki made it out of the room, Burl spoke her name.

"Vicki…you once told me, even before meeting him, that you loved him."

"Yes?"

"Have you let him know that yet?"

"No. Not yet. Not in words, anyway. But I intend to."

"How?"

"Well, I'll just say the words, silly!" Vicki laughed.

Burl processed her answer with a nod and a shrug and turned deep thoughts back to the television.

Jacob had been watching television. What seemed like an instant later he opened his eyes to find Burl standing over him, shaking him. There had been no distinct stages leading to sleep — just here one second and gone the next — and a glance at his wristwatch revealed he'd been out considerably longer than an instant.

"Looks like you're ready to hit the hay," Burl grinned down at him.

"Hit the hay?" Jacob repeated while forcing himself to sit upright.

"Another colloquialism," Burl grunted after plopping down beside him. "Which, I guess, would roughly translate in Bostonian to 'it would appear that you desire to proceed to the bed chamber!'"

"Oh, I see," Jacob chuckled around a yawn. "And you are correct," he concluded as he started to his feet.

A big hand fell gently across his shoulder to hold him in place.

"Hey, uh, Jacob, I've been thinking about this God thing and I think there's more I should say…"

Jacob might have felt put upon if not for the deep look of concern on Burl's face.

"…First let me clarify something. I'm certainly, as you're about to discover, no theologian. I can't even carry on a conversation about any religion for longer than about two seconds. Still, though, I do believe…very much so…that there is a supreme being. I choose to call this being God. I don't know about Jesus and him being the son of God and all that. I mean, as far as I know, that could all be true. I have no problem with it being true…I just really don't know. But I do know there is something much bigger and magnificent than myself that plays some phenomenal role in the universe. Basically, this belief has served me well.

"I told you I'm not much for going to church. Well, I'm not much for praying either, but that's what I wanted to tell you about…"

Jacob listened intently as Burl told him how a bad hit in a game against the Packers left him momentarily paralyzed.

"…I was praying my butt off for those few minutes, Jacob, and I got the feeling back in my legs and I was able to move my hands and arms again. Now, you can believe what you want, but I just have to believe that it was God hearing my prayers that made me recover so quickly.

"But that's not really the point I wanted to make. What I want you to think about, you see, is that I found myself in a place…in a situation…that I couldn't do anything but pray. I had no place else to turn. No place else to go. And that wasn't the last time I found myself in that kind of a mess…"

Jacob learned of the Hansen's closest neighbor, Butch Myers, and about the terrible fight between Burl and Myers earlier in the year.

"…He had me beat, Jacob. I was going down, and I knew that when I did, he was going to kill me. And again, there was nothing I could do but pray. No place else to turn. No place else to go. I believe some kind of supreme power…God…saved me, Jacob."

Burl rose to his feet and again placed his hand on Jacob's shoulder. "I don't mean to shove anything down your throat or make you uncomfortable…I just wanted you to know about my experiences with God. I'm sure I didn't convince you there is a divine power. I'm not so sure that the only thing that can prove to a man that God exists is God himself. No, I just wanted to…well, I just wanted you to know why I do believe."

Jacob didn't have to buy the philosophy to appreciate the sentiment. The words obviously did not come easy for Burl and they were clearly from the heart. A fourteen-year-old boy whose adoptive parents were a rich physician and a famous novelist and whose real father was none other than football hall-of-famer Burl Hansen, would always have people to go to — a place to turn. Yet this wasn't an opinion Jacob had to share with Burl. He could keep it to himself.

"Thank you, Burl. I can appreciate now why you believe. And I promise to never forget what you've told me."

The words seemed to set the father at ease.

Chapter Seventeen

Since Mom and Dad made such a fuss over the fish Jacob caught the day before, Bret decided to show them all what a real fisherman could do. It didn't make any difference that his mother made him take Jacob along to his favorite pond. After all, his big brother did not know the right spot to fish like Bret did.

The mid-morning weather turned out just right and Bret had a good assortment of plastic worms. After attaching a six-inch purple with sparkles, he cast once... twice...and then a third time.

After reeling in the third cast he glanced across the large pond to the place he'd encouraged Jacob to fish. A place Bret felt sure no fish had ever been caught.

"Hey, Jacob," he screamed across the substantial expanse of water, "it don't look like they're biting today. You wanna go exploring?"

Jacob responded, but Bret couldn't make out what he said. "Huh? What did you say?"

Jacob yelled back again and this time Bret caught something about patience, and "We just got here."

"He must have learned that shit from Daddy," Bret said out loud but not loud enough for Jacob to hear. He wasn't quite sure yet how much he could trust his older brother. What if big, tattling mouths like Sandy's ran in the family?

If Jacob wanted to go on trying after Bret told him the fish weren't biting, then he could just have at it. Bret could find better things to do like doing battle with a dragonfly that suddenly dive-bombed his head.

Bret dropped his rod and reel and jerked the baseball cap from his head. Spinning and bobbing and leaping, he swatted at the insistent pest while calling it all kinds of choice names. Then the dragonfly simply darted away.

"Yeah, you better run, you butt-nosed bastard!" Bret huffed with one final swipe of the grimy cap. After bending to retrieve his rod, Bret looked across the water and cupped one hand to the side of his mouth.

"Hey, Jacob! Where you at? Where'd you go? JAAAAACOBBBBB! Hey, where in the hell are you?"

Marsh thrust a grinning face into Hansen's office and chuckled, "Come here a minute. You've got to see this!"

The undersheriff had not been his normally jovial self for the past couple of days. Hansen attributed his dour mood to Grambs' suicide. Because Hansen had been in Seminole at the time of the death, Marsh had been in charge. Hansen feared Marsh might hold himself personally responsible for the tragedy. Hansen definitely had to see whatever took Marsh's mind off Herman Grambs.

He trailed Marsh through the building and out the front door. Hansen immediately noticed the source of his subordinate's amusement.

"You have got to be kidding me," Hansen grinned, shaking his head as he approached the curb.

"Is that a tinge of jealousy I detect?" Chuck Turner responded from astride a monstrous neon yellow Harley Davidson.

"Whose is it?" Hansen asked as he circled and took in several hundred pounds of iridescent iron, leather and chrome.

"It's mine. Ol' Tom Avery made me a hell of deal on it."

Marsh stepped up and pointed a finger at the fat-bob gasoline tanks. "That's some pretty fancy artwork on those tanks. Why don't you lift up your belly so I can get a better look?"

"Lick me, Ickabod!"

"It's one heck of a good-looking machine," Hansen admitted.

"You ought to paint some black stripes on it," Marsh said. "Then when you're cruising down the road, you'll look like a roly-poly humping a bumble bee!"

"Oh, that's so hilarious," Turner said dryly over Hansen's

laughter. "Hey, Burl, Avery has three more of these beauties sitting in his shop. You could have one, too."

"I'm not as convinced of that character's legitimacy as you are. Did you run the VIN for stolen?"

"It ain't stolen," Turner smirked. "I'm telling you, Burl, you need one of these bad boys!"

"I'll just settle for you taking me for a ride," Hansen smiled as he made a move for the back of the bike.

"Well, uh, hold on, Burl. I ain't that proficient just yet," Turner sputtered.

"Queasy Rider!" Marsh quipped.

Turner thrust a middle finger in Marsh's direction but never took his eyes off Hansen, "You know, really, Burl, Avery is a pretty good ol' boy."

"Yeah, okay," Hansen nodded, "Guess I ought to have him over for dinner. Let him tell the kids the story behind all those tattoos running up and down his arms."

"You know, I hate to agree with Chuck about anything," Marsh said, "but I'm getting where I kind of like Avery, too. He's okay."

"Yeah, well, I'll just keep hanging with you two. You guys aren't much to look at, but at least I can trust you."

"Hey, Chuck," Marsh practically blurted, "let me take a spin on your bike."

"Spin on this, skinny," Turner said with his finger in the air again.

When Vicki heard the back door open and shut, she started for the kitchen to fix her boys some lunch. She found Bret already rummaging through the fridge.

"Hi, little man. Where's your brother?"

"Ain't he in here?"

"No, he *isn't* in here," she emphasized. "Why do you think he would be? Didn't he come back with you?"

"Nope...the dirty dog," Bret replied as he wrapped small hands around a large bottle of orange juice.

"Well, where is he?" she laughed.

"Don't know. He left me at the pond."

"Where did he go?"

"Don't know. He was there one minute and then like... poof...he was gone."

Something instinctively maternal reared an ugly head. *Don't over react*, Vicki quickly instructed herself. "Bret, he didn't fall in the pond did he?" She asked with forced calmness.

"Nope. I'd've heard that. Jacob would make a loud splash. I guess he just left. I thought he was messing with me at first. You know, playing hide-and-go-seek or something, but I couldn't find him."

"How hard did you look?"

"Not very."

"Come on," Vicki barked as she headed for the back door. "He doesn't know his way around the ranch yet, Bret. You shouldn't have left him."

"I didn't leave him. He left me. I done told you that. Hey, I'm hungry."

"You can eat later," Vicki said, taking him by the arm and calling out for Sandy.

Vicki loaded her children in the old truck Burl used for ranch work and methodically began working her way toward the pond where the boys had gone to fish. She expected to find Jacob at one of the points of interest along the way, like the gully where they dumped trash or the boulder-strewn ridge line that Bret always enjoyed crawling around on. Jacob wasn't at either place. Nor did she find him in the green hay meadow or the wooded area on the ranch's highest hill. When they reached the pond and Jacob wasn't there, Vicki had a hard time convincing herself he'd traveled beyond the pond in the opposite direction of the house.

"Where exactly was Jacob the last time you saw him, Bret?"

"Over there on the other side," he pointed.

Vicki parked the truck and jumped out. "Show me," she ordered.

The boy ran ahead and Vicki and Sandy followed at a quick pace around the pond dike. She followed several yards behind Bret when he stopped and looked down at the ground.

"Here's his fishing pole!"

Vicki's heart iced over and what she wanted to scream came out as a low mournful groan.

He tried to soothe his wife.

"We'll find him. He's just lost. He didn't drown. Relax. Don't worry," he insisted in his calmest voice. When he hung up the receiver, Hansen bellowed for Pete Marsh.

"Get units on the section lines bordering the ranch. Then grab Chuck and anyone he can spare and meet me at the house as soon as possible."

Before Marsh could bolt from his office, Hansen took a deep breath and issued another order. "Call in Tackett and Jones. Tell them to get out there and not to let Vicki see any of their equipment." She didn't need to know he intended to employ his department's two certified divers.

Hansen ran from his office to his car and sped out of town with emergency lights and sirens engaged.

No one ever comes here. It's too secluded, Butch Myers reassured himself over and over as he strode to his pickup. His hands shook uncontrollably as he grabbed the fifth of whiskey from behind the seat and worked to remove the cap. After several desperate swigs he recapped it and tossed it onto the seat.

Myers stepped to the bed of the truck and removed the tarp he'd used to cover the boy. He cursed his luck after close examination of the cheap material. He'd have to get rid of it because of the blood. Myers carried the tarp deep into the woods and covered it with leaves and downed limbs and branches. When he got back to the pickup he poured gasoline from a plastic jug onto a rag and mopped up the telltale signs from the bed of the truck. With the task completed he spun and heaved up the whiskey he'd gulped.

"Goddammit!" he moaned. "Goddammit to hell!"

There wasn't supposed to be any blood. He hadn't intended to hit the boy so hard. He just wanted to knock him out for a little while. Myers climbed unsteadily into the cab and swigged more whiskey. He needed to clear his head. Plans had to be made on how he'd get Burl Hansen out to this secluded place — where no one ever came.

One of the hundreds of thoughts surging through Hansen's mind on the breakneck trip home was the need to call Vicki's pastor and maybe a couple of the women from her church to come and sit with her. Hansen dismissed the thought shortly after it popped into his head. Vicki would not simply sit and let someone hold her hand during a crisis. She would insist on doing her part to find him.

With that in mind, Hansen arrived home and saddled his quarter horse, Hercules, and Vicki's spirited sorrel mare, BeeBee. Many places on the ranch couldn't be searched on wheels. Riding horses would be quicker and easier than walking. Keeping Vicki actively searching on horseback would also keep her away from the pond.

Hansen wanted to stay away from there as well. He sent Marsh to supervise the diving operation and asked Turner to conduct a detailed search of the land surrounding the pond.

Neither husband nor wife had much to say as they rode. Vicki's mood remained constant, but Hansen knew she was struggling to remain positive.

"I've had time to pray about this, Burl," she'd declared upon first climbing into the saddle. "God didn't let Jacob come to Oklahoma to simply let something terrible happen to him. I'm going to keep my faith in his loving goodness."

A loving and caring God stood as one of the tenets of Judeo-Christian theology that gave Burl problems. He'd seen too much evidence against it. Of course, he kept those thoughts to himself.

When the Hansens' search revealed nothing either good or bad, they turned back for the house. The horses made the last hundred yards closely side by side at an extremely slow pace. Their riders held each other's hands and gripped tightly.

Turner and Marsh met the Hansens at the barn. Vicki asked immediately for an update, and both men said they had nothing new to report. Of course, they mentioned nothing of the pond, and Hansen sensed both knew something they didn't want Vicki to hear. When she hurried off to the house to check on Bret and Sandy, Marsh spoke first.

"I have good news, Burl. Tackett and Jones haven't found anything yet and don't expect to. They say visibility is better than usual for a farm pond and they've grid it once and were about finished with a second search when I left. They intend to crisscross it a third time just to be sure."

Hansen exhaled debilitating dread and inhaled a sweet, fresh breath of air before Turner took his turn.

"I've got the bad news Burl..."

Hansen held the breath and brought fingers up to rub weary eyes.

"...there's faint boot tracks up on the dike where the rod and reel were left... large ones...and scuff marks that trail back east of the pond..."

"Scuff marks?" Hansen interrupted with a catch in his throat.

"Yeah, Burl, like something was, uh, drug away from there. I think they're heel marks. We followed an intermittent trail to the road. They stopped there."

Hansen grabbed a pole supporting the weight of the barn's roof and let it support his as well. "What? What are you saying, Chuck?" He mumbled, knowing damn good and well what Chuck said, but refusing to accept it all the same.

"I believe Jacob was abducted, Burl. Someone grabbed him at the pond, dragged him to the road and loaded him into a car. And…" Turner paused and grimaced, "I think he was knocked unconscious. There are no signs of struggle, but there are drops of blood along the trail."

Hansen's stomach contracted violently and he held onto the pole to keep from falling down. All kinds of words came to mind, but only five made it to his lips.

"No, dear God…no…no!"

Captain Mike Walker walked into his grandfather's house with suitcase in hand to find the small living room packed with tribal members. Some visited quietly while others chanted. Some others prayed. A white man would be able to understand a few of the prayers, but most were not in English. Mike came quickly from Fort Benning, Georgia. He hoped he'd come quickly enough.

Tommy Horsehead met Mike just inside the door and relieved him of his suitcase. "How is he?" Mike whispered.

"Been unconscious since yesterday. I don't think he's suffering."

A quick glance around the room revealed several who were. Billy Harjo had for many decades been a vital part of the Choctaw community — a legend who would be badly missed.

"I want to see him," the grandson directed.

The two women attending to his grandfather stepped out of the tiny bedroom when Mike entered. They had performed their duties conscientiously. The old holy man was lying on spotless sheets and wearing ceremonial garb. His hair had been unbraided and washed and fanned-out on the pillows supporting his head. Herbs, roots, and small personal items of significance to Billy adorned his bed. The women had done well preparing him for passage to his next life.

His grandfather's eyes were closed and he lay totally motionless. He took shallow breaths, but they were not labored. Mike moved to and squatted beside the bed. He took the closest of the fragile hands into just one of his. The warmth of life had all but drained from the Alekchi's hand.

Mike hoped for more years with the old man because as a soldier he'd been guilty of putting off until tomorrow what should have been done many yesterdays in the past. Mike fooled himself into believing there would be time in the future to learn from the old man all the ways of their people — plenty of days after the army to pull from the great one all the secrets of his powerful medicine. Now, much of that magic passed down by the ancestors would most assuredly die with Billy Harjo.

Captain Mike Walker wore the green beret and knew dozens of ways to kill a man, but not one of the herbal medicines, incantations or ceremonies that enhanced the human condition. The young man did nothing to restrain the tears welling in his eyes.

Hansen asked Turner to call Vicki's pastor and sent Marsh into town to pick up their family doctor, Mark Sherrill. Hansen then walked the men to the door of the barn and watched until they were a good distance away. When they were, he turned and stumbled into the shadows and fell to his knees.

"Don't do this to him. Don't do it to us. Wherever he is, let him be okay. Bring Jacob back to us and show me once and for all that you are a loving and merciful God."

Hansen could not immediately get to his feet. Too much held him down. In the shadows he would remain until he could lead the doctor and the preacher into his house. Only then would he tell Vicki about the scuff marks — apparently from the heels of Jacob's shoes — that laid a bloody path leading nowhere.

Pete Marsh passed Butch Myers' place when he wondered if anyone bothered to let the Myers' know about the missing boy. They were the Hansens' closest neighbors and they just might…

The cop practically stood upright on his brake pedal.

What hit Marsh like a bat upside a ball was not anything as mystical as a premonition, but simply good, old-fashioned common sense. No one hated Burl Hansen like Butch Myers. No one.

"Oh, shit," Marsh spat as he spun his car in the road and sped back to Myers' drive. It wouldn't be long before Hansen drew the same conclusion. If Myers kidnapped that kid, Marsh's whole world could be turned upside down.

Suzy Myers responded to Marsh pounding on the front door.

"Where's Butch?" He had no time for courtesies or formalities.

"I don't know, Pete," Suzy said in her mousy voice with her whipped-puppy way of looking at the ground. "He left here early this morning. I haven't seen him since."

"What time did he leave, Suzy?"

"Like I said, it was early…about seven-thirty."

Marsh took a deep breath to calm his nerves. "Listen to me, Suzy. You tell Butch to get hold of me the minute he walks into this house."

All of a sudden it bothered Marsh a great deal that the woman wasn't looking at him. His hand shot forward, grabbed her by the oily hair of her head and pulled her nose to nose. "Are you listening to me, Suzy?" he growled.

"Yes, Pete," she sniveled, "I'm listening to you."

"Then look at me, goddammit!"

When she did, he continued, "You tell him to call me

immediately. And you don't answer this door again today. I don't give a shit who knocks on it. Do you understand?"

"Uh-huh," she sobbed.

Marsh stomped away confident Suzy Myers would do exactly as told. She knew all too well just how much pain an angry man could inflict.

Her sister came from town and picked up Bret and Sandy. Since then, Vicki kept busy doing some things around the house that just had to be done and many that didn't. After a while, though, she simply had to sit down.

She didn't know how long she'd been on the living room couch when she heard the back door open. Vicki tried to get up, but her legs didn't seem to be in the mood. So she sat and just waited for Burl to bring her the latest.

Burl she expected. But not her pastor, Dick Flinnish, and certainly not Dr. Sherrill. This time her legs answered the calling and she stood and started to sob.

"I lost him once. Oh, dear God, I can't bear to lose him again!"

She heard something about an injection and didn't object. She just couldn't bear it. Not one moment longer.

Chapter Eighteen

It was the odor. No, a stench. Permeating. Ugly beyond vile. If it had a color it would be black and marbled with bile green, and it was like nothing Jacob had ever smelled. But it was the odor that brought him to.

For the longest time he thought he was lying with his eyes closed. He came to realize they were open. Blinking. And seeing nothing. The darkness engulfed him. Held him in place. Kept him from screaming.

Where am I?

Why does my head hurt so badly?

Then, after a time, and how much time he did not know, memories started flashing through the horrifying darkness. While fishing…something hit him. He felt it throughout his entire body. Then felt himself being moved. There were grunts and cursing. And some moans.

Was I moaning from the pain?

Jacob didn't know. Oh, there was so much he didn't

know — so little to remember.

But such a stench. It filled his mouth and made his eyes sting. His stomach heaved and the warmth that had been his last meal erupted from his mouth and spilled onto his chest. Even the taste of vomit was better than the taste of the stench.

Jacob fought to keep from crying. He felt too terrified to scream. Any noise he made would alert the darkness of his presence and maybe stir the terrible thing that smelled so awful.

Marsh rolled over and grabbed the phone beside his bed on the first ring. He'd not slept, only tossed and seethed.

"You have no right laying hands on my woman, you son of a bitch!" The voice on the other end slurred.

Marsh sat upright in bed and cleared his throat. "Myers? Where the fuck are you? Are you at home?"

"Ain't none of your goddamned business where I'm at."

Marsh did not beat around the bush. It wasn't something he'd do at two in the morning. "What did you do with that boy, Butch?"

The long period of silence proved incriminating. "I don't know what you're talking about," Myers finally responded. "What boy?" he asked unconvincingly.

He was obviously drunk and Marsh realized the danger in spooking him. "Listen, Butch. We have to talk."

"I ain't got nothing to say to you, Pete. And don't come out here because I'll be gone."

Marsh paused and forced himself to speak calmly, kindly. "You haven't done a bad thing, Butch. The boy's a Jew and we don't need any Jews around here. But you need my help. I want to help you."

After long seconds of dead air Myers said weakly, "I don't need any damned help." Then he hung up.

Marsh spit venomous words into the receiver and then flung it across the room.

It was seven a.m. in Oklahoma. Eight in Boston. Hansen had been up all night and his discussion with the Boston PD's missing persons detective had been strained. After hanging up the phone he went to their bedroom to check on Vicki. She still slept soundly. The medication served its purpose.

He went back to the kitchen and poured himself yet another cup of coffee. In all fairness, the Swiretynskys should hear the news from him. But the telephone was no means for delivering such bad tidings. The Boston detective would go with rabbi in tow, and Hansen would wait for the ensuing call.

While dozens of others searched, the sheriff would keep an eye on his wife…and wait.

Marsh paced in his office before the call came in. Butch Myers had sobered.

"Are those phones bugged?" Myers rasped.

"Don't say another thing," Marsh ordered. The phones weren't bugged. But the proverbial walls had proverbial ears. "Call me at home in ten minutes."

For once Myers was punctual. Marsh picked up the phone in his kitchen. The one in the bedroom lay scattered in pieces.

"It ain't about the boy being a Jew," Myers began. "I don't intend to kill the boy. I have a boy of my own," he insisted. "I just want Hansen. He's the one I want dead."

"Okay. Okay Butch. Let me help," Marsh blurted in response. "Let me meet with you and talk about this face to face. We have to plan this out. Too much is at stake here, Butch," he pleaded.

"I ain't ready to talk. I need more time to think."

"Where's the boy, Butch?"

"I want your help, Pete. But I ain't willing to say where the boy's at. Not yet, anyway. I'll call you tonight…sometime after ten, there at your house. Will you help me then?"

"I'll help you."

"You'll help me kill Hansen?"

"If that's what it takes, Butch…I'm here for you."

Marsh hung up the phone and fell into a nearby chair. He wouldn't kill Burl Hansen. That would not be necessary. But Butch Myers would die, and probably the boy as well.

"I want my son found, you bastard!" Was the way Joe Swiretynsky started the long-distance call.

Hansen blinked blood-shot eyes and exhaled, "We're doing everything possible, Dr. Swiretynsky."

"I knew nothing good would come of this preposterous scheme of sharing our Jacob," Swiretynsky spat. "I was against it from the start and intend to hold you personally responsible for any harm that befalls my son."

"I understand your pain and fear. Believe me, we too are hurting and…"

"You do not understand our pain. Do not pretend to think for one minute that your feelings for Jacob can come close to the love we have cultivated for fourteen years…"

Swiretynsky shoveled it out, and Hansen took it, feeling he deserved it. Swiretynsky insisted he would be on the next flight out of Boston. Hansen somehow convinced the doctor to give him twenty-four more hours before coming to Oklahoma.

"Stay with your wife, Dr. Swiretynsky. Be with her; comfort her. I'll keep you informed." Joseph Swiretynsky broke into heart wrenching sobs before the line went dead.

It could be a mistake, a risk, but a risk Marsh had to take. Surely, his keen judgment of character could not fail him a second time. If his intuition proved correct, he could certainly use the help. If it didn't work out, killing just one more wouldn't be that hard to do.

Luckily, Marsh found Tom Avery alone at his cycle shop working on the engine of a customer's bike.

"Do you have you a minute to discuss this past weekend?" Marsh started the conversation.

"Sure," Avery grinned as he grabbed a rag and wiped grease from his hands.

"I didn't stick around to listen to Chuck Turner give you his standard orientation speech about what we represent...what we stand for. I've heard it a hundred times before. I know he was careful to point out that although we are a clandestine organization, that doesn't mean that we're white supremacists or an anti-government entity.

"I'm sure he emphasized that if we are anything, we are a second line of defense against our government's current enemies, foreign and domestic, that might threaten our way of life under the Constitution."

"That's what the man said," Avery nodded.

"Does that satisfy you? Is that what you were hoping to find?"

"You ask that as if there other options," Avery observed.

He seemed a quick thinker and bright. Marsh liked that. So he took the plunge. "Yeah, there's more. A lot more. There's the Inner Circle."

"Inner Circle?"

"An enforcement arm, if you will. I head it up. The commander has his job, and I have mine. You see, although we are not characteristically white supremacists, we do believe there are race related issues and people of color and religions other than Christianity that threaten our way of life…like black and Hispanic gangs…and Native Americans who are bleeding our welfare systems, while at the same time building their own empires as sovereign nations…and Muslims who are free to come and go unchecked any place they want in these United States. I could go on and on, but won't. The point is we are the part of The Battalion that takes action against radical, unlawful, or unethical actions of minorities against the majority. We are the ones…"

"I want to be part of the Inner Circle," Avery interrupted solemnly.

"Aren't you wondering what kinds of actions we take?"

"Let me tell you, Deputy. Now this might just get me kicked out of our little army, but that's okay. Because before you came here and started talking, I was of half a mind just to close shop, get on my bike and ride off into the sunset. Because The Battalion isn't what I'm looking for. The reason being...I'm about half-assed white supremacist my own self.

"I believe the *afro-Americans* are trying to take our jobs and our women. I think the Jews have already taken over our banks and industries. The Indians...they ain't at all acting like a defeated nation. And Muslims? We shouldn't have any of them here. Not a single goddamned one. So, quite honestly, you can't take enough *action* to satisfy me."

"You would have to prove yourself."

"Give me a task. I'm a soldier, Deputy."

"You be here at ten tonight and be ready to go anytime after that. There may be a job to do and I might be here to pick you up," Marsh said before turning to leave.

At first he thought it only his imagination. The longer he listened, he knew it was real. As real, as terrible, as loud as the stench — things rustled in the blackness. Scampered in the dark.

Rats.

The faint clicking of claws on the cold rock floor could be imaginary. Maybe he really didn't hear gnawing. But they did scurry. And they did scamper.

Jacob had no idea how long he'd been in the darkness. Days for sure. Maybe even weeks. He might have slept.

He might not have. He really didn't know. He did know that he had not moved an inch and did not intend to. He didn't want the rats to find him — to crawl across him — to nibble at exposed flesh.

All he did was shiver and breathe the dank and contaminated air. He thought he would grow used to the smell. He didn't. It seemed to grow increasingly pungent. He thought his fear would grow to a point where it could not grow anymore. Just peak. But it didn't.

And now, he could no longer control his bowels. Hot, watery, acidic waste filled his jeans and Jacob began to sob. Softly at first. But then uncontrollably. Louder and louder and…

Suddenly a creaking noise sounded overhead, followed by a piercing squeak. And then like the other creatures of the dark, Jacob scampered away from a sudden and bright beam of light.

He heard no noises. No sounds of life. For those reasons Myers had not been willing to open the recessed door in the planked floor of the old school house. The last thing he wanted to find was a dead boy about the same age as his Randy lying at the bottom of the ladder. Myers had been to the point of running away when he heard the muffled, dreadful sobs.

When he jerked the heavy door open and shined his

flashlight into the hole but did not see the boy, Myers gasped, "Hey! Boy! Don't be moving around down there! For God's sake, Boy…stay still."

Myers planned on tying the boy up so he couldn't move about. But it hadn't seemed necessary when he'd carried him down there nearly twenty-four hours earlier. Myers thought at the time he'd hit him too hard. He feared the boy close to death and unable to move. Knowing he could now move made Myers' skin crawl. There was something down there no kid should find.

"Can you hear me, son? You stay still. Hear me?"

Myers fought off the urge to crawl down the ladder. In his state of stark sobriety, he didn't trust what he might do if he came within touching distance of the teen. No, Myers couldn't climb one more time into that awful smelling crater without bringing the boy out with him. Myers simply needed to take a drink. No, several drinks. Sobriety just wasn't compatible with this line of work.

Myers trotted across the room and picked up a small brown bag and an army surplus canteen. He wasn't thinking straight. It would be best to shut the door again and get the hell away from the old school. Without the boy as a captive, he'd never get Hansen.

"Here, son," he said, dropping the bag and green plastic canteen into the basement, "here's you a little food and some water."

Myers tried to quickly shut the door but didn't do it

quick enough. A tortured voice wafted up from somewhere in the dark to make him cringe.

"Why are you doing this to me?" a small and shaky voice cried.

"This ain't about you, and I'm sorry you've been hurt and scared, but I won't hurt you again. And you'll get out of there soon enough. I swear you will. But, boy, I got something I gotta do. I don't really like it, but I got to repay evil with some evil. I'm sorry you had to get involved in it, but, well, uh…sometimes life just shits on you."

Myers didn't want to talk anymore and he certainly didn't want to be subjected to the frightened voice again. He gave the door a shove and let it slam shut.

Jacob retained just enough wits about him to keep his eyes on the ladder while there had been light enough to see it. The moment the door came crashing down everything immediately went black, and Jacob rushed on hands and knees toward the image of the ladder imprinted in his mind. He misjudged the distance and instead of finding it with his hands he rammed the heavy, anchored structure with his already throbbing head. He collided with enough force to send him backwards and to the ground.

Jacob struggled back to his hands and knees and scrambled around frantically on the floor searching for the ladder. His search might have only taken seconds, but it felt like it took an eternity to locate the ladder. When he did find it, he scurried up several rungs and then stopped.

He didn't want to go all the way to the top because he didn't know where the man with the gruff voice went. Maybe he sat perched at the top just waiting and listening for Jacob to climb the ladder. Jacob did not believe for a minute the man had no further intentions of doing him harm. So for now, Jacob didn't want to climb to the top. He just wanted off the floor. He felt fairly certain the rats couldn't reach him here.

There had been a hint of fresh air the few minutes the door had been open. No trace of it remained now. If possible, the evil smell seemed worse on Jacob's elevated perch than it had on the floor.

The beam of light that illuminated the ladder revealed nothing else. Jacob knew no more than he had about the dimensions of his pitch-dark cell or what, if anything, filled the black recesses.

It remained eerily silent for an undeterminable length of time. Nothing moved above or below. The sound that eventually broke the silence was not loud but still so terrible that Jacob's hold on the ladder tightened to a death grip and he squeezed his eyelids closed to shut out the image the sound evoked. The faint scraping sound he heard could be nothing other than the paper bag being drug slowly across the cold, damp floor.

Hansen and his wife sat solemnly on their patio, staring into the darkness brewing on the horizon.

"It's heading this way," Hansen mumbled, thinking out loud.

Vicki nodded. Hansen didn't expect more. She had had little to say all day long. The expression on her face mirrored the churning, blue-gray fury building in the western skies. The wicked fingers of lightning that stabbed at the not so distant hills brought chill bumps to Hansen's skin and caused his heart to pound.

Would Jacob be exposed to the storm?

Hansen averted his eyes from the weather to Vicki and found her staring back. They locked eyes for only a moment before both turned back to the horizon. What raged beyond was easier to face than what raged within.

Tom Avery locked the doors to his shop earlier than usual. A savage wind accompanied by pounding rain assaulted the tin roof of the structure and did nothing to calm his jittery nerves. After replacing his greasy overalls with only a slightly cleaner pair of worn jeans and a black sleeveless T-shirt, Avery strapped his holster and twenty-two to his right leg. The top of his steel-toed boot hid the small gun.

A tiny cell phone with a freshly charged battery fit unobtrusively in the front pocket of the jeans. The last item he slipped on was a denim shirt. Avery left it unbuttoned.

He depended on the shirt to conceal the fifteen-round nine millimeter he tucked into the small of his back.

Lastly, he dug to the bottom of an old trunk of clothing he kept hidden in a small room at the back of the grimy building. After finding what he sought, he brought it to his lips to kiss it for good luck before dropping it into the top of his left boot.

A booming crash of thunder caused Avery to jump and bellow a full breath of profanities. He'd lived through earthquakes in California and hurricanes in Florida but had only heard of the violence that could result from stormy nights in Oklahoma.

Chapter Nineteen

Myers drove the last nail in place before attaching the hardware he'd picked up earlier in town. He still hadn't gotten to the bottle yet and his hands shook badly throughout the entire process. Regardless, his finished product still looked pretty damned good. It would have to be painted later. Then it would look real damned good.

Myers moved on wobbly legs across the dirt floor of his dilapidated work shed and fumbled to unlatch the door.

"Hey! Randy!" he shouted into the darkness toward the nearby house.

The rickety screen door screeched opened and then slammed shut before Randy called out.

"Yeah, Dad? What is it?"

Suspicion filled the young voice…or maybe dread.

"Come out here. I have something to show you."

The teen entered the shed hesitantly. Myers knew his son wasn't used to his old man working behind closed doors. Or working at all as far as that went.

"Over there," Myers nodded toward his workbench.

Randy looked in the direction of the nod and his eyes widened. "Man! That's for me?"

"Well, me and your mama don't play basketball," Myers chuckled as he walked past the new backboard and rim leaning against the work bench.

While Randy knelt to examine the handiwork, Myers pulled a new basketball from a sack in the corner of the shed.

"Heads up!" he said before tossing the ball to his son. "I'll get that thing painted and up on a pole for you tomorrow."

"Tomorrow?"

"Yeah. Tomorrow…I promise."

At first it came as only a whispering thought that competed with the echoing sound of the rats devouring the sack of food somewhere deep in the blackness. Yet it grew in intensity, over the stench, over the terror, until the single word sounded like a siren in Jacob's mind.

Bait.

The word sounded loud and clear, but not the meaning behind it.

Bait.

But for what? The rats? That couldn't be. If anything,

he might be their prey.

Bait.

Jacob released the grip his left hand held on the ladder and used it to rub his aching head — to help clear the pain shorting out his ability to grasp the apparently important message his numbed mind tried to conjure. After a while, the words came back like a shout in the darkness.

"…This ain't about you…I got to repay evil with some evil…"

Bait!

Jacob's left hand rejoined his right on the ladder and slowly — at first — he started working his way toward the door above.

"No!" he whispered as he put more effort into his ascent. By the time he reached the top, the word matured to a scream.

"NOOOOOOOOOOOOO!"

With an open palm he hit the door with all the strength he could muster. When it didn't budge, he put his shoulder into it and drove upward once…twice…and a third time. Still it did not give.

"I won't let you do this!" he screamed. Convinced he could not get out through the door, he started back down the ladder. Even if he had to go through the rats…and through the darkness…he had to look for another way out. The terrible man with the gruff voice intended on using him as bait to trap Burl.

Jacob started to cry on his way down the ladder but

he didn't stop. He could not stop — could not let himself stop. By the time he reached the floor Jacob sobbed uncontrollably.

He paused for just a moment at the bottom to steady himself. Then, with his arms extended in front of him, he began to inch forward. There would be a wall. Jacob would find it and work his way around the room. Maybe there would be a door or a window.

He inched forward and groped in the darkness for several seconds before his fingers made contact...and recoiled...from a sticky and damp obstruction. Trembling, he reluctantly reached again and felt the uneven roughness of a rock wall.

For long minutes he leaned against the wall, finding the coolness somewhat of a comfort. Just when he thought he might stop crying, something scampered across the tops of his feet.

"Go away! Leave me alone!" he screamed, kicking out in all directions.

The defiance and strength in his words coupled with the action of fighting back somehow provided the encouragement he needed to press on. He would work to his right feeling and examining the wall from the floor up to as high as he could tip-toe. If a man who meant him no personal harm would go as far as to club him, abduct him, and put him in such an awful place...what would he do to his father?

Jacob made it to a corner and started down the adjacent

wall. Every few feet he screamed a threat at the rats, warning them to stay away. It seemed to work. Nothing else scampered across his feet. He worked a good way along the length of new wall when his right foot collided with something on the floor.

He screamed and jumped back several feet. When there were no sounds of anything large moving towards or away from him, Jacob drew a deep breath and bellowed another threat before slowly shuffling his feet toward whatever lay before him.

When he reached it a second time…he again recoiled, but then kicked out with his right foot and made contact with something soft but unmovable. It gave, but it did not give way. It felt of such mass and weight that he would not be able to kick it out of his path. It could be a large bag of something that could possibly be of use.

Jacob bent at the waist, leaned forward and reached with splayed and shaky fingers. The fingers of his right hand fell ever so slightly on…hair.

The stench now disturbed came up and over Jacob with a choking intensity that sent him stumbling backwards. A cry came from deep inside him and seemed to lodge in his throat. Choking and gasping, Jacob wheeled and ran full speed into the darkness… away from his gruesome find. He ran and screamed and choked until he ran headfirst into the far wall.

Withering on the ground, dazed to near unconsciousness from the collision, Jacob formed screams into a mournful plea…

"Help me...*someone*...please...*someone* help me!"

Captian Mike Walker at some point drifted off to sleep while sitting beside his grandfather's bed, holding one of Billy Harjo's languid, fragile hands. The grip now being asserted by the hand awakened Walker. The holy man suddenly applied an amazing amount of pressure.

Even more surprising, ancient eyes that had reportedly been closed for many long hours now opened and stared intently at a fixed spot on the ceiling. Billy's head cocked to the right to thrust his left ear forward. Walker had seen the old man do this hundreds of times in the past. It was Billy's way of putting his best ear forward when concentrating to listen. The Alekchi looked as pallid as ever and now he seemed to be fighting for every breath he took.

Walker turned to look at the nearby clock. It was nearly ten-thirty. Then he too gazed at the spot on the ceiling that held his grandfather rapt. Nothing appeared there for Walker's eyes to see. Walker could hear the rain pelting the roof and the booming thunder that accompanied it, but he sensed it nothing of the natural world that the dying medicine man strained to hear.

The stench grew worse than ever. It seemed as if it

chased after Jacob, caught him, and covered him like a putrid blanket both sticky and wet.

Jacob lay on his left side with his knees pulled up to his chest. His arms wrapped around and cradling his head, trying to shut out the sound of the rats and the thoughts of the decaying body. Although it had no effect on the dreadful thoughts, it did for a moment block out all sounds except for the pounding of his heart.

After a short while, though, there came another sound. It took Jacob some time to realize what he was hearing. In this horrid place, apparently underground with a structure covering it, the crash of muffled thunder could still be heard.

As a small boy, thunder frightened him. It never failed to conjure up childish images of awful beasts battling in the sky and frightful monsters whose booming voices warned of just how close they lurked. For a moment the thunder brought back the childhood anxieties. Jacob remembered how he used to flee from his own bedroom to the safety of his parents' bed. This memory prompted another.

His father would hold him and rock him. In a tone of voice that soothed Jacob's fears, Joseph Swiretynsky would remind him of what the father shared with the son in storms of the past — that thunder was God's voice and God's way of letting the frightened know that even in pouring rains and thrashing winds and deepest darkness… that God remained near. Thunder, his father had said, was the voice of God saying, "I am here with you."

Remembering the words of long ago brought to mind more recent ones. Words about *no place else to turn...no place else to go.* In Jacob's mind Burl's voice seemed to come from someplace in the darkness...

"I'm not so sure that the only thing that can prove to a man that God exists is God himself."

Still curled into a ball with his head tucked and protected, Jacob dwelt on the words...and on the stench... the rats...the darkness...and on the thunder. Maybe he did have someplace else to turn.

"I don't know what to call you," he moaned, "but if you do exist...please make the smell go away...please get me out of here."

Paper thin eyelids slowly closed over the staring eyes and the hand gripping Mike Walker's fell limp. The fragile body that had up to now been still started trembling, and the grandson began to tell the grandfather good-bye.

Just as Walker thought Billy Harjo took his last breath, the old man began to chant. To Walker's bewilderment, the skin long void of life's color started to flush. In the following moments, Harjo's chest began to rise and fall with force and regularity as his hands clinched into fists.

Marsh calmed himself before picking up the ringing phone. He could not let Myers sense his consuming anger. Now only minutes away from midnight, he'd been pacing about his home since ten, waiting for this call.

"Hello," he said pleasantly.

"Are you going to help me?" A voice slurred.

"Butch! Hello man. Say, where are you?"

"At a pay phone. Are you still going to help me kill Hansen?"

"I said I'd help you. I'll help you. Where is the boy?"

"He's with the fuckin' Indian! He's in that goddamned basement. Meet me there in an hour."

Marsh disconnected and started jabbing at the numbers that would ring Tom Avery. "Oh, I'll meet you there you, bastard," he hissed while Avery's phone rang, "I'll even be early."

It began so subtly that it caused no alarm — just a barely noticeable draft. Soon it caressed Jacob's skin like a gentle breeze. Though it came from the dark above him — from a source he could not see — Jacob did not fear it. Even as its motions intensified, Jacob sensed no threat. Whatever created the action seemed to whisk away the choking odor, replacing it with fresher, cleaner air. Something from above…in the darkness…seemed to fan Jacob and ward off the evil smell.

Jacob dropped his arms from around his head to hear a sound emitted by the fanning motion…rhythmic… powerful…reverberating.

Am I hallucinating? Jacob feared he'd finally lost what little sanity he'd managed to retain. The gale of fresh air and the sound being made could only be produced by a large set of powerful wings.

Maybe he had lost his mind. Or maybe what he heard and felt was real. It didn't matter. Either some internal defense mechanism had engaged to make Jacob believe the smell disappeared — or something mystical and magical actually hovered over him. It didn't matter which. Jacob didn't care.

Only one fact mattered. Jacob received part of what he'd asked for. Perhaps he would get the rest. At least now, he'd been given hope.

Jacob didn't hesitate to speak forcibly out loud. He didn't care what else might hear him. "Thank you! Oh, thank you so very much…dear…God!

Marsh circled the block once and didn't see any other cars on the street or anyone out and about on foot. On his second pass, he pulled into the alley and shut off his lights. He let the unmarked cruiser idle toward the dingy cinderblock building located midway down the block. Just before coming to a stop, Marsh remembered to flip the two toggle switches under the dash. One disabled the brake lights, the other the dome light.

Marsh didn't even come to a complete stop behind the motorcycle shop before Avery jerked open the front passenger door and jumped inside. Neither man spoke until they were out of the alley and creeping through the deserted city streets.

"You gonna tell me what's going on?" Avery spoke the first words. He sounded calm, even relaxed.

"I guess I better," Marsh smiled. He admired the man's cool demeanor. "After all, you might change your mind and decide you don't want any part of this business."

Marsh paused for Avery to comment. When he didn't, the undersheriff pushed on, "Do you have a gun on you?"

"Got one down in my boot."

"What caliber?"

"Twenty-two."

Marsh leaned forward, reached under the seat and retrieved a .357 revolver. "Here," he said, handing the gun across the seat, "You're going to need something a little bigger for this job."

Avery flipped out the cylinder and examined the rounds and then snapped it back in place. He tucked the big revolver into the waistband of his jeans. Only then did he ask, "Okay. So what's the job? This suspense is fucking killing me."

"When I selected the initial members of the Inner

Circle," Marsh began, "I was careful to pick people who had strong ties to one another, life-long friends, relatives, even a husband and wife team. The nature of our responsibilities demands that we be loyal to each other. That we trust each other."

"Why are you bringing me in then?" Avery questioned. "I ain't got no ties to a single son of a bitch within a hundred miles of this place."

Marsh turned his eye from the road to Avery and snarled a smile. "Exactly. You see, as it's turned out, my selection process was not without flaws. One of the members of the Inner Circle has, well, stepped way out of the circle. Now, he has to be stopped, and I don't think stopping him is going to be a one man job. Because of who he is…and family ties…and life-long friendships…I don't feel that I can count on anyone else in the Inner Circle to help me do what has to be done. So I need you because you don't have any ties. And if you carry this out, I'll know I can trust you and that you are at least loyal to me."

"Tell me, Deputy, are you saying in some roundabout way that there's going to be a killing involved?"

Before responding, Marsh slowed the car so he would be able to study Avery's face for a response. "We are going to have to kill Butch Myers…and Burl Hansen's fourteen-year-old son. Then we're going to have to dispose of the bodies. Like, I said, it's a big job for just one man."

"So it was Myers that grabbed the boy," Avery cackled. "Okay. Let me guess. We are going to kill Myers because he's an idiot who's threatening to ruin everything...and we are going to kill the boy because he's a witness and might know things we don't want others to know."

"Do you have a problem with any of this?"

"I hear the boy's a Jew."

"Does it matter?"

"Just makes it easier. I got no more use for Jews than I do Muslims," Avery growled with icy emphasis. Then he cocked his head and squinted his eyes at Marsh, "On the subject of Hansen, I'm curious. Is he a member of The Battalion?"

"Oh, no," Marsh chuckled. "The commander and I have kicked around the idea of inviting him in several times, but we always come to the same conclusion. He'd have no interest in joining."

"Why do you think that?"

"Burl believes that for every true problem there is a system in place to solve the problem. He believes that the vast majority of the time, the system will function as designed and the problem will be alleviated. Burl would probably say that if a problem is perceived for which there is no system in place to counter it, that would be proof enough that no problem exists.

"I like to call Burl a practical idealist. If asked to join the militia, his response would undoubtedly be, 'Why do we need a militia...when we have the National Guard and the Army and the Marines?' Burl is a damned good man, but he'd be a sorry soldier."

"That's too bad. When the shit hits the fan, I wouldn't mind having the big bad dude covering my back."

Marsh nodded his head in agreement before getting back to the matter at hand. He told Avery everything about Darrell Baker, Shelly Rafell, Max Bemo, and how Butch Myers blabbed to Herman Grambs. Then he explained how he intended to dispose of Myers and Hansen's kid.

But Marsh strategically kept some things secret.

Chapter Twenty

"He's already fucking here," Marsh exclaimed as the cruiser's headlights fell on Myers' battered truck.

"What do we do now?" Avery asked.

Marsh's plan revolved around them arriving first, taking care of the kid, and then ambushing Myers. "We'll improvise. Just let me do the talking and do what I tell you."

"Can do."

Marsh pulled in and positioned the car so the headlights illuminated the entrance to the old three-room school building. Myers stepped into the doorway. He brought a hand up to shield his eyes from the bright lights, but otherwise didn't move. Marsh remained in the car a few seconds to make some mental adjustments to his plan.

"There's a spare flashlight in the glove box. Grab it," he barked at Avery before opening the door and stepping out. Marsh left the car running and lights on.

"Hey, Pete, who's that you brought with you?" Myers called from the door as he made a visor of his hand and blinked into the headlights.

"It's Tom Avery," Marsh called back.

"What the fuck's he doing here?"

Myers didn't sound nearly as drunk as Marsh wanted him to be. "He wants to join the Inner Circle, Butch. This is his test."

As Myers processed the development, Marsh started for the front door, motioning Avery to follow. They didn't stop until they were mere feet in front of the solidly built man blocking the doorway.

"How do you know we can trust him?" Myers said to Marsh while glaring at Avery.

"Let me worry about that, Butch," Marsh said without managing to keep an edge entirely off his words. "Do you have a gun on you?"

"I got several in the truck. Why you asking?"

Marsh had to bite his tongue to keep from lashing out. He reassured himself that retribution for all this man endangered would come soon enough. Hoping to alleviate the palpable tension, the deputy chuckled, "Hell, Butch, if we're going to get Burl out here, we better damn sure know we have the firepower to bring him down. Believe me, with his kid involved, it's going to be like trying to drop a bull elephant. We got to be prepared to put a whole lot of lead in old Burl."

The levity had some effect. Myers exhaled a long

breath and let his shoulders drop slightly. "Okay. Okay. I'm sorry, Pete. I'm just a little nervous."

"No problem, Butch. We just got a big job to do here. So, let's get it done. Is the boy still in the basement?"

"Yeah, I was just getting ready to get him out. He's been down there too long. I shouldn't have put him down there in the first place."

Marsh turned to Avery. "The door to the basement is in the floor just inside the first room…Go take care of the kid."

Avery nodded and started around Myers. Big hands — that had almost been famous — formed into fists as Myers stepped to his left and blocked Avery's advance.

Myers had done some drinking but stopped short of being real drunk. He'd certainly drunk enough to take the biting edge off what he'd done…and had left to do. Thank God he didn't drink more or he might not have discerned that "take care of" isn't necessarily the same as "take good care of."

"I'll get the boy out of there," he said to Avery through gritted teeth.

"Butch," Marsh said harshly, "that boy's not coming out of there. Not now. Not ever. Now, get out of his way."

"No way. Fuck you, Pete." Myers shook his head

violently to both clear away alcohol induced cobwebs and emphasize his defiance.

Avery tried shoving past him. Myers brought a hand up and pushed Avery several feet backwards.

Obscenities flew simultaneously from Marsh and Avery as Marsh pulled his service revolver and Avery jerked the gun from beneath his shirt. The barrels of both guns quickly aligned with Myers' face.

"You have fucked this up enough you ignorant bastard!" Marsh bellowed. "Now, get the fuck out of the way, or I will shoot you where you stand. I swear to God I will!"

"I can't let you kill that boy, Pete. I don't want that on my conscience!"

Marsh thrust the barrel of the revolver to the side of Myers' head. The metallic click of the hammer being cocked reverberated throughout Myers' entire body.

"That kid has to die, Butch. He knows too much. Do you think he hasn't discovered the body down there with him? Do you want to go to the pen? Does lethal injection appeal to you, Butch? And what about your family? What happens to them if you go to prison? What happens to that son of yours if I have to kill your stupid ass right here and now?"

The basketball goal came to mind. It wasn't painted and it had to be put up tomorrow...he'd promised. Myers shuffled out of Avery's way on suddenly weakened legs. He turned from the headlights' glare to gaze into the darkness. He tried not to hear the clomping of Avery's heavy boots falling on the plank floor…*or the creaking of the heavy door being pulled open...*

"Listen to me Butch," Marsh whispered urgently.

…or the falling of those heavy boots on the rungs of the ladder…

"That man's not like us Butch. Although what he's getting ready to do is absolutely necessary, you and I couldn't have done it."

…and the calling out of the young voice…sounding hopeful at first…

"That's the real reason I brought him along Butch. I need him to do what has to be done. I need him to do the thing you and I won't do. Can't do."

…and the sudden, terrified gasp from the realization that it wasn't help climbing down the stairs…

"But now, I'm going to need your help Butch. I need you to help me make this whole mess look like it was Tom Avery's fault."

…or the screams…

"I have to kill him when he comes out of there. Will you help me Butch?"

Myers stared into the dark and tried not to hear any of it. Not the screams growing more frantic by the second. Not Marsh's plea to kill one more time.

Suddenly a quaking explosion of a gunshot erupted, then a tortured cry. Then came a second shot, which was followed by the most awful thing Myers had yet to hear…

silence…the permanent kind.

"He's killed the boy Butch. Will you help me kill him now?"

Myers couldn't speak. But while wiping tears from his face he did find the strength to nod.

The color had returned to his face while his breathing grew increasingly stronger. Just when Mike Walker allowed himself to believe his grandfather might recover, Billy Harjo started to convulse.

Again thin eyelids popped open to reveal the faded pupils. This time they reflected what looked to Walker like stark terror. The look remained only a moment before the eyes again rolled back into their sockets. Violently, horribly, Billy Harjo gasped for a final breath.

It was over.

The mouth fell slack. The eyelids remained open.

And Mike Walker began to sob.

Marsh crouched beside the doorway with gun in hand. His nerves felt like someone set them on fire, but his gun hand remained steady enough. When Avery stepped out into the beam of the headlights, Marsh straightened and thrust the gun to Avery's throat.

"What the fuck?" Avery gurgled.

"Don't even flinch," Marsh growled. Then to Myers, "Get his gun. Hurry, get the goddamned gun!"

Myers grabbed the .357, and Marsh violently shoved Avery off the steps. Myers jumped down after him and jammed the revolver into the startled face. Marsh backed off several yards while keeping Avery in his sights. He could now breathe a little easier because Myers did as told. So far, so good.

"I did what you told me to do," Avery bleated.

Marsh backed up even farther. The fear in Avery's voice made him uncomfortable. Fear could make men take desperate risks. "Shoot the motherfucker, Butch! Shoot him now!"

Myers gave Avery a shove and pulled back the hammer. Without hesitation he turned the gun on Marsh.

"The boy didn't have to die!" Myers screamed before pulling the trigger.

Marsh felt no searing pain. He saw no bright flash of light and didn't hear a thundering noise. But he did hear a metallic click. The gun misfired.

Marsh wheeled on Myers and pulled his trigger. Out of the corner of his eye he saw Avery reaching for the small of his back.

Marsh's shot went wide, and Myers pulled his trigger a second time. Again, it did nothing but click. Marsh didn't know why, but Avery must have unloaded the .357. This time Marsh jerked off a round at Avery. The tattooed man flinched and spun.

Marsh's third round struck Myers in the chest. The fourth one hit just left of his navel. Marsh then wheeled and leveled on Avery, who stumbled for the cover of darkness. Marsh jerked the trigger twice more but couldn't tell if the bullets found their mark. Avery had disappeared into the night.

Myers lay sprawled on his back just inside the glow of the car's headlights. He did not move and the gun lay at his side.

Cursing, and with his hands starting to shake, Marsh emptied his spent rounds and fumbled with reloads when a hail of bullets thundered at him from the darkness.

Marsh dove for the muddy ground and scampered on hands and knees for the cruiser. More rounds peppered the ground around him. Avery had an automatic, and Marsh feared, a fifteen-round magazine. Marsh rolled to safety on the far side of the car just as the shooting stopped. He could hear twigs snapping and the rustling of underbrush. Was Avery moving closer or farther away? Or was he circling?

With sweat rolling down and into his eyes, Marsh tried to control frenzied breathing as he again fumbled to reload his revolver. That done, he rolled onto his stomach and peered around the front tire of his car. Nothing moved in the dark, and Marsh struggled to put together a plan of action. Now, everything was truly fucked up.

Hansen lay in bed beside his wife, listening to her steady, sedated breathing. Sleep for him, what little there had been, proved fitful at best. When the phone beside the bed rang, he grabbed it before it could ring a second time.

"Hello," he whispered, glad now that he hadn't given into the urge to take some of the pills the doctor prescribed for both him and Vicki.

"Sheriff Hansen?" A faintly familiar voice asked with a gasping wheeze. Static on the line suggested the call was coming from a cell phone.

"Yeah, this is Hansen," he said while pushing up from his side to sit up in bed.

"This is Tom Avery," the voice struggled. "Don't say anything. Just listen. I'm hurt bad and fading fast…"

Avery was in pain. Hansen could hear it in his voice. The words sounded weak, metered, and came in moans and groans.

Hansen didn't interrupt, but pushed off the bed and hurried out of the bedroom.

"…Do you know where the old school is, out east of Finley on county road one-fifty?"

It took a second. Hansen had not been out there in years. "Yeah, I know where it is. Does this have something to do with my son?" he snarled into the phone.

"Yes. Yes," Avery moaned. The connection crackled and grew weaker. "There's a lot I have to tell you, and so little time. I don't know how much longer I've got. I'm under a bridge on the dirt road that leads to the school. I think I'm south of it…not real sure. You have to get out here…So you'll know, I'm…"

Hansen could not keep from interrupting. "What's happened? What the hell is going on Avery and how is it tied to Jacob?" Hansen interrupted, unable to keep from doing so.

"Just…get out here…and come alone. You can't trust anyone…Your undersheriff is in on it…a conspiracy… you're in danger…I'm hit…Marsh…watch him."

"Is Jacob all right?" Hansen asked loudly.

Avery responded only with a gasp for air and a guttural moan.

"Avery? Avery, can you hear me?" Hansen shouted into the phone. "What kind of bullshit is this? Marsh is in on it? What the hell is going on?"

There was no answer. The line had gone dead. Hansen threw on his clothes and strapped on his gun belt. Before going out the door he grabbed the phone in the kitchen and punched in a number.

Hansen had absolutely no idea what was really going on. Avery could be up to anything. Did he truly think Hansen would believe Jacob's abduction was part of a conspiracy involving Pete Marsh? Bullshit.

It took several rings, but a groggy voice finally responded on the other end of the line. "Yeah? What? Who is this?"

"Chuck, wake up. I need help."

"Burl? What's up? Is it the boy?" Turner asked.

"Yeah. I think so. I just got a call from Tom Avery. He sounds bad. I think he's been shot. Says he's under a bridge on the road to the old Pleasant Valley schoolhouse. Can you meet me out there?"

"Sure. I'll be on the way in less than five."

"Hey, Chuck," Hansen said before his best friend could hang up. "He said Pete is involved. I, uh, don't know what to make of it."

A long pause came from Chuck's end. "Chuck? Are you there?"

"Pete…involved?" Chuck finally muttered, "Avery must be out of his mind."

"Yeah. I don't know what he's up to," Hansen nodded. "I'll try to raise Pete on the radio when I get in the car. I'll bet he's still working. I'll have him meet us out there."

Marsh lay beside his car and thought and waited and thought some more…until he thought and waited too long. The car started making a funny sound. Marsh could now smell antifreeze and he heard the hissing sound of steam spewing from the radiator. The cruiser had overheated.

"Fuck!" Marsh screamed into the night. Still, though, he didn't dare move. Avery could be just waiting for Marsh to show himself. After several more long minutes of indecision, the car's engine started to knock and then it died.

For an undetermined length of time, Marsh laid on his belly in the mud with his gun trained on the shadows where Avery disappeared. He could hear nothing but crickets and his own breathing. Occasionally, the storm that moved through earlier lit up the skies to the east.

Just when Marsh began to believe things couldn't get any worse, Burl Hansen's voice boomed over the police radio in the car. The sheriff was calling for him. Marsh considered pushing to his feet, but then thought of how the bullets hit all around him in near misses. Avery could still be out there just waiting in the shadows.

As far as Marsh cared, Hansen could just keep on calling. Even if Marsh could get to the radio, just what the fuck would he say to his boss?

Hansen was nearly a half mile away from the deserted schoolhouse when he came to a rickety wood-planked bridge spanning a wide ravine. He pulled to the side of the road and reached for his flashlight when the graveyard-shift dispatcher called his unit number.

"Go ahead," Hansen responded as he carefully watched for any movement around the bridge up in front of him.

"I tried both Pete's home and cell numbers. Uh, I can't raise him, Sheriff," the dispatcher advised.

It didn't make sense. Pete didn't answer his radio either. At this time of night, Pete either worked or went home.

"Ten-four," Hansen grumbled.

"Do you want me to get another unit out to back you, Sheriff?"

Hansen considered the offer for a moment before deciding. "Negative. Chief Turner is in route."

Turner would be all the help Hansen would need.

Hansen got out of his car and took several deep breaths. Nerves played hell with his stomach. The thought of an ambush toyed with his imagination, although he couldn't think of any reason Avery would want to ambush him — unless he was somehow involved with Jacob's disappearance.

Hansen slowly and carefully approached the bridge with his flashlight on and held at arm's length away from his body. If anyone shot at the light, they might miss him.

"Avery? Tom Avery?" Hansen shouted as he scanned the beam of light across the landscape that dropped off steeply to the left and right of the one-lane bridge. "Are you out there, Avery?"

The grass on the left side wasn't nearly as tall as that on the right. The brush wasn't as thick either. Hansen started off the side of the road and down the left side. To make sure he had solid footing, he shined the bright beam to the ground directly out in front of his feet. There he spotted blood on the grass. Lots of blood.

"Avery! It's Hansen! Can you hear me?"

No response came. Hansen wasted no time getting

down the steep embankment. The trail of blood was thick and easy to track. Hansen followed it to the still form lying beneath the bridge.

Avery lay stretched out on his back. When the flashlight's beam fell directly upon him, a bloody hand feebly raised a pistol and pointed it toward the light.

"Is that you, Hansen?" Avery strained to ask.

"Yeah, it's me, Avery. Toss that gun away." Hansen had pulled his sidearm and now pointed it at Avery's forehead.

Avery tried to comply but managed only to drop the automatic at his side.

Hansen kept his gun trained on Avery while moving to the downed man's side. Once there, he kicked the blood-caked gun out of reach and holstered his before dropping to one knee to check the damage.

Avery had an awful gaping wound high on his left shoulder. Hansen had seen few shooting victims but hunted for years and knew an exit wound when he saw one. The round would have entered his back. Blood also practically spouted from a small hole in his shirt down on the lower left side of his abdomen. This one looked like an entry wound.

"What the hell happened? Is Jacob out here?" Hansen asked.

"Pull off my left boot," Avery moaned.

"Huh? What the hell…"

"Pull off my fucking left boot," Avery moaned through gritted teeth.

Puzzled, Hansen gently began working the boot off Avery's foot. In the process, something shiny fell out of the top of the boot and landed in the wet grass. Hansen reached and retrieved a badge. The words, "Alcohol, Tobacco, and Firearms" were engraved on it.

Hansen studied the badge for several seconds. It didn't seem possible. "You're a federal agent?" he asked, astonished.

Avery nodded while gasping for a breath, "BATF. Real name's Boyd Mackey… here trying to infiltrate a militia group. Marsh heads up a…a…killing squad. Calls it the… Inner Circle."

Hansen straightened and shook his head in disbelief. "Bullshit! This is all bullshit!" The badge didn't really mean a thing. It could be a fake or even stolen. "I don't believe you. I really don't know who the hell you are or what the hell you're…"

"They killed the kids you fished out of the lake… Bemo, too."

"No. No. You've got something all wrong," Hansen shook his head. "I know Pete too well. We've been together for…"

"And they've got your son."

Hansen's shaking head ground to a standstill. The denials caught in his throat.

"He's in the cellar of the old school," Avery, or whatever the hell his name was, said with a voice starting to weaken even more. "The door is in the floor of the first room."

Hansen shot to his feet. "Is he..." He just couldn't complete the question.

"Get to him...hurry."

Hansen started away. "I'll send an ambulance," he called over his shoulder.

"Hey!" Mackey exhaled, "Marsh is still out here someplace...Watch him...kick my gun back over here to me... and...don't go down in that cellar...before calling out your name."

Hansen put the bloody gun back in Avery's hand. He had made it up on the road when the man frantically started shouting something else. Hansen couldn't make out what he said, but thought he heard the word "Turner." It made sense — the two men had done business and grown friendly.

"I've already called him," Hansen shouted to comfort the wounded man. "He's on his way!"

Chapter Twenty-One

Jacob sat upright with his legs tucked beneath him. He gently swayed back and forth, praying, and straining to see the door far above him. If the rats were moving, he couldn't hear them. The terribly loud gunshots in the confined space all but deafened him. His ears still rang. His head still throbbed.

Earlier when the man came down the ladder, Jacob believed for a moment it might be Burl. He began to scream when he realized it wasn't. The man clamped a rough hand across Jacob's mouth and pulled him close… hugging him. He'd then whispered in Jacob's ear.

He'd tried telling Jacob that everything would be all right…that he was a friend…that he wouldn't hurt him. Jacob didn't believe the man and continued to struggle and scream although the hand across his mouth muted the effort.

Then the man did a strange thing. He gently placed his cheek against Jacob's forehead and whispered, "I'll get your father here. I promise. Just hang on a little longer."

The man claimed to be a police officer and introduced himself as Boyd. Then he took his hand away from Jacob's mouth.

Boyd told him to hold his ears tightly, but Jacob hadn't understood and didn't do it. There followed a blinding flash. The sudden explosion came so completely unexpected that Jacob shrieked in response. Boyd clamped his hand over his mouth again, but it proved unnecessary because it suddenly occurred to Jacob that the eruption sounded like thunder. Right beside him. All around him. Thunder. The voice of God. The noise of the second shot didn't affect Jacob whatsoever.

In the seconds that followed, Boyd offered more words of encouragement. Then he did something else strange.

"I'm going to position you in front of the ladder…" he whispered while moving Jacob into place.

"…Watch the door. Don't take your eyes off of it…"

He placed something in Jacob's hand and positioned his fingers the way they needed to be.

"…if someone comes down that ladder other than your father…start pulling the trigger."

Then he was gone.

Moments after that Jacob thought he heard more thunder. Or maybe, it was just the ringing in his ears.

Now, Jacob just sat and rocked and stared up into the darkness. The small gun in his hand felt comforting, and Boyd had encouraged him, but still all seemed far from being right. Jacob remained very much frightened, in pain, and hungry beyond description. Worse yet, the stench came back

When Boyd first opened the door to make his descent, he frightened away the thing with wings that fanned Jacob with a cool, fresh breeze. Jacob long decided that whatever fanned him from above wasn't a hallucination or a dream. Whatever it was, it had been real. Jacob now chose to believe God sent it there. God granted him a miracle.

Now he silently prayed for another. He wanted Burl to get there, and get there fast, and get there safely, and get them both far away from this iniquitous place. With the knowledge Jacob processed of the dangers lurking at the top of the ladder, he understood that for all that to happen…it would take yet another miracle.

Chuck Turner monitored the county department's radio frequency and heard Hansen call for the ambulance. Turner hissed a line of profanities as he reached for his microphone. What in the hell was happening? He desperately wished he'd gotten to Avery before Hansen did, but the Arrowhead Ranch stood twenty minutes closer to the old school than Turner's house in town.

"Burl, this is Chuck," Turner huffed into the mike, not caring to bother with proper radio calls or procedures. "What's going on out there?"

Hansen didn't use radio etiquette either. "Avery's out here. He's been shot up pretty badly. I'm heading now to the school. Avery says Jacob is in the basement. There's, uh, more, Chuck...but I don't want to discuss it over the air. Hurry up and get out here."

"County One," the dispatcher cut in, "Do you need more help out there?"

After a pause, Turner heard Burl respond, "Do we have anyone close?"

This time Turner cut in abruptly, "County Headquarters, this is Chief Turner. I'm real close and will run code three. I should be there in two minutes."

Damage control would most definitely be needed. It would be bad enough just dealing with his old friend. He didn't want others out there.

Turner breathed a sigh of relief when Hansen came back on the air.

"Headquarters, just hold off on any more help. Chief Turner and I will handle this."

Hansen skid his car to a stop on the dirt road in front of the school. Marsh's cruiser sat directly in front of the school with lights burning.

Hansen sprang from his car, but fought back the urge to bolt for the building. Instead, he stood surveying what lay before him, considering all Avery had said. Hansen simply could not imagine Pete Marsh ever doing harm to him or anyone close to him. Still, too much was at stake for Hansen to take any chances at this point. At the moment he had to consider all possibilities. Jacob's life could depend on it. Hansen pulled his service revolver but held it down to his side.

"Hey! Pete!" He called, doing his best to sound normal. "Pete! Where are you?"

No answer came in return. Everything was eerily quiet. Although the lights were on, Marsh's car wasn't running. Hansen thought it strange he would kill the engine and leave the lights on.

Nothing about the situation felt right, but Hansen couldn't give a damn. From what he'd been told, Jacob was waiting, and Hansen had wasted enough time being careful.

Although he wanted to, he didn't run. He just walked as fast as he could while scanning the area with the flashlight. When he came along the left side of Marsh's car, he shined his light inside. Nothing looked out of place. Just a few long strides later Hansen's beam of light fell across a form on the ground to the front and right of Marsh's cruiser.

Hansen involuntarily came to an abrupt stop. "Fuck!" After a deep breath he moved to the man on the ground. Hansen realized while still feet away that it was Butch Myers and there was nothing anyone could do for the man now. Dead eyes stared up at dark skies still brewing with clouds.

Because both his mind and heart raced, Hansen bolted

toward the old building and hit full stride before reaching the front steps. Once inside, he slowed just enough to locate the cellar door with his flashlight beam. Hansen jerked the door open with such force that it popped the old hinges and sent them flying into the darkness.

Marsh thought he had it all worked out. He would say Butch Myers called him at home late in the evening. Phone records would back him up. Myers called to confess how he and Tom Avery kidnapped Jacob in hopes of getting a chunk of the money everyone knew Burl Hansen earned playing big-time football.

Myers decided, Marsh would say, to come clean when he learned of Avery's plan to kill the boy whether or not they collected the ransom. Marsh would relay how he had schemed with Myers to meet at the school to arrest Avery and rescue Jacob.

Sure it would reflect badly on Marsh for not calling for a back-up and because he accidentally killed Myers by cross-fire in a shoot-out with Avery. Marsh might even lose his job. But that was a hell of a lot better than going to prison for life or having poison pumped into his veins. And when the investigation turned up the two bodies in the cellar? That, too, could be easily laid at the feet of Myers and Avery. Admittedly, it wasn't a perfect story. It had some loopholes. Still though, Marsh could have made it work before Burl Hansen showed up on the scene.

Marsh lay on the ground listening to his radio and cursing his luck until Hansen called for an ambulance. Avery wasn't waiting in the dark for him to move. He was half a mile away. At that point Marsh had jumped up and darted into the shadows on the far side of the rock school house. Within those shadows, he worked on yet another lie until Hansen barreled into the school and all hell broke loose.

Jacob had heard the boots pounding on the floor above him. They sounded angry. He hadn't expected the door to be opened so quickly or violently.

When no familiar voice sounded, Jacob blinked at the faint light in the opening and started pulling the trigger. He didn't know how many times the little gun fired, but he pulled the trigger until it did nothing but click.

Hansen fell to the floor and didn't move until he heard the clicking and the faint sobs. The bullets had whizzed by his face and head before he remembered Avery's last warning.

"Jacob!" he screamed out, "It's me! It's Burl!"

"Burl?" A voice, frightened and small, repeated his name from the depths of the awful smelling darkness.

Jacob dropped the gun and tried getting to his feet but he couldn't move.

"Burl!" he yelled this time with conviction.

A huge form blocked what little light shone from above.

"It's me, Jacob. I'm coming down to get you."

In another minute Jacob was hoisted from the floor and wrapped in powerful, hugging arms. He couldn't keep from crying. Obviously, Burl couldn't either.

Hansen put Jacob on the ladder first and then strained to climb it while pushing upward on his weakened and very heavy son. Once he'd pushed Jacob out of the cellar opening and onto the floor, Hansen crawled out and collapsed beside him.

"Are you okay? Do you have any injuries?" Hansen huffed.

A shaky voice responded, "I'm all right…now."

Burl struggled to his feet and fumbled in the dark for Jacob's hand. He'd lost both his flashlight and gun when he'd fallen to the floor to avoid being shot. With no little effort, he got Jacob to his feet and led him toward the door and fresh air. Burl could only imagine the source of the stench in the cellar.

Father and son made it outside and embraced again in the dimming lights of Marsh's car. Hansen stood and hugged Jacob without words until the sound of the familiar voice made Jacob jerk violently in Burl's arms.

The voice caused Hansen to stiffen.

"Burl," Pete Marsh called again from behind them.

Hansen turned and moved Jacob behind him. "What the hell is going on, Pete?" He tried to keep his voice even. Burl grew suddenly wary, but remained hopeful Pete was still on his side.

"It was, uh, terrible, Burl. I guess I really fucked… uh, I'm sorry…messed things up. It just all happened so quickly…"

Hansen studied Marsh for any sign that he intended to harm them, but detected nothing unusual in the man he'd grown to trust. Marsh's gun was holstered and if anything, he just seemed distraught. Hansen began to breathe a little easier, but kept his place between his friend and his son.

"…Butch called me at home. It was him and Tom Avery that kidnapped your son. They wanted a ransom. Butch had found out that Avery planned on killing Jacob no matter how the whole mess worked out. Myers didn't want any part of that, Burl."

It was possible, Hansen reasoned. Things went bad for Avery — he took a couple of bullets and started putting together a lie to buy some time. Chances were he was crawling through the woods that very minute in an effort to get away. The badge had been a fake.

"What happened out here?" Hansen asked as he motioned with his head at Myers' body, hoping Jacob wouldn't look in the direction of his nod. A quick look at Jacob convinced Burl that of all the worries he had, Jacob seeing the body wasn't one of them. The boy's head hung down, his eyes nearly closed and he struggled to take in great gulps of fresh air. He looked asleep on his feet.

"When I pulled up, Myers and Avery were wrestling over a gun. It all...it all happened so fast. One second they were wrestling, the next second Avery has another gun in his hand and is shooting at me. I returned fire and I guess...Oh, God, Burl, it was horrible...I hit Myers in the cross-fire. But I think I got Avery, too."

Hansen wanted so much to believe his friend that he worked to make himself do so when something just too obvious hit him like a kick to the groin. *Who had given Jacob the gun?* Avery, in a round about way, had warned Hansen about the gun.

Hansen averted his eyes for a moment to look at Marsh's county car. Why hadn't the undersheriff used his radio at some point to call for help or notify headquarters of his situation?

When Hansen turned his eyes back to Marsh, his stomach lurched. Marsh seemed to be studying him intently. The expression on his face had drastically hardened.

After several seconds of strained silence, Marsh shook his head and grinned sadly. "You're not buying any of this, are you, Burl?"

Hansen considered all he could say and settled on, "Pete, can we get the boy out of here?"

"Did you, uh, talk to Avery, Burl? You know, there's a part of this fucked up situation that I don't really understand either. I guess he gave your boy a gun? Why would

He do that? Who the hell is he, Burl? I can't figure out why…"

"Pete," Hansen interrupted, "my son has been through enough. I'm taking him home."

Marsh casually moved his gun hand to rest on the grips of his holstered firearm. He brought the flashlight up in his other hand to menacingly shine in Hansen's face.

"Don't think so, Burl," he said with what sounded like authentic sadness.

"Pete, whatever's happened…it's over now. I have an ambulance coming for Avery. He's a federal agent, Pete. It's all over."

"Maybe not, Burl. I think he's dying. Probably already has. If he doesn't, well, hell, I'm already in bad trouble. But if he does die…that just leaves you and the boy as witnesses."

Hansen flexed the muscles in his legs to loosen them up. "Listen to me, Pete," he said, forcing his voice to be calm. "Surely, you don't mean to…"

In mid-sentence Hansen sprang to action. While lunging forward, he pushed back behind him, shoving Jacob to the ground. Jacob screamed out in surprise, and Marsh bellowed a threat while pulling his gun from the holster. At least fifteen feet separated the two men when Hansen made his move. Just as the tip of Marsh's barrel cleared the holster, Hansen leaped the remaining feet. He collided violently with Marsh, who reacted even more violently.

Marsh pulled the trigger.

Hansen felt what immediately seemed like a horse kick to his guts. Simultaneously he experienced the sensation of gasoline being poured into his stomach and ignited.

The two men careened full-force into the side of Marsh's car. The much smaller undersheriff was smashed between sheet metal and three hundred pounds of flesh and bone. They went from the car to the ground, and Hansen came to rest on top of Marsh but could do nothing but lie there. Hansen felt himself slipping into unconsciousness with one consolation. Marsh lay motionless beneath him.

Turner struggled back up the steep bridge embankment moments after hearing the gunshot. It came from the direction of the school.

Minutes earlier the man he'd known as Tom Avery raised a gun to shoot Turner, but had no bullets left to fire. Turner pulled a gun full of bullets and Avery introduced himself as Boyd Mackey while quickly becoming more hospitable. He told Turner all he'd relayed to Hansen about The Battalion, the deaths, the whole shebang.

Mackey's badge and true identity completely shocked Turner. He wouldn't have thought any undercover agent could infiltrate his organization, but this Mackey proved himself an amazing cop with a truly damaging story to tell. Turner wondered, as he left the agent lying there, if

Burl Hansen yet encountered anything to substantiate any part of the story.

The gunshot made Turner think Hansen probably had. The best Turner could hope for was that the fired bullet took care of a problem he really didn't want to deal with.

The last thing Jacob expected Burl to do was shove him to the ground. One second he'd been standing beside Burl, dazed from the pounding in his head and concentrating on nothing but breathing the delightful night air. The next second he was falling backwards. Jacob felt confused even before the gunshot sounded that seemed to shake the ground he lay on. He tried to put it together in his mind as he lay sprawled on his back, staring into the dark sky. Burl, Marsh, and Jacob were there alone. The bad guy must have come back and shot at them.

When he pushed upright into a sitting position, his eyes were drawn to Marsh's glaring flashlight on the ground. Jacob climbed to his feet and stumbled for the light, calling Burl's name as he went. Burl did not respond. The drained battery in Marsh's car restricted the headlights to a faint glow.

Jacob grabbed the flashlight and started a sweeping search of the darkness. When the beam revealed the two men on the ground, Jacob could not understand why Burl lay draped across Marsh, but he didn't let his confusion keep him from running to them.

Burl was not moving. Jacob screamed out his name, grabbed his massive shoulders and rolled him partially off the skinny undersheriff. Only then did Jacob notice the blood. It soaked Marsh, but Jacob quickly determined that the blood spouted from a bubbling hole in Burl's shirt.

Jacob fell to his knees and lowered his face close to his father's. "Burl! Can you here me? How did this happen, Burl?"

Only a sudden and intense anger kept panic at bay. When Burl failed to respond, Jacob looked up into the pitch-black skies and all but shouted, "Are you really there? Did you really help me? If you do exist, and you were there with me, then why is this happening now? Hear me again. Please…one more time. Let him be okay. Get us out of this. Please!"

Jacob felt Burl's arm move. It was draped across one of Marsh's legs, and Jacob realized the arm moved only because Marsh began to stir.

Jacob didn't know why, but it seemed obvious Burl had attacked Marsh and had been shot in the process. Jacob instinctively knew he must get Burl and himself away before Marsh came completely around. If he could get Burl out to his cruiser in the road, Jacob would drive them out of there. He'd never driven, but he knew the basics. Start the engine. Drop it into gear. Stand on the accelerator.

Jacob hooked his hands beneath Burl's huge arms and

started to tug. It took amazing effort to simply budge the man. After pulling with all his might, Jacob stopped every few inches to catch his breath and reestablish the hold underneath Burl's arms. But he did make progress. He covered at least a quarter of the distance to Burl's car before he first heard the faint whine of an approaching siren.

Chapter Twenty-Two

Hansen regained consciousness to look up into a nearly full moon. It was still partially covered with wispy clouds, but the skies were clearing. The moon provided enough light for Hansen to make out Jacob kneeling next to him. The boy mumbled words Hansen couldn't make out.

"I can't understand you, Jacob," he groaned, "Speak up."

His son jumped. The sound of his voice must have startled him.

"Burl!" Jacob shouted with relief. "I dragged you here to the car and I was trying to lift you to get you in, and all of a sudden you started groaning really loud and the bleeding got worse, and I thought I'd done you even more damage so I started…I was…I've been praying for you, Burl."

"Praying?" Had he heard his son right? Hansen's gut felt like someone had removed his intestines with a fork, stomped them real good, and then shoved them back in place with an ice pick. He'd known a lot of physical pain in life but nothing like this. The pain could be playing tricks with his mind.

"Yes, sir, praying. You told me that only God can truly prove his existence. Remember?"

Hansen remembered saying something along those lines. He nodded. It hurt worse to talk.

"Well, I think he has. Something astonishing happened down in the…"

Just yards away Pete Marsh groaned loudly.

"Jacob!" Burl said urgently. "Get in the car. Use the radio to tell Chuck to step on it. Tell him we're in danger and need another ambulance."

They were only feet from the car. When Jacob jerked open the door, the interior light illuminated the spot where Burl lay helpless.

"Burl!" Jacob screeched a second later. "The wires to the radio have been torn from beneath the dash. It won't work!"

"Are the keys still in the ignition?" Hansen gritted his teeth because of the scorching pain.

"No!"

"You son of a bitch!" Hansen shouted in the direction where Marsh lay moaning. He called Jacob back to his side. "Help me sit up. I want to lean back against the car."

Hansen thought it impossible to feel any more pain.

The act of sitting and scooting proved him wrong. He didn't realize the extent of his injury. When he did, it frightened him.

"Jacob, listen good," he rasped from his new position up against the car. "Down the road to your left there is a bridge. It's less than a mile away. An ambulance should be there by the time you can get there..."

"I heard a siren in the distance," Jacob interrupted excitedly, "I couldn't understand why it suddenly stopped. It's already there!"

"Then you've got to hurry. Tell them to come quickly...and call for more help."

Jacob, wide-eyed and jittery, gave Hansen's hand a squeeze and bolted away.

"Hey!" Hansen called out after him, "Don't stop for *nothing* or *nobody*. You got to get there as fast you can." Hansen wanted Jacob as far away as he could get. Nothing he needed to see could possibly happen here. "And, Jacob! Keep praying son! Keep praying!"

Jacob broke into a run, feeling awkward and sluggish. The farther he went the worse it became. He wasn't much of a runner in the best of conditions. Having been deprived of sleep and food and water, only fear kept him putting one heavy foot in front of the other. Burl depended on him like no person ever had or would ever do again.

His head pounded. His lungs burned. Every jolting step brought pain to a different part of his body. Still, he rambled on with the moon lighting the way before him.

He had just begun to feel he might run forever, and had forever to run, when he crested a hill and saw the glow of pulsating red lights reflecting off trees and terrain in front of him. Without warning, blinding headlights and the whine of an accelerating engine bore down upon him.

Jacob moved to the side of the road but didn't slow down. The car, however, skid to a stop in the loose gravel up in front of him. Turner bounced from the car and intercepted Jacob, taking hold of both his arms.

"Where's Burl?"

"Back there," Jacob huffed, "at that old building. He's been shot! He needs help!"

The police chief turned Jacob toward his car, "You come with me," he ordered.

Jacob remembered his instructions. "No! I have to get to the ambulance."

The grip on his arms tightened, uncomfortably and emphatically, "We need to get back to your father."

Jacob spun out of the grip and side-stepped the even less agile Turner, "I have to keep going!"

Turner lunged but missed, and Jacob lurched away.

"Jacob!" Turner called angrily, "Get back here!"

Jacob kept going but called out over his shoulder, "Go help him! He needs you! I'll get the ambulance!"

Jacob heard cursing and the spinning of tires on gravel. With the ambulance now in sight, Turner's taillights disappeared over the little hill Jacob had labored to climb.

Hansen helplessly watched Pete Marsh struggle to his feet. "Why?" he called out to the man he'd considered a close friend.

Marsh retrieved his firearm and limped toward Hansen. The moonlight reflected his scowl. "Don't make this any harder than it has to be…for either of us," he barked.

The headlights of a fast approaching car instantly lit up what had become a deadly playing field. Hansen's heart leaped in his heaving chest. It must be Turner. He only had to buy seconds more of time.

"It's over Pete. That's Chuck."

Marsh turned his head and blinked into the blinding light. The sudden smile baffled Hansen.

"Oh, no, old friend," he chuckled, "It's just the beginning." Then Marsh brought up his gun and took aim at Hansen.

Hansen heard the car door open and slam shut and he bellowed to Turner, "Chuck! He's killed Myers. He shot me and intended to kill Jacob!"

Hansen expected a response but didn't get one. He jerked his head to locate Turner. In the glow of the lights he saw only a silhouette…standing motionless.

"There's a survivalist group, Chuck. They're white supremacists. They killed the kids and Bemo," Hansen cried.

The only response came from Marsh. "I'll be damned. You don't know, do you? Avery didn't tell you!" Marsh laughed.

"Didn't tell me what? Chuck? Talk to me, Chuck!" Hansen pleaded. An unexpected sinking feeling joined with his fear and pain.

"Yeah, talk to him, Chuck," Marsh goaded. "Tell him how it was all your idea to begin with."

For torturous seconds there were no words. Then Turner's voice sounded weakly, "It wasn't supposed to be this way, Burl."

Hansen wanted to say more, but, "No…no…" was all he could manage. This had to be some terrible nightmare. Not Chuck Turner, too.

"Yes…Yes…" Marsh said softly as he walked closer and stuck the pistol to Hansen's head. "…afraid so, boss. I do honestly wish it didn't have to end this way for you."

Hansen didn't think he'd hear the shot. But he did. Then a second one. And a third. The blood splattered his face, blinding him, but he heard Marsh hit the ground.

Hansen didn't have the strength to clear the blood from his eyes. He could hear gravel crunching under approaching footsteps.

"Burl," Turner's tone sounded soft and sorrowful, "It was supposed to be just a militia. We were not survivalists or supremacists. We intended to be a second line of defense should our government crumble in these times when we're surrounded by enemies and hated around the world. We wanted to protect our community when the terrorists regroup and strike again.

"I want you to know, and the investigation will bear this out, I didn't know a thing about what Pete and his group was doing. Avery told me all just minutes ago. It was the first I heard about it. They were working right under my nose…committing atrocities…in an organization I built to protect citizens. I'm sorry. God, I'm so very sorry."

Hansen heard Turner take a deep, labored breath. "Your son is all right. I think Avery will be, too. Burl, please forgive me. Please ask Vicki to do the same. I've called an ambulance for you. You hang in there…You're the best friend I ever had."

Hansen heard yet more crunching gravel and then the sound of a man walking into the brush at the side of the road.

"Chuck? Hey, Chuck! Come back here, old friend," Hansen coughed. "Come back and let's talk…Chuck?... CHUCK!"

This time Hansen heard only a single gunshot.

Chapter Twenty-Three

Before ever attempting to open his eyes, Jacob realized he was in a bed. Safe. Sound. Secure. His body felt relaxed and comfortable under crisp sheets with just the perfect amount of blankets. He breathed both fresh and clean air.

He had to open his eyes in stages, blinking back the brightness of sanitary white walls and ceilings. When he finally managed to keep them open, the faces hovering over him remained blurred beyond recognition. Already he felt his face being caressed with anxious hands and peppered with enthusiastic, loving kisses. Jacob recognized his mother's perfume and the tickle of his father's beard. Voices he hadn't heard in what seemed like a lifetime called his name, expressing joy, and releasing their tension.

When he found his own voice, it sounded raspy. His mouth felt sandpaper dry. "Where am I?"

Joseph Swiretynsky's face came into focus. "You're in

the hospital and you are doing wonderfully," he replied.

Jacob processed the words while pulling his arms from beneath the covers to return their affection — to grip their hands and hug their necks.

"You slept nearly thirty hours," Rose Swiretynsky cooed. Jacob felt the moisture on her cheeks.

"It was the concussion," his father added.

For several more minutes greetings were exchanged while Jacob's vision and memory cleared. The last thing he could remember before waking up to a world of light and love was being helped into the cab of the ambulance at the little bridge. The memory sat him upright in bed.

"Burl! Where is he? Is he all right?" The sudden motion brought dizziness and a slight pang to the back of his head.

"Burl has come through two complicated surgeries and is in the intensive care unit, darling. But his condition has been upgraded from critical to stable," Rose reassured while his father tenderly positioned him back on the pillows.

Jacob pushed back off the pillows. "I want to see him."

"Rest a while longer," Joe said while again gently forcing Jacob to lie still. "You can see him this afternoon before we depart."

"Depart?" Jacob tried to sit up yet again, but a determined hand on his chest held him in place. "From here? From the hospital? Or from…"

"Departing for home. For Boston," Joe emphasized.

"But I've only been here little over a week. We had planned on me staying…"

"We are going home, Jacob. Today." The tone signified finality — concrete absoluteness.

Jacob turned to his mother. A solemn but committed nod of her head indicated complete agreement with her husband.

"Where is Vicki?" Jacob wondered out loud while attempting to deal with his disappointment.

"With her husband," Joe said coldly. The "where she belongs" was clearly implied.

"But," Rose quickly inserted while glaring at her husband through squinted eyes, "she has been in every hour to check on you."

"Does she know I'm leaving so soon?"

"She knows," Rose replied gently.

Vicki rapped softly on the door before pushing it open. The sight of Jacob sitting on the side of the bed brought back the memory of how to smile. Despite the fatigue that consumed her, Vicki darted across the room. Dr. Swiretynsky stepped from her path with a tangible reluctance. Taking Jacob in her arms brought back the tears. There had been so many. How could there possibly be more?

Vicki summoned the contents of her heart with the

only words that felt appropriate. "I'm sorry Jacob. I'm so very sorry."

After all, hadn't it all been entirely her fault? She brought him here — despite everyone else's warnings and objections. How could she have so wrongly interpreted the will of God?

"Oh, Vicki," Jacob emphasized with an embrace of his own, "You owe no apologies. What happened was no fault of yours."

"I was so selfish, Jacob. I just had to meet you. I just had to see you. I made up my own mind and heart without..."

Jacob abruptly dropped his arms and pulled out of her embrace. Vicki didn't know what expression she'd find on his face but felt relieved that he was not looking at her but at his adoptive parents.

"May we have a few minutes...alone?" He asked in his gentle manner, that warmed Vicki's heart from the first minute she'd laid eyes on him.

Rose moved instantly to comply with the wish, but her husband stared coolly at Vicki for several seconds before trailing his wife. Vicki did not blame him for his behavior. She deserved the animosity.

The door closed behind the parents, and Vicki tried to pick up where she'd stopped. "I guess I justified what I wanted by calling it God's will. I just wanted you to know...I wanted you to see...I felt that if you could be here and witness..."

How could she put it without sounding pompously

ridiculous? That she intended to point him in the right direction? That she planned to see his soul saved because she considered the God and religion he'd been raised with inadequate? It would be impossible for her make Jacob understand that under the pretense of doing God's will she actually tried taking over God's role.

The past week and a half had changed him. For one, he now had a whole new perspective on the analogy of someone squirming like a fish on a hook. He'd actually observed a fish doing so. He did not like seeing Vicki do the same. Jacob reached out and took her hands in his and interrupted her heavily laden babblings.

"Vicki, I do honestly believe that it was God's will for me to come here. You were the conduit for his workings."

"You do? Really?" Her expression brightened, but just a fraction.

He instantly made the decision not to tell her everything. The dark and swollen bags under her eyelids and the angry redness in her eyes signified a need for just good news. She did not need to hear from her son that he once believed the concept of a supreme spiritual being to be no more than a fairy tale.

"Yes, really! One thing has occurred that stands head and shoulders above all else…I've met my family. God had to want that to happen. Why wouldn't He? And as for the last couple of days, well, let's just say, I know God so much better than I ever did before."

The expressions now brightened to the point of flowing. It became apparent that a pretty face still lived beneath the residue of the recent torturous hours.

"He was with you in that terrible place?" she asked.

"It was truly a miracle. The next time we're together, when you're rested, I'll tell you a most magnificent story."

Vicki reached for Jacob. "I want you to know that I love you," she said as she pulled him into a hug. "I've always loved you."

Jacob didn't hesitate. "I love you too…Mom."

Tubes and wires ran from Burl in all directions. He bore the color of oatmeal and the tube running from his nose seemed to interfere with his breathing. But he was awake. He even managed a weak smile when Jacob entered the small cubicle of glassed walls. One heavily muscled shoulder protruded from the sheets. Jacob rested a hand on it.

"How are you feeling, Burl?"

"Not good enough to dance…not bad enough to die!"

An apparent strength in the voice alleviated Jacob's

worries. The big man would do just fine.

For several minutes, only the humming of the machines beside his bed filled the void. Then Jacob gave the shoulder a squeeze. "Thank you for rescuing me, Burl."

An even longer period of silence followed. "Thanks for praying for me, Jacob. I don't know that I'd have made it this far without it. I'm so glad you…well, that you, uh…" The voice trailed away to even more silence.

Jacob knew what Burl wanted to say. By now he also knew that matters of the heart were not easily transformed into words by Burl Hansen.

"I was terribly frightened in that cellar, Burl, and I wasn't very brave. Truly, I had absolutely no place else to turn."

"Not brave?" Hansen rasped, "You're standing here aren't you? That means you didn't give up. That took courage, Jacob."

Jacob glanced around to confirm their privacy before moving closer and leaning down to Hansen's ear. "Burl, I believe there was an angel down there with me. Or something, anyway, with wings. It fanned me and warded off that terrible smell. I know as well as I'm standing before you right now, that I wasn't hallucinating. It wasn't a dream. It was like, well, maybe a huge bird with great wings…Do you think I'm crazy?"

Burl's eyes wandered past Jacob's face to stare up at the ceiling. "Great wings," he repeated thoughtfully while seeming to concentrate hard on some memory. Moments later his eyes turned back to Jacob. They seemed livelier.

"Crazy? Hell, no. I don't think you're crazy. I have no problem believing in angels or any other...phenomenal occurrence...that can't be explained."

Jacob sighed with relief and stood upright. He would have no more doubts about the thing in the cellar.

"I guess you know I'm going home today."

Burl averted his eyes to the far wall and blinked them several times. Still, they revealed a glimmer of moisture. Several seconds later he struggled to bring a hand from beneath the covers. Burl laid his hand on top of the one Jacob rested on the broad shoulder.

"Hey, uh, you know, I want..." Burl stammered before pausing to clear his throat and concluding, "Well, I'm not good with this kind of stuff. I hate goodbyes."

"I would have never guessed," Jacob chuckled while trying to nonchalantly wipe at his own eyes.

Burl took a deep breath, held it, and then slowly let it go. "They play a lot of football up your way. Have you ever been to a pro game?"

"No, sir."

"You know, Boston isn't that far away. Why don't we plan to take in a game...just you and me? Let's say, in November, before it gets too awfully cold. But hey, up there winter hits a lot earlier than down here. I remember playing up there in October one year when it was still like summer in Chicago and…"

Jacob listened as he matched the smile on his father's face and tried to convince himself that November would be here before he knew it.

ABOUT THE AUTHOR

Keith Remer is a former police officer, a retired Army colonel and now teaches leadership courses to college students. He is an Oklahoma rancher who enjoys good scotch, fine cigars, and long trips on his Harley Davidson with his wife, Carrie.

You can learn more about the author and his upcoming novels by visiting www.KeithRemer.com

LaVergne, TN USA
19 January 2010
170402LV00002B/1/P